FIRST A LADY

JADE CARY

JOIN MY NEWSLETTER

I'd love to keep in touch with you! Join my newsletter so that you never miss out on a thing!

Join here: http://bit.ly/2IMNHBA

DEDICATION

To my life, my love, my breath. Baby, I love your way.

August

*C*heers and chants of 'Four more years!' flowed like a wave over the stage from the convention floor of The Ernest N. Morial Center in New Orleans, growing louder as the appearance of President Matthew Douglas Coolidge grew near. Special Agent John Marin stood behind the president backstage as the first lady wrapped up her speech. Coolidge was an easy, accessible man who genuinely liked and respected the agents who served at his pleasure. Marin had the president's back, literally. It was his job to stand behind the Commander-in-Chief, see what he saw. And what he saw now, what both men saw, was Lady Grace Ashton Coolidge sing the praises of a very popular third-party president, and a man she clearly admired.

"It is often said that the greatest men have the greatest challenges, and I have seen more truth in that statement over the last three and a half years than at any other time in my life," Mrs. Coolidge said.

She was a popular first lady, possessing class and sophistication, a great sense of humor, and genuine empathy for others that *few before her achieved no matter how hard they worked. Her porcelain features and searing ice-blue eyes belied a strength of character and a wicked sexiness that no one in Washington missed. She was a woman who knew what and who she was, yet she never used it to get ahead, get her way in things—and that, perhaps more than anything, drove the power-hungry in D.C. crazy. She got things done simply by being who she was—no tricks, no games.*

A fierce advocate for children and a staunch enemy of the corporate greed that preyed on them, she had won fans and had gained a number of enemies in the four years the power couple had occupied the White House. English by birth and heritage, and the daughter of a Duke, Grace Coolidge was often entertained by the peerage when she traveled abroad, and she took the good-natured ribbing in the press about her lineage with typical good humor. A teacher by education and core competence, she was in favor of, and fought for, sweeping education reform.

"I see the challenges Matt will face in the next four years as hills to climb," the first lady continued, "mountains to traverse. The view, the vistas, can and will be shared by all of us. There is no greater act, no greater honor than serving as President of the United States, and being rather prejudiced, I believe there is no greater man than my husband to fill that role."

Secret Service agents lined the front of the stage, and they flanked both sides. As Marin scanned the crowd he was able to locate several agents buried amongst the delegates. Nodding in satisfaction, he closed the curtains and turned to an agent who was stationed with him. The man was not there. Not wanting to leave the president, he decided he'd wait a minute before alerting the others. It was a minute he would come to regret.

"And I believe I can speak for him when I say he serves at your pleasure." The first lady paused for effect. "Ladies and

Gentlemen, your president, my husband, Matthew Douglas Coolidge."

The hall erupted as Matt Coolidge walked out on stage to the hip-hop hit, "This Is How We Do It". Mrs. Coolidge applauded and smiled and allowed her husband to come to her, and when he reached her he bent down and kissed her, first on the cheek, then on the lips—just a peck, but he lingered there, his eyes dancing, his pride in his wife showing in every move, every gesture he made. His hand made circles on her lower back, and then drifted farther down, just for a second, and released her with the tiniest of pats. Weeks later, after news outlets and reporters tried to make sense of the senseless, the media would grasp onto that one thing, both tender and erotic; familiar, as only a husband could be with his wife. That Matt Coolidge behaved like a newlywed after five years of marriage was the stuff of fairytales. It was what America would hang on to; it was all they were left with.

The crackle of static in John Marin's earpiece brought his eyes to the closed curtains again, and he parted them to allow the first lady to pass. He would radio about the missing agent, he thought to himself, as he peered out to the stage where Matt Coolidge raised his arms in an attempt to quiet the crowd. The president was to speak for forty-five minutes, and Marin knew the man wanted to get to it. It had been a long four days, and he wanted to return to Washington and governing the country. The amount of time it took for all of this to weave through Marin's mind was mere seconds, but that was all the time he needed to see the gun raised in the hand of the agent standing in front of the stage—the one who stood beside him moments ago—unmoving. Marin scanned the crowd, followed the agent's eyes like a defensive tackle follows a quarterback's, to see what he saw. And Marin realized, too late, that the agent was looking directly at the president. A second agent stood on the opposite end of the stage, his gun raised as well.

"What the fuck?" Marin muttered as he pulled his gun.

It would later be reported, via hundreds of eyewitnesses who were there, that the president had a convulsion and fell to the ground. Some reported that the president 'danced joyously on stage' to the music and the prospect of another term in The White House. What most did not know was that, as President Matthew Coolidge raised his arms to quiet the crowd, a bullet fired from a standard Secret Service issue .357 SIG Sauer pistol pierced his heart, and a second, fired from the other side of the stage, pierced his head above the temple, entered his brain, and killed him instantly.

As the agents backstage, and those scattered amongst the crowd, tried to locate the shooters, panic ensued, driving thousands to the floor or rushing to the exits.

Marin, seeing that the president could not be saved, acted as only he knew how to: he fell over the first lady and shielded her from the gunfire on the convention floor. And as an eerie quiet settled in the hall, he picked up a dazed Grace Coolidge and carried her to safety.

2

Nine Months Later

*A*s presidential libraries, went, it was modest—and, if one were honest, the most beautiful. Set on three-hundred acres of Coolidge family-owned land covered in well-maintained lawns, natural gardens and copses of trees that changed into brilliant color in the fall, The Matthew Douglas Coolidge Memorial Library, located in President Coolidge's hometown of Queensbury, New York, was unique. First, it was small—a mere eight-thousand square feet over three stories. Second, unlike other presidential libraries that were more modern looking, this one was an original stately nineteenth century home that had been in the late president's family for generations. The drive from the main road between towering oaks gave visitors a view of the entire library set back on the property, surrounded by an elevated stone terrace with batwing stone stairs leading up to the main entrance.

The five surviving First Ladies of the United States flanked Grace Coolidge as they stood for pictures on the steps of the newly renovated library. Once photos were taken, the current and former presidents gathered for pictures with Grace, and then the first ladies joined. These were photos Grace would treasure forever, and it was not lost on her, or the country, how historic a gathering it was. The widow of the first Libertarian president, flanked by three democrats and two republicans, who all still spoke to each other, was unprecedented. Grace wondered how long it would be before a picture like this was taken again, or would the country revert back to the duopoly it had coveted since 1864.

The days since that horrible August night had been a blur. Handling the affairs associated with the library and settling into her new life outside The White House left Grace little time to grieve the devastating loss—to the country and to herself. She missed Matt, even if their last couple of year had been less than close, less than all she'd hoped. What she hoped now was that Matt was proud—proud of the short but profound legacy he left a grateful nation; and proud of her for honoring him as best she could.

Grace was the only first lady amongst the group whose husband predeceased her, and the former presidents and first ladies had been wonderful to her—this day, and the days leading up to the library dedication. As final pictures were taken, and the current and former presidents and their wives were ushered into limousines, only Dolly Breitbart remained.

At eighty-two, Mrs. Breitbart was the oldest of the living first ladies, and the wife of the forty-first president, Jonah Breitbart. She was the one Grace felt closest to. The two women had met on several occasions throughout Matt's career, and President Breitbart had been a great and diligent supporter of Matt Coolidge's presidency, often advising the young president on policy and foreign affairs, which was Jonah Breitbart's specialty.

"I wanted a few minutes with you away from the others, Grace," Dolly Breitbart said. "How are you holding up, kid?"

Grace smiled. Dolly called everyone 'kid', but where Grace was concerned, the endearment held some truth. Now, at thirty-five, Grace was fifteen years the current first lady's junior. Still, she never felt beneath these strong, proud women.

"I'm fine, Dolly." They took the stone stairs down as a Secret Service agent kept a respectful distance. "I'm glad this is over and done with."

"I hear you," the older woman said. "My God, it seemed Jonah's library took forever."

"You were so involved, too, weren't you?"

"As were you with this one, dear," said Dolly. "And you know, if you want it done right, you have to be on top of everything." The ladies followed the walkway toward the gardens. "Have you managed to get back to London on occasion?"

"I have, quite a bit, actually," answered Grace.

"And how are your folks?"

"They're lovely, thank you for asking."

"They look wonderful. I didn't get a chance to talk to them inside—so much going on." Dolly looped her arm through Grace's.

"I'll spend a week or so with them in Vermont after the memorial in October."

"Nice. I'll be there for that; Jonah, too. What else have you got cooking?"

"I'm dedicating the new U.S. embassy in London in October as well."

"Say hi to the ambassador for me," Dolly laughed. "And I am sorry."

"He's all right."

"You're too kind."

Grace laughed and patted the elder woman's hand as she led her down the sandstone path toward the rose garden.

"I want you to know how extremely proud I am of you, Grace," Dolly said. "You have handled the last year with such class, such grace—no pun intended. You've done your duty, you've conducted yourself without scandal, you've supported Bannish—which isn't always easy to do..." They passed a hedge of boxwood that served as a dramatic entrance to a plot of roses.

"He's trying to follow Matt's dreams," Grace said. "It isn't easy."

"No, it isn't. Oh, Grace are these the ones?" Dolly Breitbart opened her eyes wide in awe.

"Yes. One thing Matt always said was that he wanted a plot full of Lady Grace roses on the grounds of his library." The area between the walkway and a hillside covered in English lavender and whisper-pink azaleas was filled with rows of the dark pink roses with the subtle light pink edges. The plot was hemmed in by a two-foot high privet hedge.

"Romantic. And smart. And the smell!" Dolly leaned down and inhaled a particularly fragrant one in full bloom. "Oh, how gorgeous, Grace."

"Want one?"

"Oh, I'd love it. Is that kosher?"

"Who will stop us?" Grace turned toward one of the agents. "After all, we are first ladies, and we have *carte blanche*."

The agent moved swiftly toward the ladies at Grace's beckoning. "Can you cut this somehow for us? Do you carry weapons of that nature on you?" Grace inquired with a sassy arch of her brow.

"Yes, ma'am, I do," the agent answered amidst titters from Dolly, who was always amazed at the charm of one so young. Grace Coolidge could charm a man right out of his birthright; she'd said so to Jonah more than once.

"Oh, the air is absolutely filled with that gorgeous scent, Grace. Such a gift, to all of us." Dolly whiffed another open flower as the agent bent to cut the selected bloom. Grace crouched down to hold the stem for him.

"Careful of the thorns, ma'am," he said as his penknife sliced through the green stalk, and Grace wondered why the snap of the stem against the blade was so loud, like a firecracker. Her next thought was why the agent appeared to be listing sideways. Grace's final thought, before everything went black, was why she and Dolly were suddenly thrust underneath him as blood seeped from his chest all over Grace's cream Chanel suit. Pink rose petals showered down upon them, their sweet fragrance filling the dead air.

Oh, not again, thought Grace.

And then, nothing.

October, London

They were arguing again. It wasn't serious; it never was.

"Oh, again, Grant? It wasn't enough that Grace and I missed the opening."

"That wasn't my fault," Grant Harrison huffed at his wife. "No one asked the two of you to go gallivanting 'til all hours of the morning while I bloody worried half to death."

"Poor Harry," Grace teased with a pout. "We'll come tomorrow."

"That would be fine with me but see if you can't get through to old coddle puss there. Jane, for God's sake," Grant Harrison begged, seeing the dark look on his wife's face. Both he and Grace knew what that meant and where it could go if all in attendance didn't tread very lightly.

Grant Harrison and Grace Ashton Coolidge had known each other since primary school, and when he married Julie Ann Needham ten years ago, Jane, as everyone called her, became one of Grace's dearest friends, surpassing in some ways Harry himself.

"Janey, let's do go tomorrow. I've been dying to go to the LPO for months. And I hear the new conductor is very handsome." She glanced sideways at her longtime friend, the London Philharmonic's new, and youngest ever, conductor.

"Don't you start, Gracie," he muttered sourly.

"Oh, Harry, don't be cross. We'll be good, we promise. Won't we, Jane?"

"No," snapped her dear friend, still smarting. Grace, frankly, had already forgotten what started the whole row. She got up and went into the kitchen of the Harrison's London flat and retrieved a new bottle of wine. She stared out the tenth-floor window overlooking Hyde Park and the Thames, the London lights shimmering off the still water like stars on glass. The Harrisons were dear old friends and they had taken good care of her since the assassination in New Orleans a year ago, and again after the shooting at the Coolidge Library in May. Grace had been in a fog, and it had started to lift a bit, after months at the country house and the love and attention of many friends. She would get through this next hiccup as well. And in thirty-seven months, the United States would have its next national election. It felt like decades. Charles Bannish, Matt's VP at the time of the assassination, became president, and was officially elected in November. Surely, he would be running for a second term. With almost a year under his belt, his polling numbers weren't bad.

Not that Grace didn't have other pressing concerns right now. This month she would help open the new U.S. embassy in London, and then travel to the states for a memorial tribute to Matt, a year after his assassination. She was excited and nervous and dreading the trip all at once. Under pressure from the Libertarian Party to stay involved, make appearances, and campaign for party hopefuls, she would do all of the above while attending parties and fundraisers in New York prior to the memorial in Washington, D.C.

"As long as you're in New York, could you...?"

"Such a nice tribute they're planning for Matt, Gracie. I'll hold a dinner!"

"Oh, do come for the opening of the new Cathcart exhibit at the Met, Mrs. Coolidge!"

It seemed to be never-ending. They all thought they were helping, these East Coast friends and supporters of hers and Matt's. Grace knew they were all sorry to see her flee—and that was the exact word used—to London when the dust settled after the assassination. But she couldn't stay. She could barely breathe; how could she remain in Washington, much less New York, where Matt was a two term Republican Senator before switching parties and running as the Libertarian candidate five years ago? Even Charles Bannish tried to get her to come back to 'town'. He'd even floated the idea of a U.S. ambassadorship in some remote location where she couldn't get into too much trouble. And just when she was beginning to find her sea legs, begin to reconcile what had happened to the most popular president since Kennedy, and begin once again to find hope, someone shot at her at the Coolidge library dedication. A Secret Service agent had been killed, Dolly Breitbart suffered a broken wrist when the agent tackled her to the ground, and for the second time in nine months, Grace came away from a shooting without a scratch. How many more deaths would there have to be before change, the kind of change she and

Matt had always dreamed of, brought order again to the country she loved? How much more could she take?

She felt like she had nine lives; her time was coming due, surely.

Grace grabbed the bottle and a corkscrew and padded back into the great room. Jane and Harry were dancing cheek to cheek to some old show tune. How she loved seeing them together. Despite their bickering earlier, they were a couple in love, and they were very dear together. Watching them in each other arms, she recalled a happier time with Matt, when he would take her in his arms for no reason other than to show his love. When did that all end? It seemed to happen slowly, over a period of time she could not retrace. A sliver of envy pierced her heart at the sight of her friends.

"Oh, for God's sake," she snapped with a smirk.

At Grace's exclamation, Grant Harrison slapped Jane's fanny sharply, and growled in her ear, "Now, I'm ready to make up, darling."

Jane saw something in Grace's eyes and stilled in her husband's arms. "Oh, Gracie. We're sorry we quarreled. Grant, she doesn't need this." Jane walked over to Grace. "Do forgive us, darling. How insensitive of me."

"Oh, stop babying me, Jane. And get that earnest look off your face, Harry, or so help me...! I am fine; perfectly fine."

"Of course you are." Jane took the wine out of Grace's hand while Harry got her seated. Grace had a fresh glass of wine in her hand seconds later. And as the friends chatted, and then pulled her into a circle for a dance, Grace thought about all she had going on. She'd kept herself so busy she didn't know which way was up half the time. Next on the list was the dedication of the new U.S. Embassy in London.

Maybe after that, she'd skulk off to Fiji. Surely no one would find her there.

———————

JOHN MARIN HATED TOURISTS. He was watching a bunch now, on the deck of some rental, the captain of the Sea Witch laughing and passing out rum drinks while the Funky Bunch tried to fish off the bow and snorkel drunk. Marin didn't come to St. John, U.S Virgin Islands to hear and see the crew from Duck Dynasty getting down. He came for the quiet, for the peace; he came to forget.

One of the women in the group stood in her white one-piece and waved at him, swaying on her feet as the boat bobbed in the wake of a Jet Ski that came too close to their boat. Marin raised his bottle of Mount Gay Extra Old and took a swig, the taste of vanilla and caramelized bananas silky smooth on his tongue. A sailfish breached the water beyond the cove, and all on the boat saw it except White-Tank. She wasn't a bad looking woman, and she seemed a little drunk herself, which he didn't mind. A man stood, belly hanging over his loud madras shorts, and he slipped a meaty arm around the woman before offering his own wave at the only other boat anchored in Hurricane Hole. Marin lifted his bottle again, took another swallow, and allowed the rum to slide down his throat and numb him further. Kicking back in the cockpit of his Winsome 43-foot sailboat was what John Marin did best—in fact he was becoming an expert. Perched on the edge of the bow, he had a clear view of the cove he called home, a place that never saw the heavy winds that other parts of the island did.

Steel drum island music drifted over his ears, coming from the tourist boat, the passengers swaying and gyrating, drinks sloshing over red Solo cups and onto the deck of the boat as they whooped and hollered over each other. They were entitled, he supposed. After all, there was no place more beautiful, more remote, or more forgiving than St. John. He just didn't want to hear it, from anyone. This was his own private island, where no one spoke unless spoken to, and nothing and no one knew him, except for the drinks he so lovingly consumed and the women he so ardently fucked.

He set the rum bottle down and dragged his hand through hair that had grown to his shoulders, from the military-short style he'd sported in a past life. The hair on his face, kept trimmed, stopped itching him long ago. His skin, pale as only blonds can be from birth, had turned coppery bronze after almost a year in the Caribbean sun, hardening his already weathered look. His wardrobe consisted of board shorts and tank tops or the occasional long-sleeved Henley if a chill kicked up. That hadn't changed since he shucked his suits and all other remnants of his time in the Secret Service a year ago and came to St. John with close to five million dollars in the bank from the sale of his D.C. home, his car and all his worldly goods. He purchased the sailboat, used, for $200,000, bought a few pairs of shorts, some shirts, a pair of Top Siders and some flip-flops. He even sprung for a hat, all purchased on the island. He'd arrived with the clothes on his back, and his guns. Those he'd never let go.

He came to the island to forget. Forget how he never saw the carnage coming, never saw the betrayal, never saw that a man like Matt Coolidge could never survive a country that had gone soft off government love, and that it would take generations of Matt Coolidges to pull America out from under the muck it had allowed itself to get mired in. John

Marin just never...saw it, and that was the most difficult thing of all to accept.

He set the bottle of rum down on the deck and fell backwards into the warm Caribbean. He sunk down, down, down and looked up through the clear turquoise water at an equally clear sky, wondering if this was how he'd die, under the weight of the sea, where he heard nothing, saw nothing, felt nothing. Or would he die an old man sitting at the bar in the Jaded Mermaid in Coral Bay, beard to his waist and tall tales on his tongue. He decided, as his chest began to ache, and the pressure filled his head, that he wanted to go, just like this, and he didn't want to wait years for it to happen.

The sooner the better.

4

*I*t had been a while since Grace Ashton Coolidge had been summoned anywhere, but to be sitting in the office of the United States Ambassador to Great Britain at Winfield House in Regents Park cooling her heels was beyond the pale. She knew, of course, what this was about, so to be made to wait for Brandt Delacroix's arrival like a naughty schoolgirl in the headmaster's office made her feel nothing more than just that. Grace supposed it could be worse; she could have been sitting in some Scotland Yard office with a detective or constable who could not begin to grasp the delicacy of the situation, nor her conflicting feelings on the matter.

Winfield House on the quietest of days was still abuzz. Secretaries scampered about, men in uniform came and went, and when she arrived she saw two men sitting at a table inside the foyer of the main entrance to the residence. Grace thought they were there to escort her to wherever the ambassador was hiding, but they only stood and nodded to her as she passed. They wore dark suits, stern expressions and familiar bulges under their jackets. They scrutinized her with cold eyes. An icy chill slithered down her spine after locking eyes with one in particular. Hair shorn close to his head, he was balding—too young for that, Grace had thought. But it was the cold eyes that had her looking away, hoping the men were there on other business that did not include her.

It would have been a simple matter of time before she would meet with Delacroix, as she was to appear and say a few words at the new embassy dedication in less than two weeks, and she figured he had an agenda lined up for her. Then she would travel to the United States, where she would appear at a memorial for Matt, a year and two months after the assassination.

Disappearing after that dreadful day was bad enough; she never spoke to the nation as a newly widowed first lady, never did the interview on *60 Minutes*, never spoke to the Washington Post. Even Andrew Morton, the famed biographer and historian, was ordered to keep his distance once she returned to England. She never got her goodbye to a nation that took a chance on a good man and had him for four years. She never got to thank them for their trust and their kindness and their acceptance, their willingness to change, to say goodbye to the old ways and ring in the new. She never got closure, nor did the citizens of a country she loved and thought of as her own, her dual citizenship notwithstanding.

The shooting at the library took up two news days and then it was over. The fallen agent received appropriate coverage, and great fuss had been paid to Dolly Breitbart's broken wrist. And, as sad as she was for Dolly, and as broken hearted as she was over Agent Adelson, Grace had been eternally grateful for the lack of publicity for herself. And now, as two more obligations for the United States loomed close, Grace knew that her participation would come at a price, and Charles Bannish elected the seemingly indefatigable and pompous Brandt Delacroix to deliver the bill.

Grace's thoughts drifted to the two men sitting in the foyer. Were they U.S. Secret Service? The Military? MI5? Private security? Exactly how much did Brandt Delacroix know regarding her, if anything? No one knew what she knew—at least no one here, right now. And she needed to keep it that way, until Washington. The men looked like security. So, it was all but done then. She was getting it whether she wanted it or not.

Grace breathed a weary sigh and took a sip of her tea as the sounds of footsteps brought her head up in greeting to the man himself. He looked like a leprechaun, he truly did; red hair, a pink, ruddy face, and all five-foot-eight-inches of him, he came sweeping into the room as if he'd already put out three brush blazes and stopped a war. It was barely noon.

"Grace! How nice to see you. I'm sorry to keep you waiting." He took both her hands in his after she stood and kissed both her cheeks. "Sit, please. Finish your tea."

"I'd have thought a meeting about the dedication would take place at the embassy, Brandt," Grace said, batting her eyes in confusion as she sat and crossed her legs. "Goodness, I haven't been to Winfield House since Matt and I came for a visit in his first hundred days."

"I know. It's been a long time." An awkward silence ensued, which gave Brandt Delacroix enough time to get a bit red in the face, which wasn't difficult. "But, this meeting isn't about the dedication, per se."

"Oh?"

"Since the shooting at the library, you've hidden here in

your flat and at Shannonfield House without benefit of the same protection afforded the other surviving first ladies."

"By my own choice, Brandt," Grace reminded.

"Yes, well, that stops now."

"I beg your pardon?"

Brandt Delacroix held up a tiny hand. "Forgive me for being stern, Grace, but this isn't up for discussion. You've refused agents while here at home, but you will not be allowed to refuse protection once at the embassy for the dedication, nor while making the trip back to the states for the memorial for Matt." Delacroix sighed. "Grace, please don't fight this. They simply won't let you do these things if you don't agree."

"That is ridiculous."

"No, it isn't. One, you are like family to the president, so he is not taking no for an answer. To be clear, you are like family to me, too, so I am fully on his side." Delacroix had been the ambassador now for five years, and he had taken on a slight British accent. Appointed by Matt Coolidge, Charles Bannish inexplicably saw no reason to relieve the man of his post and bring in someone sturdier, not to mention more qualified. "He said he will deliver the dressing down of your life if he gets wind of so much as a whimper from you on this," Delacroix finished with flair, taking joy in passing that along to her direct from the mouth of Charles Dargavel Bannish.

"Charles Bannish is always finding a way to hover over me, as if his comforting arm could take away past events," Grace snapped.

"That isn't what he's doing, and you know it. Secondly, without protection you bring danger to the embassy dedication and the memorial, so this is not up for discussion."

"So you've stated."

"Yes, well...either agree to protection, or you stay home, and Bannish will get the current VP to speak, or Elton-friggin'-John. Hey, Prince Harry just married an American. We'll get her; anyone but you. And he is serious, Grace."

"Fine. How long will I have to endure this?"

"Until your obligations to the U.S. are over, at the very least."

"So, even here, in England?"

"Yes. You are still a national treasure, even if you long not to be." Delacroix shook his head and finally sat in the white silk chair opposite her. He took her hands. "Surely you must know this, Grace."

"Yes, well..." She extricated herself from his grip. She would not be so quickly charmed by this swindler, Grace sniffed indignantly. It would take more than Brandt Delacroix's soft hands to bring her around. Thankfully, this seemed to be about standard operating procedure and nothing more. "And why, dear Brandt, would I trust the U.S. Secret Service, when they killed my husband?"

"Two rogue agents, darling. Surely the entire department can't be blamed." Delacroix paused and shrugged. "Nevertheless, they've undergone a complete overhaul. You have nothing to worry about."

"I have everything in the world to worry about." She felt the pinprick of tears in her eyes. Damn, damn, damn! She would not cry in front of this man. She would not. The one charming missive, the one she found in her purse a week ago—and how it got into her purse she couldn't begin to guess—was very specific: *WE KILLED HIM WE'LL KILL U 2*.

So, yes, she trusted no one, especially the United States Secret Service.

"I will not take an agent from the Secret Service, Brandt, and that is final."

"Then we're done here. I'll tell the president. He'll be disappointed. He was looking forward to seeing you. Relax and finish your tea." He started to walk away, then turned around. "Prince Harry it is."

Oh, you sonofabitch! She wanted to screech. "Brandt, wait." Grace couldn't miss the smirk he tried to hide, and it infuriated her. Still, she needed to do this; she needed to go back to the U.S. Do her *duty*—for closure, if nothing else.

"Yes?"

"What if I...what if I find my own security? I'll hire someone I can trust."

Brandt Delacroix was silent for a long time and glanced toward the door, a gesture Grace did not miss. So, she was right. It made her trust him, and what sat outside that door, even less. She did not know why, and she would spend time after leaving Winfield House figuring it out. For now, she would stall him any way she could.

"I won't take a Secret Service agent," Grace reiterated. "I am no longer first lady."

"In the eyes of the United States, you are." Delacroix tapped his red lips with a chapped pointer. "I'll look into it and then take it to the president."

"I'll find someone. It's what I'm comfortable doing."

"I'll get back to you, Mrs. Coolidge." And with a curt nod, he turned and left the room.

"JOHN, ANOTHER?" Rafe asked from behind the bar, waving the empty beer bottle in front of his face, pulling him out of his fugue.

"Yeah, sure, thanks, buddy."

"Food?" Marin shook his head. "Well, I'm going on break in a minute. Jen's coming on."

Jen. She came with the bar, and since he was comfortable here, unlike at the others in town—tourist places, all of them—he had to deal with her. Nice girl, Jen, was. They'd had a thing for five minutes, and when she got clingy, Marin stopped it cold. God bless her, she tried. But no nookie was better than clingy nookie, so he held her at arm's length, smiled at her a lot, and asked after her two kids from two different men before he got too drunk to see her in a way that landed them in bed together every time. One kid was running around now, chasing after a runaway Hot Wheel he'd scooted across the floor. The car rolled under Marin's feet, and the boy ran over, looked up at the familiar face, smiled, and crawled along the dirty wood floor in search of the car. Marin lowered the tip of a flip-flop and kicked the car out into the middle of the floor again. The boy looked up at him, smiled, tapped his fist against Marin's offered one, and ran off.

John Marin had the gift of being able to fit in anywhere. Nondescript at first glance, it took people a while to see past the rugged face and tight-lipped countenance and notice the handsome man beneath. His size was, at times, an asset; at other times it could drive people away. He could attract people as quickly as he could repel them, and that talent sat in the depths of his eyes, and the cold countenance he wore on occasion. At other times, people—especially women—were drawn to that same strength seeking comfort; his warmth and an uncanny ability to protect and nurture just by sharing the same air space was a gift. Mostly, though, he was Switzerland until someone who didn't know him mistook him for weak, and then he'd prove that quiet rarely meant weak. Had he been a sociopath, he'd have been an extremely dangerous one. Instead, he carried groceries for the elderly, opened doors for the ladies, and took shit from no one.

It was early; The Jaded Mermaid was still relatively empty. A few locals occupied a table by the door, and one other old-timer sat at the end of the bar, muttering about the weather and politics, only to disappear inside his rum punch again. In an hour or so the locals, fresh off their fishing boats, would drift in, find seats at the bar or at tables inside or out, and the place would jump until about two a.m., since it was Saturday. It was perfectly acceptable to attend church hung over; it was not prudent to take a boat out starting at five a.m. for a day of fishing still half-drunk and still heavy headed. Marin knew these people, for better or for worse. They were his people now, and for the next hour, Marin had some peace and quiet to look forward to. He felt a good drunk coming on. Maybe he'd stay in town tonight; maybe he'd return to the boat, secure in its slip in the marina, and see if he couldn't coax one of the female tourists to his deck for a nightcap.

He noticed the bottle of beer in front of him, not remembering Rafe setting it down. That was happening a lot lately, the drifting in and out. He should probably read a book, or look at a newspaper once in a while, do the crossword. Keep the mind sharp. He played with that thought for a minute, then let it go—as he did most things.

"Hey, John."

"Mmmm." Rafe stood next to him.

"Phone."

"Huh?"

"You have a call. In the office. I'm going outside for a cigarette."

John Marin had given up his cell phone and an email

address long ago. He'd received one or two calls here since, had no idea who from. He'd never returned them. There was no one he needed to hear from, and no one he needed to reach. He never felt completely good about that, since he had a family. He almost told Rafe to go hang it up, but curiosity and a beer haze got him up off the bar stool. He passed Jen on the way into the office and gave her a smile. She looked inordinately good tonight, but he shook that off. He didn't want to have to wean her off him for one night of fairly decent sex.

He entered the office and didn't bother closing the door. The phone receiver lay on a sticky veneer-topped desk overflowing with papers and Styrofoam cups of coffee; one had dots of mold floating on the surface.

"Yeah," he said when he placed the receiver to his ear.

"Mr. Marin? Mr. John Marin?"

"Yeah."

"Right. My name is Sterling Jarvis and I am the personal secretary to Lady Grace Ashton Coolidge." Marin shook his head, and it took him several seconds to realize that *sec-re-tree* meant *secretary*. "Mrs. Coolidge," the man went on, "requested I contact you regarding an offer of temporary employment for the month of October."

"Mrs. Coolidge?" Marin said.

"Lady Grace Ashton Coolidge, yes, the former first lady of..."

"Yes, I know who you're talking about."

"Splendid, splendid, indeed. As I was saying..."

"Uh, mister..." Marin broke in.

"Jarvis. Again, I am Lady Grace's..."

A-gane. "How did you find me?"

The man cleared his throat. "Well, now about that..."

"Never mind. Jarvis, is it? I'm not looking for employment."

"Would you like to at least hear the offer?" the man said in an affronted tone after a pause of several long seconds. When Marin didn't answer, the man went on.

"Lady Grace is scheduled to attend several events in the states this month, and she would like to..."

"Mr. Jarvis..."

"...hire you as her personal protection. You see, well..."

Marin was about to hang up, but something in the man's voice made him stop. Suddenly he wanted to hear more. And he realized, as he waited for the man to speak again, that it really wasn't the man's tone or inflection or his words, or the man himself that made John Marin want to hear more; it was Lady Grace Ashton Coolidge.

He fell on her body, covering her amid the chaos in the convention hall. When the shooting stopped and the screaming continued, he lifted the delicate and petrified first lady into his arms and carried her through a throng of people running from, or running into, the fray. He found a limo, one of many in the presidential motorcade, keys still in the ignition, windows bulletproof, abandoned. He tossed her into the backseat, got into the driver's seat, and drove. He drove until they were far from New Orleans, far from the city, out in the middle of nowhere, surrounded by the loamy smell of swamp and something herbaceous. It was only then that he got out, opened the back door, and pulled the sobbing, near catatonic woman into his arms. He held her, rocked her until she quieted; until she had nothing left to give.

Days later, after he'd been arrested, roughed up, and jailed, when it was determined that he had nothing to do with the assassination, and that he'd broken protocol in order to save the first lady, he appeared in front of the interim director of Homeland Security—for the acting one had been fired—and spoke about what he saw; two members of the Secret Service opened fire on the President of the United States, killing him.

He often thought of her, wondered how she was doing; one minute her husband was alive and patting her rump, the next he was laying in the middle of a huge stage with two bullets in his body—two. That's all it took. The first lady couldn't hold him as he took his last breaths, never got to say goodbye, never got closure. But it wasn't that; the country had been humiliated not by jihadists, but by two of their own, sworn to protect. America, at the time he left, never saw their first lady, never got to mourn for her or with her. She simply...disappeared.

And Marin still didn't know if the two agents were alive or dead, in custody or free.

"...an issue with the U.S. Secret Service, and well, she is reluctant, as you can probably understand, to attend these functions unescorted. Mr. Marin? *Mr. Marin*?"

"I don't do that kind of work anymore."

The man sighed. "Lady Grace is not comfortable with the options being offered."

"Which are?"

"U.S. Secret Service, at the moment. She inquired if private security was acceptable, and they seem reluctant to grant her request."

"Who is *they*?" Why was he asking? He didn't care. "Never mind, Mr. Jarvis. I'm not your man." And then he hung up.

The next night, as Marin sat at a table with a few locals and a country music star who had a home on the island, Rafe appeared at his side.

"Not sure when we became your fuckin' switchboard, pal, but you got another call. You selling condos in the Sahara now?"

"Tell him I'm not here." Marin wasn't going to play this

game with the former first lady's Mr. French. He wasn't interested. Period.

"It's a woman." Marin stopped breathing for a second, and then lifted his beer bottle and read every word on the label—twice. He was stalling, trying to decide what the upside was to taking the call. He had a whole list of cons.

Does she have this amazing voice, like royalty? Does she sound like sex and gin and cigarettes? Can you tell she's beautiful over the phone? He could have asked all of these questions, but he didn't. Instead, he got up and went into the office. He stared at the receiver for several seconds before he picked it up and held it to his ear.

"Yes?"

"John Marin?"

"Yes."

"Hi. It's Grace Coolidge."

Marin swallowed hard. That voice, the accent, was all it took. *No, no it wasn't.* "Ma'am."

"Please, no formalities. It's Grace."

"Listen, uh..."

"Please."

Marin stared out the grimy office window as rain pelted the ground and the roof, sounding like the hooves of a hundred horses, her whispered plea stabbing him straight in the heart. "Mrs. Coolidge..."

"I...I need you."

And with those three words, Marin's heart quickened. He slammed his eyes shut.

"I realize you've spoken to Sterling, and he did give me the unfortunate news that you weren't available, but I thought I might try. You see, I've been in London for the past year, and I am being called back to the states for some events this month. I'm also to participate in the new U.S. embassy dedication in London."

"Mr. Jarvis told me already. And I told him..."

"I know. If you would please just hear me out, and then if it's still no, I'll understand." Her words came out breathy, self-conscious, afraid.

Marin sighed. "Of course, I'm sorry. Go ahead."

"I remember so little about that night, but amid all the chaos and horror, the one thing I do remember is you." Marin gripped the receiver. "At my most terrified, I knew that nothing would happen to me because you were there."

"Ma'am..."

"They won't allow me to go to the U.S. without protection, and I won't...I cannot trust the Secret Service. I'm at a loss."

After a pause of several seconds, Marin said, "Well, you've been through a time." A little drunk, he was having trouble thinking on his feet, but he couldn't do better than that? "Maybe you've done enough for the good ol' U.S of A. Maybe you stay in London."

"I'm afraid I'm obligated one last time."

"We all make our choices, Mrs. Coolidge."

Marin thought she'd hung up, and then he heard an audible sigh on the other end of the line. "Grace." Her disappointment was palpable. "So, it's still no."

He couldn't. There was just no way. "I'm not in that line of work anymore," he said. "I'm sorry."

"So am I." And then she did hang up.

"That was easy," he said aloud when the dial tone reached his ear. It was for the best. He was in no position to protect anyone; he could hardly take care of himself.

Three days later, he was bent over a scrub broom washing the deck of his boat. As he scrubbed, the birds hovered overhead and managed to shit on every spot he'd just cleaned. He was about to give up and take out the rum when a shadow blocked the sun from his face. Figuring it was Garvin, the Kiwi who occupied the slip next to his, he didn't even look up when he said, "Give me ten, Gar, and we'll soak up some rum and see if we can't get laid tonight." The delicate clearing of a throat brought Marin's head up.

She stood on the dock in a white linen dress that hugged her gently from her creamy, slender shoulders to the tops of her shapely calves. A matching wide brimmed hat and over-sized sunglasses hid most of her face. Her perfume— patchouli and honeysuckle and the Caribbean—drifted over him on a gentle breeze and settled on his tongue. Her hair, the color of wildflower honey, and once long enough to brush her shoulders, was short, wisps fanning out behind her ears, which were adorned with simple sapphire studs that glimmered in the sun. She stood before him now thinner, smaller, less formidable than he remembered. But despite a year and a few subtle changes, John Marin would have known the lady anywhere. He squinted into the sun when she moved a little to her left. And then he shook his head.

"Holy shit."

"Well," Grace Ashton Coolidge said. "That's certainly no way to say hello."

5

*M*arin stood straight and leaned his scrub broom against the edge of the boat. The woman stood there like she had a right, like she was entitled. Like she belonged. Her posture, that regal head held high, showed a confidence the rest of her betrayed.

"You don't understand 'no', do you, Mrs. Coolidge?"

"I understand it quite well. Accepting it...well, that goes to a flaw in my character that could use a little work."

"What the hell are you doing here? Are you crazy?" At those terse words, he watched her beautiful face fall, and he regretted them immediately.

"No," she said. "I'm desperate."

No. Dammit, no! "Well, you came a long way to hear me repeat myself, Mrs. Coolidge, something I don't like doing on the best of days."

"Grace."

"Right." He looked past her to the end of the dock. A large, dark haired man in a black suit stood at attention, looking as out of place on the island as a subway car. "Who's the goon?"

"A poor imitation of you."

It came to him then—the smell of gunpowder, sulfuric, acrid; her perfume, feminine, sexy; the tang of the fear and adrenaline coming out of her pores as he struggled between rushing the stage to save a man who was already gone and saving her. He smelled it again, that sublime and familiar odor of desperation, fear, and aching vulnerability.

"Go home, lady. I don't exist." He was getting mad now, felt it bubbling inside him, unfamiliar after living an entire year in a place where anger was a waste of time. She just stood there, staring at him, so he picked up his broom and resumed scrubbing. When he looked up again, she was gone.

And that, oddly enough, infuriated him more than if she'd stayed.

The following day, he almost ran into her when he came out of the market with an armload of groceries.

"I'm starting to get irritated, Mrs. Coolidge."

"Grace."

"My answer is still no."

"Why?" She struggled to keep up with him as he walked across the small parking lot. In a pair of strappy heels, he guessed that wasn't easy.

"Told you already." He walked fast, crossing the small road to the marina, where his boat still sat in a slip at the end of a long dock.

"I'm willing to pay." Her voice shook with every running step she was forced to take to keep up with his long stride.

"Good to know."

"Oh!" Marin heard the squeal and then a grunt. He didn't want to, but he glanced behind him. She was limping. Goddammit! He warred between hoisting her over his shoulder and moving on, but he knew if he picked her up, if he touched her, he'd never let go, and then he'd end up taking this fucking job. He turned and kept walking.

"Mr. Marin. Oh! Oh, wait. *Wait!*" she snapped. Her tone pushed him beyond irritated. He stopped and spun on her.

"You're testing my patience, woman." He took two more steps toward her, putting him so close that her gauzy turquoise blouse brushed against his chest. Grace shifted her weight to her left, balancing herself with the toe of her right shoe barely touching the ground. She kept a hand atop the same white hat she wore the day before, and those same overlarge sunglasses shielded her eyes—from the sun, and unwanted attention.

"Go home, Mrs. Coolidge, while you still have your dignity." He continued to his boat. The unsteady click-clack of heels on the wood dock told him she would not be deterred, despite the limp and the necessity to step over the numerous cracks on the dock so she wouldn't catch her heel. She'd hurt herself, twisted her ankle in those damn shoes, he was sure of it. Not one to be dismissed, she was insisting on the last word. He'd give it to her because he didn't care one way or the other—former FLOTUS or not, John Marin was at the end of his rope. He had nothing left to lose.

He hopped up and over the side of his boat, then turned and stared down at the out of breath woman, wincing as she favored her right ankle. She'd made the decision to push him to his limit, and by God, she'd regret it.

"Here's the thing," he said with a glower and a raised finger. "I don't work for you anymore, I don't work for the U.S. government anymore. I've tried the polite way, I've tried nice."

"Have you?" Undeterred, she shaded her eyes from the sun despite the colored windshields she wore on her eyes.

Marin laughed. "You don't belong here, Mrs. Coolidge; you or your goon."

"Well," she said, balancing herself on a dirty, dew moistened storage box and kicking off her shoe. "Certainly not the first time I've heard that. In fact, Senator David Howell said the very same in my ear after asking me to dance at the inauguration. Imagine?"

Separated from this woman by the bow of a boat and half a dock, he almost turned away, went below until she disappeared. But at her words, at that simple two-dozen word backstory, he saw it all. On the surface she was determined and fierce, but underneath all that bravado, that feminine bluster and the British charm that got her what she wanted more times than not, was pain. It was deep, it was dark, and it sat in her eyes like a neon sign. With all the resources in the world that were available to this woman, she managed to track him down on a small island in the Caribbean and beg for his help. Why him? Why now, a year after the assassination?

Goddamn, she was *beautiful*; there was just no other word for it. He'd always thought so, but something happened in the last year that settled that beauty into her bones—as if, as first lady, that beauty was unsure if it had the right to belong to her. Most of all, Marin noticed, she was as her name suggested: *Grace*. Every inch of her. She had it from head to toe. The way she carried herself, her sense of humor, the gin-and-cigarettes voice. She had it all. She had been the perfect first lady: charming, smart, accessible, and one of the youngest first ladies in history. Marin put her at thirty-four or five now. She'd been through hell, and it still sat in her ice blue eyes like a permanent stain. But that wasn't his problem. He no longer did this kind of work. It was time to get tough.

"Lady, you don't want me."

"Yes, I do."

"Why? Why me?"

She stood on one foot, favoring her injured ankle. In her white linen slacks that showed off a good deal of ankle and a breezy turquoise blouse, she looked like the typical tourist on vacation, and not the most popular first lady since Jacqueline Kennedy.

"You know why you. I wouldn't have survived that night had it not been for you. I was ready to run out on that stage and throw myself in front of my husband, even as he ceased being the president the moment that first bullet left the gun's chamber, and you stopped me. One minute I was under you, and the next I was crouched in the back of a car with you in the driver's seat. I thought I'd lose my mind, and you made sure I didn't."

"Is there a particular reason why you feel the need for protection?"

"I don't—at all. I'm being forced into it, I'm afraid. They won't allow me to participate in the embassy dedication or go to the U.S. without it. They want me to take Secret Service protection, and I've refused. Then they—"

Marin held up a hand. "Who is 'they'?"

"Well, the current president, ultimately."

"You've spoken directly to him?"

Grace paused for a brief moment. "No. No, I haven't."

"Who have you spoken to?"

"The U.S. Ambassador to Great Britain, Brandt Delacroix. He's pushing me to take Secret Service protection, and he won't commit to allowing private security—as if it's his bloody choice."

"Not a fan?"

"No," she smiled. "Not a fan."

Marin stared at her for a long time. None of this sat right with him.

"Maybe you say no to this trip."

"I can't." Her chest rose and fell in a resigned sigh. "I've come all this way, as you pointed out, to make you an offer, and it is this: one week. Meet me in New York on the sixteenth of October, where I will attend parties and dine with old friends and political colleagues, and then come with me to Washington D.C. and help me get through one evening without losing my mind. Name your price."

Marin growled and slammed his hands on his hips. He stared out at the open sea that lay beyond the harbor. The life he had now was simple, just the way he liked it. This woman, what she was asking, was complicated. Her presence here pissed him off; her insistence was wearing him down, and that was making him very angry. Her goon stood, as he had the day before, at the end of the dock. Why was he even struggling with this? He didn't want to do it, yet as he looked down at this woman, at that beautiful face, he found himself needing to protect her as much as she needed protecting. Grace stared up at him and waited for an answer, as if she knew she had one coming, and it would be the one she was looking for.

"Sonofabitch!"

One shapely brow shot up and she gave him a sardonic smirk. Marin catapulted over the side of the boat and swept her up in his arms. Grace let out a delicate gasp and draped her arms around his neck as he lifted her higher and deposited her over the side of the boat onto the freshly scrubbed teak deck.

"Lose the other shoe right now, before you go ass-over," he said as he untied the ropes holding the boat close to the dock. Marin shot a final glance at the goon, who had not so much as blinked, despite the fact that he just hoisted his mistress over the side of a boat without a second thought. With ropes untied, he vaulted onto the boat and stared down at her, not believing he was considering this. "And you'll lose the goon, too," he said as he started the motor.

"He's not so bad," Grace said, removing her hat and setting her huge sunglasses atop her head.

"If I'd been in charge, you wouldn't have set your pretty shoes on the dock by yourself, forget about going out to sea." Marin maneuvered the boat out of the harbor. "He's not a cousin or anything, is he?"

"A distant one, I do believe."

"He goes."

"Fine."

Once out of the harbor, Marin raised the sails. Grace leaned back on the bench seat, her expensive white sandals tossed haphazardly on the deck at her feet. Marin went below and came out a moment later with a bag of frozen corn and a hand towel, which he used to secure the frozen vegetables to her ankle. Grace tipped her face up to the sun, her porcelain skin already pinking.

"Put your hat back on. This sun is strong. And keep that on your ankle. Looks like it's swelling."

"All right," she answered, and under her breath, she said, "You're already taking care of me."

"Don't sit there like a cat who just caught the canary, Duchess. You might live to regret this visit. Your goon should be horsewhipped."

Grace sat up straight and flushed. "You weren't supposed to hear that."

"I know." And then he smirked. It was rare that she'd seen John Marin crack. As a senior member of the Secret Service staff, and Matt's top man in his detail, Grace had been in close proximity to him often in her four years in the White House. She found him sharp, articulate, and incredibly devoted to the president. She also found him...something. She could not put a finger on it, exactly. He was quite handsome, the kind of handsome that curled a woman's loins. His smile was crooked, his indigo eyes were hard and unreadable, yet when she was with him in the back of that limo, out on that deserted stretch of road while her husband lay dead on a convention stage, she knew nothing would touch her; not while he was with her. That alone made John Marin incredibly appealing. She felt it again, now, sitting on his boat as they sailed into open water. He would protect her with his life until she was out of his sight again. It's how he was wired. That was why she wanted him.

As an agent, Marin had kept his dusty blond hair short and conservatively groomed. Now, after a year as a beach bum, for that was how he looked—tan shorts and a forest green Henley that did not hide one inch of his muscular chest and broad, powerful shoulders, and a short-cropped beard—his now sun-bleached hair was long enough to band into a ponytail. This did nothing to make him look any less formidable, or less tightly wound. The sleeves of the Henley were pushed up, revealing a crop of coppery bronze hair along a pair of strong forearms that expanded and contracted as he steered them out to sea.

Marin gripped the wheel so hard his knuckles were white. He was haunted, daily—even in this paradise—by the sounds of screaming and gunshots, and by visions of the president lying supine on the stage, dead before Marin even knew what was happening, and the devastating helplessness he felt. It only took a moment, and it was a moment he had missed. Why, then, would he put himself out there again? Goddamn her! He did not want this; he knew it deep down, yet he felt himself giving in to this incredible, unbelievably striking woman. Where did this sudden need to protect and shield her come from? There were others she could hire, but John Marin knew that none were more qualified than he. But those others hadn't allowed a sitting president to die on their watch. And those others didn't have the almost uncontrollable desire to take the former first lady up off her seat and kiss her until she climaxed.

He looked over at the beautiful woman, now a widow— a frightened widow who was being asked to return to the scene of her husband's massacre and celebrate his life and his service to his country. To return to, for lack of a more formal explanation, the very country that murdered its president, and do it, not for the patriotism she felt, but for the people who loved her as first lady, and to finish out an obligation she'd been robbed of a year ago.

It was only a week, she said. Could he possibly find some sort of redemption in so short a time?

They were silent during the fifteen-minute sail to a quiet cove surrounded by green forested rolling hills, the water a turquoise blue like Grace had never seen before. She watched Marin lower the sails and ease the boat into the first of two coves. As she looked over the side, she could see tropical fish swimming below, the water so clear and the fish so brightly colored.

"Oh, isn't this beautiful."

"This is where I live," he scowled. "This is what I'd be leaving to come work for you."

"I understand your reluctance. I wouldn't wish to leave, either."

Marin came around and sat on a teak storage bench across from her. He leaned his elbows on his knees and looked straight at her. His penetrating stare made her quiver inside. She wanted to look away. She just couldn't.

"I'm not reluctant. I said no because I don't do this kind of work anymore, and I don't appreciate being cornered like this."

She opened her mouth to speak, and when he arched a warning brow, she snapped it shut.

"That's first. You're used to having your way, but the world is a different place now, and I am a different man."

"And we've come out to this beautiful cove so you can scold me on my bad manners?"

"You didn't hear me when I said no, more than once, so yes, I'm scolding you on your bad manners. You don't know me, lady. I have nothing to lose here, and you've lost just about everything, so let's cut the bullshit."

Grace steadied herself and raised her chin proudly, feeling nothing of the kind. "All right, let's do. Your name is Judson Branch Marin. You were born in Cody, Wyoming on November 31, 1974. They call you John, after your grandfather. You are the only son of rancher Edmond the second, and Kathryn, nee Judson, and the eldest of five—the only boy. In 1998, your family sold off all the beef cattle and turned your property into one of the most popular dude ranches in the country. The Big Five. Sweet.

"You were a star at just about everything at Cody High and left as soon as you could for the United States Army. You became a Ranger, graduating first in your class. In 2005 you started a security firm, Marin and Associates. You hired and trained an elite group used in campaigns all over the Middle East. You saw how fruitless it all was, however, and sold the company in 2011. You joined the Secret Service and you were the Department of Homeland Security's first choice to cover the president. Matt was lucky to have you.

You're forty-four years old, and you haven't called home since the assassination, even though you're very close to your parents and four sisters. You have a very healthy bank account and no debt." Grace leaned forward and met his now angry glare. "I know you, Mr. Marin, and I want you."

Grace sat back, not out of pride at having done her homework so thoroughly, but because of the fiery rage on John Marin's face. She understood; she did. But, dammit, she needed him.

"You looked into me."

"Of course I did," she sniffed. "It wasn't difficult."

Marin was up off the storage box and had Grace on her feet in a flash. The bag of frozen vegetables fell to the deck, and Marin kicked it away. It opened, scattering frozen corn across the freshly scrubbed teak. Marin jerked her up on her toes and paid no attention to the wince on her face as her weight came down on the bad ankle.

"Let go of me," she ordered, her eyes blazing, her mouth pressed into a thin line. She hissed the order while she balanced on one foot, babying her injury.

"No, ma'am. You need to know what you're getting with me."

Grace locked eyes with him and saw something besides anger lurking their depths. It was primal, arrogant, proprietary. The man was all alpha, yet she was not afraid. In fact, she couldn't remember a time when she was more aroused. His nostrils flared, as if he could smell it on her. She glanced at his right hand, so large that her entire upper arm disappeared inside it. She shifted her eyes back to him and raised a perfectly shaped brow. It was time to break the tension. "I bruise easy," she murmured.

An overwhelming urge to put Grace Ashton Coolidge across his knee and tan her hide suffused his whole being.

That profound thought was followed by the startling realization that he might actually be hurting her, and in a way neither of them would get much out of. That was not his style.

"Dammit," he hissed, setting her down on the padded bench that wrapped around the stern of his sailboat.

"You're very upset with me, and I am sorry, truly." Her upper arm throbbed, but she refused to give him the satisfaction of rubbing it. "But I would expect that you, of all people, would wish for someone like me to check into things before putting one-hundred percent of my trust into an endeavor. Wouldn't you?"

Marin looked out to sea and took a deep, cleansing breath. And then he chuckled and shook his head. "Yeah, I guess so." Then he looked down at her. "I'm sorry. Did I hurt you?" It was then that he was reminded of her ice-blue eyes, so incredibly haunting and beautiful. They glistened in the tropical sun, and he wanted nothing more that to take back what he'd just done.

"No."

He brushed his fingers over her upper arm, where he'd grabbed her. It was red. She'd bruise, all right. He saw that with great clarity. He slammed his eyes shut. "Dammit. I'm sorry, Grace."

"Make it up to me. Help me," she whispered.

Marin stared out to sea again. He didn't even know why he was hesitating at this point. He took her in, a new admiration forming in his mind, not to mention his heart and points further south. It was right that she'd checked into him. Good for her. "As Special Agent to the President I made $160,000 a year."

"My heavens, that's not a lot."

"It is for two weeks' worth of my time."

"I said one week."

"And when is the memorial?" he asked.

"October twenty-third."

"And the dedication?"

"The fourteenth."

"If I take this job, Duchess, you won't be leaving this island without me, understood?"

Grace had to think about this. Such a mandate would mean bringing John Marin back to London. She was being forced into accepting protection so she could fulfill two more obligations before either considering a position dangled in front of her by President Bannish, or slipping into obscurity and taking a humble teaching position at the local village primary school, while living out the rest of her life in the Sussex countryside. Going directly to New York would make the threats to her irrelevant. Out of sight, out of mind, so to speak. If they went directly to New York from here, John Marin would be none the wiser. No, this caveat of his simply wouldn't do. Dammit! She should have waited a week to come here and beg, but as she'd told him already, she was desperate.

"Yes, of course," she answered after he raised an impatient brow at her.

"Good. And I want the money in advance, whether I work a month or five minutes."

She hesitated a fraction of a second before she said, "Done."

"What else aren't you telling me?"

Grace hesitated only a second before answering. "Nothing. That's it. I can't speak at the memorial, or at the U.S. Embassy without protection. Once the memorial in D.C. is over, your job is done." She clasped her hands in her lap.

"You sure?"

Grace hesitated. "Yes, of course." She felt instantly bad for lying to him, but what other choice did she have?

"All right. You will do exactly as I say; in other words, for the time that I am with you, I'm in charge."

Grace nodded.

"I sit next to you when we travel, and I sleep where you sleep." When her eyes came together in question, he amended. "Suites, no separate hotel rooms, or you'll rent an apartment. I'm in your space, not across the hall. I'm not your escort, I'm paid protection. That will be my only role, and that's how we'll both treat it."

"Fine." She swallowed hard, wondering suddenly what she'd gotten herself into.

"I attend every function you attend—I don't give a shit if it's lunch with your mother—and you stay on my hip when we're in public, no exceptions."

"All right." Her heart pounded; her core followed blindly.

"You'll hire a driver of my choosing, so I can have eyes on you and not on the road."

"Agreed. Is that all?"

"In short, Mrs. Coolidge, I lead, and you follow."

Grace vibrated at his words, and she was instantly ashamed. He was the exact kind of man she had no business admiring—yet admire him she did. He was rough-hewn and dominant; she was refined and civilized. He seemed to tower over her at well over six feet to her five and a half, and he was tough as nails. She was nothing of the kind, or so she believed. She sniffed to hide her embarrassment as it suffused her face like a stain. "I have a few rules of my own."

"I'm in charge."

"Yes, so you've said." Grace examined her nails. Pronouncing them flawless, she cleared her throat. "I will be attending a lot of functions, and I will need you to dress the part, so I'd like to meet in New York a day or two ahead of my scheduled functions so you can be outfitted appropriately. Of course, that expense will be on me." She scanned him up one side and down the other. "I don't imagine you have suits or a tuxedo stashed away in storage."

Marin straightened, and a black cloud suffused his entire being. "Mrs. Coolidge, you didn't hear me."

Grace batted her eyes in surprise. "Beg pardon?"

"You're under the impression that I'm the kind of man who can be manipulated. Is that what you think?"

"Of course not." Affronted, she placed a delicate hand to her chest.

"Then I'll say it one more time: you don't leave this island without me by your side, which means that unless you're flying to New York from here, I go where you go. And I'm not going into this without some preparation. Clear?"

She looked up at him, suddenly wondering at the wisdom of asking this rough, uncivilized man to protect her. God, he was infuriating, yet she needed him. And for some reason, what he thought of her mattered, seeing her vulnerable mattered, knowing her somewhat as opposed to not at all, mattered. She sighed in acquiescence. "I would like you to cut your hair, and shave your beard," she blurted.

"No."

"Sorry?"

"I said no. Anything else?"

Grace blinked several times in surprise and then chided herself as to why she was. John Marin was who he was, and that was why she wanted him, and no one else. "Not at the moment, no."

Marin sighed. "You shouldn't have come here, Mrs. Coolidge."

"Grace. So you've said. Is it possible to move on, or do you plan to beat this dead horse for the next week?"

Marin gave her a tight-lipped glare. "Two."

"Two, of course," she capitulated. "Thank you."

"Don't thank me yet. You may regret this."

"I just may," she grumbled.

"Back out now, then. No hard feelings."

"No," Grace said, shaking her head. She crossed her arm over her body and propped an elbow there. She slid a thumbnail delicately between her teeth and closed her eyes, raising her face to the sky. Raw emotion crossed her features. This wasn't hubris; it was relief. Something wasn't right. The quiver of her lips was impossible to miss. Her golden blond hair was short and thick and swept back off her face. In repose, like this, she looked regal, like a young Grace Kelly. He loved long hair on a woman, loved the way it flowed through his hands when he kissed her, or made love to her, but he was so mesmerized by this hair on this woman that he fisted his hands in his lap to keep from reaching out and lacing them deep into the pile of honey that just brushed the nape of her swan neck and swept up like a wave on top of her head. It made her look every inch the sophisticated lady. A pair of simple diamonds glittered in the tropical sun against a pair of delicate lobes, and the flowing fabric of her turquoise blouse undulated over her body in concert with the current of the serene Caribbean that surrounded them. He should say no; he should change his mind, right here and right now, and tell her no thank you and good-fucking-bye. Aloha on a steel guitar.

"Grace." She did not answer or move. *Sonofabitch.* "Duchess, look at me."

Her breath shuddered on a sigh. Her lips, pressed together, formed one thin line, and a single tear escaped from her closed lashes. Those same words caressed her ears on that deserted road outside of New Orleans when she felt catatonic in the wake of the brutal death of her husband.

Look at me. I said look at me, Mrs. Coolidge.

She had, then, and it had saved her.

Marin crouched down in front of her. He took her hands in his before she could swipe away that single, telling tear. "Open your eyes and look at me."

Grace shook her head in an attempt to throw off the sudden flood of emotions that came upon her like a tidal wave. She could not stop it—the sting along the bridge of her nose, the quiver of her mouth, the moisture that sat in her lashes and would soon slide down her face if she didn't get hold of herself. She never allowed herself this kind of emotion; why now? Why, oh why now? After some time, she opened her eyes and raised her chin.

"You're safe with me. I won't let anything happen to you."

"I certainly hope not," she whispered, "at $215 an hour."

"You can always say no, Duchess, and believe me, I won't suddenly show up in London to talk you into it."

She realized too late how she sounded and attempted a subtle backpedal. "I did that math in my head. I was trying to impress you."

One side of his mouth quirked up. "I'm impressed, ma'am, and that's not easy to do."

6

They spent two days in London shopping, and Marin was glad of it, for he took the opportunity to train the former first lady. Grace learned that this was far different from Secret Service protection. In the White House John Marin was one of several invisible agents who swept in to act at the first sign of trouble. Now he was an army of one and required her to think about what she was doing and follow some rules.

"As ungentlemanly as you might think it is, I won't carry your bags while we shop. I need to keep my hands free."

"I walk between you and the street, always. No exceptions."

"When I issue an order, you act immediately, or I will move you physically."

"My hand is on you at all times. You don't feel me, you stop."

Stunned at his lack of anything in terms of clothes, Grace outfitted him completely, from head to toe, for events from casual to the most formal. One large suitcase, a garment bag and a carryon would hold it all, and Marin didn't argue. He insisted Grace trust him with her life; he in turn had to trust her with his wardrobe.

Despite his reluctance to spend time shopping with a woman, he found Grace charming and funny, open and accessible to the sales people, and he enjoyed watching her face when he'd come out of the dressing room in clothes she'd chosen for him.

"That one, yes," she'd say, then, "But only if you like it."

Her scrutinizing gaze as he stood on a pedestal while a tailor measured him for his suits and tuxedo made him want to cooperate—and coming from a man who hated shopping at the grocery store, that was something. Grace had excellent taste, and with every new outfit, he felt like someone important. He liked her approval, her nod of acceptance of one outfit over another. And he enjoyed the breaks they took inside warm pubs off the beaten path, where she went unrecognized and unbothered by the patrons. He enjoyed their quiet conversations, her stories of living in the White House, and her memories of growing up the only child of a Duke and an American artist. Marin listened and spoke little about himself, a habit from his days working private security and in the Secret Service.

Marin had all the locks in Grace's London flat replaced, and a security system installed. He blacked out the windows to the street so that she could see out, but no one could see in. Once finished in London, they moved to the country.

Shannonfield Manor sat on one hundred acres just outside the village of Plaistow in West Sussex, south of London. It was not what John expected. The country house was old, warm and simple. The exterior of the house was trimmed in vertical wood, while the inside was a maze of small cozy rooms with old wood beamed ceilings and fire-places, a large kitchen, six bedrooms and eight bathrooms.

The property had beautiful outdoor grounds, three guest-houses and a pool. Except for the rain, he couldn't hear a thing.

Marin liked her flat in London but felt most comfortable at Shannonfield Manor. It reminded him of home—not that an old English country manor was anything like a log ranch home on two thousand acres. It was the peace he felt, the smell of horses and grass and land, and the way the woodsmoke from the many fireplaces had permanently infused every room in the house.

Grace kept a small staff at the manor. Sterling Jarvis, Grace's personal secretary, was a stiff, efficient man who seemed loyal and devoted to her. Jarvis hovered over Marin like the outsider he was, and Marin found he possessed the smallest amount of patience for it, and it was waning fast. An elderly housekeeper, Mrs. Mathilda Whipple, and her husband, Jasper, were the only other staff. Grace treated them like family, and he could see that she was very comfortable here, under their care.

Grace watched him through the window as he walked the property with Jasper Whipple, the manor caretaker, her gaze like butterfly kisses against his neck. The woman was stunning; there was just no other word for it. He didn't have much use for the porcelain, delicate types. With his big body, he was always afraid he'd break them. But this one, with the way she carried herself, the Queens English accent, her quiet dignity and natural sophistication, had him seeing things differently. Like an ethereal angel standing guard over a domain she seemed to neither need nor want, her intense scrutiny pricked at him like a frond of stinging nettles, and forced his back a little straighter, and tightened his resolve to see her safely through the next two weeks. She was the former first lady of the United States, and the widow of the late president. The need to shield and protect her, a trait long buried over the past year, felt disproportionate to the job he was hired to do. Grace Ashton Coolidge was a client, and that was it. The historical fondness he had for her, and her husband, was beside the point and, Marin was certain, had absolutely no bearing on his attraction to her. She was off limits, forbidden, yet he couldn't stop thinking about her when they were apart, and couldn't take his eyes off her when they were together. None of that mattered. She was a client; she was a job. That was it. That was all.

That Jasper Whipple had to repeat himself more than once on the tour forced Marin to shake off all personal thoughts of the lady in the window and concentrate on the task at hand.

GRACE SAT in the drawing room with a stack of papers in front of her and a fire blazing in the fireplace, when Marin came in about an hour later. Sterling Jarvis stood over her shoulder in conversation. Marin's presence was larger than life, his countenance one a man possessed when he was fully in charge, of himself and everyone else. Warmth slid down Grace's chest, and her heart quickened at his sudden arrival, like a stealth fighter: one minute, silence; the next, a bomb drops.

"You have a security system," Marin said. At the brusque interruption, the secretary looked up, muttered, "Excuse me," and left the room.

Marin stepped aside to let the man pass. Grace found herself spending great amounts of time trying to read him, figure him out, read the tea leaves. Was he angry, or just efficient? Did he like her, or was she just a job to him? How odd that she gave a damn how he felt, one way or the other. He was here to see her through the next two weeks, nothing more. Why, then, did she want to see him smile at her, just once?

She removed her reading glasses and nodded.

"Show me where it's set up."

Grace took him to a room between the kitchen and dining room. A numbered security pad and a separate pad that appeared to take a hand or finger print was next to it on the wall, and a bank of screens were set up, numbered to correspond to the various cameras that were set up throughout the property. They were dark.

"When was this installed?" Marin asked.

"Shortly after Matt took office, in case we wanted to spend time here. Turns out Camp David was closer."

"So Homeland Security was in charge?"

"Yes."

"And it was never finished."

"I suppose not," Grace answered. "I spent so little time here after Matt was elected."

"I'll look into it. You have a good system here, and we should be using it."

Grace walked along the wall of screens. "What is all this?"

"Well, the idea is that the screens are on all the time and correspond to the cameras that have been installed on the property. An agent would sit in the room as long and you and the president were here and watch. I'm guessing plans for fences were in the works."

"I believe so, yes." Grace pointed to a screen. "What's this one for?"

"I'll know more once I get everything working."

"I suppose my lack of knowledge regarding any of this goes to my reluctance to show too much happiness while I was here, afraid we'd never return if Matt thought it meant something to me." Grace shook off her complaining with a laugh. "You seem to know what you're doing with all this."

Her revelation about her husband shook Marin for a minute, and then he, too, shrugged it off. He wasn't here to analyze the Coolidge marriage, but something between anger and sadness settled in him nevertheless.

"I don't, but I have people who do. We'll be staying in the next day or two until I get this up and running."

"But I wanted to go into London tomorrow."

Marin narrowed his eyes at her. "What for?"

"A little shopping. Does it matter?"

"Yes. Unless it's vital, it'll have to wait. This is more important."

"That certainly isn't necessary," she said, trying to keep her sudden anger in check.

"I'd feel better about it."

"Well, Sterling can accompany me, then."

"I go where you go, remember?"

Grace sniffed. "You're being very difficult, it seems."

"No, I'm not." Marin pinned her with a glare. "I don't like repeating myself."

"So you've said—more than once." Grace smirked at her own *bon mot*. "Do you enjoy being this confrontational?"

"No, actually, I don't, Duchess, but repeating something I've said once already is annoying. Repeating something I've said five times is infuriating. Don't make me keep doing it."

Grace crossed her arms and studied him. *Duchess*. She smiled inwardly. His overbearing manner threw her off and, she was loathe to admit, she liked it; it made her feel special, and oddly normal. He was a man who would not defer to her, as he was forced to as an agent. She snapped out of her thoughts as the annoyance of imposed restriction crept up on her; she felt it plenty during her four years in the White House. But she also felt a sense of relief, and she had no idea what it meant or what to do with it. All she knew was that she felt better—safer—with John Marin around.

MARIN SAT at the desk in the library at Shannonfield House, three days from their departure to New York, and two days from the embassy dedication in London. A fire crackled in the fireplace, the smell of woodsmoke in the air. A cup of tea sat on the desk in front of Grace's now-vacant chair at the side of the desk, creamed and sugared the way she liked. His coffee, strong and black sat in a mug to his right. He could hear Grace outside the library in business-like conversation with Sterling Jarvis. Her perfume lingered, flowers and musk and *her*. And as he tried to concentrate on the work before him, he realized that a protectee's perfume had never entered his sphere, until now. He didn't like it. As if to mock him for such a lie, his cock stirred.

She was different here. Relaxed, easy, in good humor. They'd sat in companionable silence all morning, each going over the nine-day itinerary; he, with a fine eye, looking over hotel and apartment choices, venues in which she was scheduled to appear, and the homes of personal friends who insisted on throwing parties in her honor. Given the timing, Marin wanted to make sure the places in which Grace was scheduled to appear were secure. As first lady, her schedules had been handled for her, advance teams were dispatched ahead of time to secure hotels and venues. As a civilian for the last year, she'd simply gone wherever she wanted. She had some habits to shed, and a few to adopt before he was comfortable going to the U.S., or the embassy for the dedication.

"Lady Grace would like your thoughts on staying in Maryland for the D.C. portion of the trip," Jarvis said, standing the doorway.

"Why?" Marin said, looking up from his work and wondering why Lady Grace couldn't poke her own head in and ask herself.

"I think she would like to be out of the city. She feels more comfortable. She's maintained an apartment there since—" Jarvis shifted his eyes away, as if what came next was forbidden conversation. "—since leaving The White House."

"That should be fine," Marin said, knowing from experience how tragedy affected the victim's loved ones, too. Sterling Jarvis clearly cared for Grace, and in an odd way, that made Marin able to tolerate him a bit easier. The man wasn't all that bad. He shook off the sentiment with a terse, "I'll need blueprints for the building."

"The entire building?"

"The entire building."

"Very good."

"And, I need a legal pad, Jarvis. Do we have one anywhere?"

"Bottom drawer to your right, I believe."

"Thanks." Marin opened the drawer and shuffled some papers aside. A manila envelope, folded and banded around what felt like a brick of documents, sat on top of what he needed. He set the bundle on the desk and pulled out a yellow pad of paper. As he was putting the envelope back in the drawer he saw, written on the front in Grace's distinctive script, 'S.Y.' and below that, 'I. Devon'. It meant nothing to

him, so he tossed it back into the drawer and got back
to work.

———

IT WAS LATE AFTERNOON, and Marin hadn't looked up since
late morning. He'd skipped lunch, recalling vaguely that it
had been offered and promptly rejected in favor of
another cup of coffee. The only thing keeping Jarvis
around, to Marin's way of thinking, was his skill in that
department. He'd never had better coffee in his life. He
heard Jarvis rattling around outside the office and looked
at the clock—3:47. Teatime. Marin laughed at the absur-
dity of taking time out in the late afternoon for tea and
cake, or sandwiches, but on this day, he was actually
looking forward to the break. He was hungry, his eyes
ached, and he hadn't seen Grace much all day. Jarvis
carried in a tray holding the fancy flowered teapot, three
matching cups and a plate of sandwiches ringed with tiny
muffins.

"I'm going to wake Lady Grace for tea. She's having a
nap. Fancy a cup, Mr. Marin?"

"Today, I would, Jarvis. Thanks."

"Good. Be back in a jiff." As he turned to go, the phone
rang, and Jarvis about-faced and picked up the extension on
the library desk.

"Shannonfield Manor, Ashton House," he answered.

Marin stood, stretched and came around the desk to
grab a sandwich.

"Inspector Devon, yes, of course...the lady is indisposed
at the moment. May we return?"

Marin stopped in mid-reach of a cucumber sandwich
and turned to the secretary. *Devon.* "Very good," he contin-

ued. "We'll return straight away." Jarvis hung up the phone. "Excuse me while I go wake Herself."

As soon as Jarvis left the room, Marin returned to the desk, opened it, and extracted the bundled envelope. 'I. Devon' had to be 'Inspector Devon'. That was now clear to him. S.Y., however... It took Marin a full minute before it came to him: Scotland Yard. He opened the envelope and dumped the contents on the desk. He used a pen to unfold the first piece of paper that fell out because, folded or not, one word got his attention. In large, bold black font, was the word *KILL*.

WE KILLED HIM, WE CAN KILL U 2

Marin looked up, red clouding his eyes. He set his hands flat on the desktop and looked out the window into the misty countryside. "Sonofabitch!"

"YOU MAKE a terrible lady's maid, Sterling," Grace said, entering the library. "Do join us for—" She stopped cold when she saw the desk littered with the familiar missives she'd packed away and tried to forget, and the absolute look of rage on John Marin's face.

"You could do with two lady's maids, judging by the condition of your roo—" Sterling Jarvis halted next to his mistress and he, too, faltered. Grace glanced at him, he glanced at her, and they both turned their eyes to the stone-faced man standing behind the desk with his arms folded. The air was thick with tension as Marin glared, first at Sterling Jarvis.

"What's this?" Jarvis asked, glancing at the paper-strewn desk, then turning to Grace.

"You didn't know about this?" Marin said.

The man's Adam's apple bobbed as he stared at the pile of missives on the desk. "Uh...er...".

"Excuse us, please. I'd like to talk to Grace alone."

Sterling Jarvis turned to Grace for permission, and jumped when Marin barked, "Now!"

The small man scooted out of the room as if dodging a snapped towel to his bare ass. Marin turned his steely eyes on Grace. Her heart slammed against her chest and she couldn't breathe. "John, I—"

"What the hell is this? Never mind, I can damn well see what it is. This is what you were afraid of. This is why you were so desperate for help."

"No, I, er...I was forced into..." Grace forced a swallow past a lump in her throat.

"Enough!" Marin gripped the edge of the desk until his knuckles turned white. "You lied to me."

She could only nod in acquiescence.

"What were you thinking?"

Grace shook her head, at a loss of where to begin.

"You weren't. That's the only right answer." Brows the color of winter wheat crashed together, forming a V above the bridge of a strong nose. A pair of deep furrows creased a weathered brow, and a pair of eyes the color of new, unwashed denim bore into her. The gray mist outside did not come close to matching Marin's black countenance. Grace felt herself shrinking before him like a child about to be spanked for something she knew she'd done wrong. Her tummy fluttered and something else tingled farther south. She found it hard to stand. Biceps bulged from beneath the tight black t-shirt he wore, flexing as he leaned against the desk. Faded jeans the color of a fall sky hugged his hips, a worn black belt securing them to his waist. The gloomy chill from outside seemed to have worked its way in, as Grace drew further into her worn indigo cardigan, and her legs grew suddenly chilled under snug gray slacks before turning to jelly. Under his angry, scrutinizing gaze she felt positively shredded. She was not in fear of him; it was his approval and his regard she sought, and that was now in jeopardy.

"I—I'm sorry, John. I don't know what to say.

"I'm sure you are." Marin straightened. "And I'm sure you don't." He waved a hand over the desk absently. "This is not how I work, Grace."

"I know."

"I told you what I'd put up with. We had an understanding, didn't we?"

"So, you're leaving then?" The question came out on a shaky whisper. It was not lost on Marin, for he turned his angry eyes on her.

"That about covers it."

7

*G*race sat rigid in the chair as Marin's loud chastisements directed at Sterling Jarvis shook the walls outside the library, and she cringed as the familiar clomp of his black boots reverberated through the house as he climbed the stairs to the second floor. The ceiling above her shook as he made the journey to his room, directly across from hers, anger seeping out of every step he took.

The door to the library opened slowly, and Sterling Jarvis's face peered around the jamb.

"Dear God," he whispered. "Are you all right?"

"Yes, of course," she answered, a thumbnail secured between her teeth.

"I don't believe I've ever seen a human being that angry," her ever-capable servant reflected. "What would you like me to do?"

"Stand by, please, and do whatever he says, answer whatever questions he has. Do not lie; do not attempt to protect me, please."

"You didn't tell him?"

"Obviously I didn't."

"Whatever were you thinking, Grace?"

"That's just what he said."

Jarvis sighed. "Shout if you need me. I'll be cowering in the kitchen with Mrs. Whipple and a cup of strong and heavily sugared tea, laced with your very best brandy. Would you like one?"

Grace shook her head and closed her eyes at the gentle snick of the door closing. What would Marin do now, she wondered. Would he leave her? Had she shared all this with him, surely he would not have outright forbid her from attending the scheduled events. After all, that was why he was hired—to accompany her and keep her safe. Threatening missives or no, his tasks wouldn't change.

She wasn't thinking clearly; she hadn't since May. Telling Marin the whole truth made all of this too real. Perfectly reasonable, then, to sweep it all under the rug and get through her trip to the states with her head buried snugly in the sand. The burden she carried was tremendous. It was possible that John Marin was the one person she could trust —wasn't it?

How ridiculous it all seemed now as she stared at the papers laid out on the desk, the bold words jumping off the page at her like daggers, sending a chill up her spine and setting regret firmly in her heart.

BITCH

KILL

DIE

TRAITOR

MAY

Yes. May. The pages haunted her since the first one arrived by post several months ago, up until the last one, found tucked inside her purse, of all things, over a week ago.

What ever would she do?

MARIN PACED the length of his room. Decorated in blues, tans and browns, it was as close to the perfect man's room as anything he'd ever seen, yet all he saw now was red, rimmed in coal black. He swore aloud as he paced, the pages upon pages of threats and disparaging words meant to insult, hurt and frighten the former first lady looming in front of him like hovering ghosts.

The woman needed to be shaken until her teeth fell out, but that didn't lessen the terror she must feel now and had felt for however long this had been going on. He'd been out of touch with everything, including news from the U.S., for a year. God only knew what Grace had endured in that time, with no one, to his knowledge, to whom she could turn, except Sterling Jarvis. The hapless assistant knew what was going on, and he did nothing. But that wasn't entirely true: Jarvis had called him on his lady's behalf.

Marin had been trained to see certain things, and he knew when someone was lying, or keeping something from him. He knew there was something else. Why hadn't he pressed her, if not on the boat, then once he got here, when there was no going back? A year away from reality, and a brain muddled by decent rum could put a man off his game. Marin ran his hand through his hair, pulling it from its banded queue. The rubber snapped and flew across the room, landing on the plaid down comforter on his bed, on top of which sat his suitcase, the tags still on. He should be packing right now—and fuck yes, he was keeping the clothes. Goddamn her!

He stalked to the diamond leaded beveled glass window

and looked down onto the grounds. One hundred acres, no fucking working security system, and Grace kept this major detail from him for almost a week. How could he possibly protect her when she hid things like this from him? More importantly, why did she do it?

He growled into the quiet room, and he noticed for the first time that someone had lit his fireplace for him. It was getting toward evening, and the last couple of nights, coming into a warm room, a fire already burning and a bed of coals hot enough to ignite the new logs he'd toss on top was nice. It was civil—Jarvis's doing, no doubt.

Truth was, the longer he stood there, looking out over the fog that now covered most of the property, the more he saw that the reason for her terror would remain, even if he left—and leave he should. But he wasn't leaving Grace, and he knew it. Deep down, she probably knew it, too. As he stood looking out over the expansive property, unsecured so that anyone could just stroll right on up, he vowed he's stop babying her.

"Fuck," he muttered. His name on a soft whisper had him turning to face the lady herself, standing in the doorway, her arms crossed over her middle and a look of terror in her eyes. She looked small, and contrite.

"Tell me what I must do to fix this," she said with a shuddering whisper. Wrapped in that worn cardigan, a thin pink t-shirt barely skimming the top of figure hugging slacks, she looked like a scared teenager, no longer the strong, sexy, confident woman he'd come to know. In her eyes, John Marin saw fear—not like the night her husband was assassinated, but damn close. He would not be manipulated, he told himself, as the slightest pain settled in his chest. Marin shook his head. He felt himself weakening, unable to tear himself away from this haunted woman. Her porcelain complexion had lost all its peaches and cream and had gone gray. Unshed tears gathered in her lashes, threatening to fall. God, how he wanted to take her in his arms and soothe her, then throttle her until her eyes rolled back in her head. Her face changed, as if he'd spoken his thoughts aloud.

"Get that look off your face, Duchess." He stalked toward her, stopping just short of snatching her into his embrace.

"What look?"

"I'm not interested in the doe-eyes and the wobbling lip. What did I tell you I'd do if you broke the rules?"

"You...you said you'd leave, 'be gone' is how you put it, I believe."

"And what makes you think I won't do exactly that?"

"I believe you will, if I don't try and stop you."

"Yeah? And how will you do that?"

"I don't know," she said, her voice barely above a whisper. And then all thoughts of leaving her went right out the beveled windows when Grace Ashton Coolidge took two steps toward him and fell into his arms.

Marin slammed his eyes shut as his arms went around her, encircled her before he thought it through, and tightened before he could pull away. He had no business comforting her. What she needed was a stiff and unyielding hand across her backside half a dozen times—his preferably. The very idea caused his cock to stir in sync with a shot of electricity that made way up his body and into his brain, where all thought ceased—at least for the moment.

"This isn't over." He intended to growl those words, show her his anger. But what came out was muted and tender, with the slightest hint of authority. She pushed away until she could look up into his eyes.

"I know."

Her face was innocent, earnest, contrite. It pulled something long-buried from him before he could stop it.

"Think about how you're not going to do this again."

Grace folded her arms and the slightest smirk crossed her lips. "Are you putting me in a time-out?"

"I think you have it coming," he said.

"Daddy's angry," she whispered.

Something so primal stirred in him that he had to take a step back. He buried his hands under his arms so he wouldn't grab her by the arms and shake the life out of her. He eased them into a stern fold. If Grace Coolidge wanted Daddy, she'd found the right one. His cock ceased stirring and lengthened, causing him to shift on his feet to lessen the discomfort. His brows crashed together.

"You think this is a joke?"

"No," she whispered.

"Good." He brushed past her and turned in the doorway. "Think."

MARIN SPENT the next few hours on the phone after leaving her standing in his bedroom, empty of his embrace and a renewed sense of foreboding. The comfort she felt in his arms, that moment of tenderness and, dare she say, forgiveness, disappeared with a two-word tease from her to lighten the mood. While she wasn't sorry she said it, she was sorry he didn't care for it. *Daddy* was all she could come up with at his countenance and attitude. It fit; she'd said it. Now she felt like a fool. She would apologize. This was serious, and she knew it.

She released herself from her own self-imposed time-out after about an hour and came downstairs to chaos. Marin had ordered Sterling to pack for the London flat immediately—or Siberia; it was all the same to Sterling. He was not being paid to watch Sterling Jarvis, he told her, and she could do without him until after the trip. And then he sent the Whipples packing as well. He would not hear a moment of Grace's protestations on the matter, and that made her all the more furious. A dozen times she found herself questioning the wisdom of asking him to stay.

Her secretary hadn't been happy. "Just for now, just until we get settled. Please, Sterling, darling, don't worry." At those words, Marin stuck his head out the library doors and set a glare upon Grace that chilled her blood. Then he turned the same one on Sterling Jarvis, which caused the man to jump, break wind, and flee to the guesthouse he lived in to pack. Satisfied, Marin slammed the library doors where, as far as Grace knew, he still remained. Left-overs she'd warmed up for supper sat uneaten, congealing in a pan.

Grace exited the shower, dried off, and slipped a soft pink printed silk chemise over her head along with a matching robe. She pulled a hairbrush through her hair and thought about the formidable man who was still quite furious with her, as if those few moments cocooned in his arms meant nothing—or worse, never happened. What was it about John Marin that made her conscious to the point of self-criticism at the very breaths she took in and out? In past dealings, for instance, if she ran into him in the residence at the White House, her first thought always was to check her hair, or breathe into her hand to check for fetid odor. And she was a woman devoted to her husband, loved him even. Yet John Marin had always made her feel tipped sideways. They didn't make men like John Marin anymore.

Refreshed and ready to fall into bed, Grace walked out of the bathroom, hairbrush still in hand, and screeched.

Marin stood against the doorjamb of her bedroom and ran his eyes down her body and back up again, settling on the wide wooden hairbrush in her hand. Grace pulled it from her hair, held it behind her back in both hands, and twisted it like a pretzel. When he met her eyes, Grace could not deny the anger that still lay there. She'd scowled at him all day; it seemed easier than begging him to forgive her. After all, she was proud, too. Now, standing before him, his forgiveness was all she wanted.

"You startled me." Grace pinned him with a glare. "What if I'd been in the nude?"

"Library," he snapped. "We need to talk."

She brought her hand up to her chest, taking the hairbrush with her. "Shall I change?"

Marin looked her up and down and shook his head once. "Not on my account."

"All right." She let out a breath only when he'd reached the stairs, taking them down, two at a time. With a huff she tossed the brush on top of her antique walnut vanity with a veiled curse, cinched her robe closed and journeyed downstairs to face an angry Mr. Marin.

Grace entered the library on shaky legs. The tea tray Jarvis had set up earlier in the day still sat on a side table, against a wall across from the desk where Marin stood in a rage hours ago. The teapot was ice cold, the sandwiches and mini muffins now hard and stale. Marin paced in front of the desk, where offensive missives had been replaced with a legal pad, a pen, her closed laptop, and a glass filled to a third with dark liquid. He held the same in his hand. A fire crackled in the fireplace. A lamp in the corner of the room and another on the desk cast calm light over the emotionally charged room.

"Sit down," he said without looking at her. Grace took

one of the chairs in front of the desk, a familiar place she took when she and her father would slip into the cozy library for a nightcap and a chat after her mother had gone to bed. John Marin looked no less formidable than her father had, and still did. Grace took the glass of whiskey between her hands and took a tentative sip.

"Before you go any further," she began, "there's more."

Marin set his backside against the desk next to her, bringing a set of wide hips and a distinctive bulge created by the crossing of his feet as he leaned, directly in her sightline. "What?"

"The carriage house."

"The carriage house?"

"Yes. You see, there was an accident."

"An accident."

"Well, it wasn't an accident, really."

"No?"

"No."

"Show me." One scan at her limited attire and he amended his order. "Never mind. Don't move out of that chair."

Grace sighed in defeat and nodded once.

When he returned ten minutes later, Grace couldn't believe that he was angrier than before, but he was.

"All right, talk." And as he thought about what he saw when he opened the double doors of the makeshift garage that separated the manor house from the stables, his face flamed, heat rising off him like a fever. The front end of the two-toned green Bentley was smashed in. Glass lay on the seats and floor of the vehicle like ice chips.

"I was none the worse for the wear, thank God, but my driver, well…"

"I can see that," he said, scanning her again. His voice

was pitched low, and even though Grace knew it was lowered in anger, her body still clenched in arousal.

Dear God.

"Well, I was shopping at Alexander McQueen..."

Marin arched a brow.

"...On Bond Street," she continued, as if that was all the explanation he needed, "And when I came out there was commotion. The Bentley was on the walk against a pole and Jamison was being tended to by a medic, and then I was whisked away by a detective from Scotland Yard."

Hands on his hips, Marin gripped them until he felt pain. "Jarvis know?"

"Yes," she answered.

"And he told no one."

"Correct, upon my order."

Marin's eyes narrowed. "Not smart."

"So you've said."

"Were the police called?"

"Yes...well, not called. They showed up."

"And what was their take on the accident?"

Grace sighed. "Witnesses stated that the driver of the car went out of his way to cause the accident."

"Was the driver cited, arrested, anything?"

"No," Grace reported sadly. "He...fled."

"Of course he did. And were those threats in your desk shared with anyone in authority, was two and two put together by anyone?"

"I didn't tell them about the missives, no."

"Of course not. That would be the intelligent thing to do."

Grace glared at him. "You're very rude."

"And you're very stupid." Marin paced the floor behind her as she stared at the drink in her lap. No one had ever

spoken to her in this way, not even Matt. Her late husband
could be cruel, but somehow her memories of their quarrels
paled in comparison to what John Marin said to her now.

"Is this it, now? Is this all you have to tell me?"

She paused a brief moment before answering in the
affirmative. Decision made, it made her feel no better,
or safer.

"Are you sure?"

Grace nodded, avoiding his eyes.

"Even if you think it's unimportant," he said, "I want to
know about it."

"There's nothing more."

"Homeland Security seen any of this?"

"No."

"Do they know any of this?"

"No," she said, a hint of desperation in her voice. "And
they mustn't."

"Why not?"

Again, Grace was silent, contemplating all the ways
things were going south. "I don't trust them."

Marin, too, was quiet for longer than Grace was comfortable with. "I don't work this way."

"I know."

"But, I don't blame you for not trusting them. I don't
either."

Grace sighed again, this time with relief. "You must
think me so foolish—and stupid, clearly."

Marin was indeed about to blast her for her foolishness,
but at her words something dark in him lightened and
tenderness came over him unlike anything he'd ever felt.
Tenderness did not come easily to John Marin; he couldn't
afford it. This, with this *woman*, was different. Despite it all,
if Grace were his, she wouldn't sit for a week.

He walked over to the fireplace and warmed his back. Grace got up, and after he uttered no objection, took a seat in one of the wingback chairs by the fire, a chill coming over her so suddenly she shivered.

"Keeping this from me was foolish, Grace, but you're no fool. And I shouldn't have called you stupid. I apologize."

Grace nodded.

"How did you expect me to help you without knowing about those letters and that someone fucking...? Sorry." Marin took a deep breath and tried again. "Someone rammed into your car. Can you explain to me what the hell you were thinking?"

"Will you be swearing at me all night?"

"Least of your worries. Tell me about those letters—everything. Start from the first one you received." And she did, ending with the last one, found in her purse.

Marin shook his head. "You need your goddamn ass spanked."

Grace jumped as if startled, and heat shrouded her entire body, beginning with an intense tingle in her scalp. His words came out of him deep and low, and so quietly that she barely heard him, yet the effect was more potent than if he had screamed the words at her in a rage, or, God forbid, actually done it. This man, standing in front of her with his appalling ego, the unmitigated gall, the alpha confidence he wore like an expensive suit that automatically gave him the right, whether he truly had it or not, to say such a thing to her—*to her*—as he warmed his bloody back in front of her fire! Something electric zinged between her legs, and she squirmed in her seat as tears bloomed in her eyes. She stared at the fire, blinking rapidly to hold them at bay.

"And I suppose you're just the man for the job."

"I am, and if need be, I'll take it. You won't even have to

pay me." Marin didn't care at this point what she thought, and in fact he was daring her to fire him. All his problems would be solved. Hers of course, would be exacerbated. This gave him all the permission he needed to take the lady in hand if he felt the need. He had nothing to lose.

"I'd like to see you try," she said, her voice shaking. Suddenly her *Daddy* reference didn't seem so off-base. And to think she considered apologizing for it.

"No, you wouldn't."

She opened her mouth to speak further, say something snippy, or conjure up some sort of affronted tone, but it snapped shut very much on its own. It took her a minute to regroup.

"You've decided to stay on, then."

Marin shook his head. Jaw tight, he wanted to lash out. He never should have said yes to this woman, yet now, standing here with his back warm, and her scent invading his very soul, he couldn't remember why his reluctance at the beginning was so strong. He had to have known, standing on that boat while she rolled her twisted ankle, perspiration glistening on her forehead and upper lip, reciting his fucking CV to him with a plea in her voice masking her misplaced pride, that he would have agreed to ride into the depths of hell for her.

"You won't do this again," he said, with all the confidence of a man who believed that exact thing to be true. Grace swallowed hard and shook her head, the heat now dissipating as a chill ran up her arms. Blast and damn that incessant jolt of electricity that insisted on caressing her in places that hadn't been touched in a while. Marin stood over her, drink in hand and a stern look on his face.

"Go to bed." He moved from the fire and stood behind her. "I have work to do."

Grace's mouth fell open until she believed her chin might crash into her lap. "I beg your pardon?"

"You heard me," he said behind her.

She stood and pulled herself up to her full height. "How dare you! I'll not be sent to bed like a bloody child." She tossed her head and lifted her chin in defiance. "You forget yourself, John."

The flicker of the fire reflected in Grace's defiant eyes. Her jaw tightened, and her mouth set into a thin line John Marin didn't much care for. He'd gone too far, and he knew it, yet he was still here—and so was she. This woman needed a strong hand, and by her body language, she knew it, too. The desire to take her across his lap was overwhelming. Naturally dominant, he only fantasized about taming the woman in his life, and the fact that his endeavors in that department weren't terribly successful spoke to why he was alone. Yet, here he stood, in the fancy library of a fancy country home, wanting nothing more than to bring the former first lady to heel in a way that would please them both immensely.

Jesus, she was beautiful. All fired up over something he said lit its own fire deep inside him. Not one to rile a woman on purpose, he found that with her he could become addicted to giving her a hard time, and then taking the fire right out of her. Her eyes sparkled; her pretty mouth was set in a defiant moue, and the stiff back she maintained caused her unencumbered breasts to present themselves through her thin garments, puckered nipples and all. How badly he wanted to pull her arms behind her back, unburden her of that robe and whatever was underneath, and pluck and suck those upturned tips until she was in tears. And then he would spank her, good and hard. The thought of his large

handprint glowing on her gorgeous ass caused his dick
to jerk.

Jesus, calm down, Marin, he chided himself. *She's a client
and nothing more.*

A client and nothing more.

A client and nothing more.

Satisfied that he'd turned a corner, despite the diamond
cutter that still plagued him by throbbing against the front
of his jeans, Marin set his drink down on the desk, and in
half a step he was in front of her. He snatched her by the
arm, spun her around and backed her against the desk. He
loomed over her, one hand flat on the desk, the other still
wrapped around her upper arm. Her mouth quivered. If she
were his, he'd have her over the desk and her gown off in a
heartbeat.

If she were his.

If she were his.

If she were his.

"Let me go." Fear flickered in her eyes before lust took
over. Grace Ashton Coolidge didn't appear to carry a
submissive bone in her body, but there was something
about the way he was handling her that turned her on.
Marin had been trained to read body language, and he read
hers now, like a third-grade primer. He could see it; he could
smell it. Despite her indignant outrage, the former first lady
did not want the upper hand—not really, not now. She'd
done wrong, and she knew it. She was a proud woman
who'd just been scolded for her actions, and then ordered to
bed. He'd taken a chance, saying what he did, and he got the
expected reaction. He cocked one side of his mouth up, but
the gesture did not reach his eyes.

"Quiet, Duchess." He jerked her up and brought his
mouth crashing down over hers. He let go of her arms and

brought one hand up to clasp her jaw and laced the other into her hair. He'd been dying to lace his big hand in that cloud of honey for days, and now that he had those heavy tresses in his fist, he pulled her head back, held her jaw still, and swarmed through her mouth with his tongue, licking, setting the pace, taking his time. Grace did not fight him, but instead fell right into line. She went limp in his arms and moaned desire into his mouth as he moved her to his liking, controlling her every move as he kissed her.

God, she was spoiled, and she was frightened. He would keep her safe, but by all that was holy, the woman would obey the rules. She tasted like roses and whiskey and something deeper, exotic, fresh. On a different night, under different circumstances he'd have her coming where she stood. But tonight, here, now, the woman needed taming. And she needed to be reassured. Why he believed kissing the life out of her would accomplish either of those goals, he'd ponder in the light of new day. For now, in this moment, Grace had been right: he had forgotten himself.

Nevertheless, Marin drifted his hand down—the one that wasn't locked in her hair—tracing the ridges of her spine until he came to the swell of her hips, flaring out from her narrow waist. He ran the flat of his hand over the swell of her firm bottom, and Grace gasped in his mouth, her eyes wide. Not taking his off hers, his hand left her hip and he brought it down with a snap, right where her bottom met her thigh. Out of line. Completely out of line. But when Grace deepened the kiss with a soft moan, Judson Branch Marin found himself profoundly lost. He'd tested the waters, and he found them the perfect temperature.

The moment he snatched her up, Grace's knees went weak and a pool formed between her legs. Her hands tightened around his biceps, hard as rock. The hand laced in her hair scalded her scalp. There was anger in this kiss, anger and determined domination. His tongue moved through her mouth, in and out, taking his time, taking control, his taste scotch and cilantro, cedar and vanilla. Her tongue tangled with his in what she knew would be a losing battle. Grace was angry and embarrassed, and she felt foolish, very foolish, yet not one thing Marin said tonight had been a lie. Out of line? Perhaps. And that seemed to rekindle her ire, yet she couldn't summon an ounce of righteous anger with which to lash out at him. And then he swatted her. And then she managed a teeny-tiny orgasm.

The kiss ended as abruptly as it began when Marin separated from her mouth by yanking her head back. He looked down at her. Her eyes asked for more; his denied her. She'd been naughty, and naughty girls didn't get kissed, he wanted to tell her. A deep furrow creased his brow, and his lips set themselves in one flat line.

"You deserved that," he growled, giving her a little shake.

A ghost of a smile formed on her pretty mouth. "Indeed."

"More of it and you might settle into a semi-obedient woman." Shock and anger warred within her until Grace threw her head back and laughed. It was a throaty laugh, sincere and without the slightest guilt or guile. Still, it irked him. He took her chin between his thumb and forefinger. "Careful, woman," he growled.

"I'm sorry. I'm not laughing at you—unless amusing me was your intent."

"It might have been—a little."

"I thought so."

"Not one damn thing about tonight was funny, lady."

"I know. Will you be giving me another thorough kissing, then, to make sure I don't forget it?"

"Keep it up, Duchess, and I will give you more than a kiss, and I'll deliver it much farther south." Marin waltzed her none too gently to the double doors of the library.

"Bed," he said in her ear. He gave her a gentle shove through the door and planted a sharp swat to the seat of her silk robe. Grace turned on him, ready to pounce. Marin pulled himself up to his full height and pierced her with a stare.

"Go ahead, Grace, say it. Tell me I'm out of line, that I have no right."

"You son of a—"

Marin placed his thumb over parted lips. "Say it, Duchess, and I'll wash that pretty mouth out with soap." And then he smiled, and a smile for John Marin was a twitch of the mouth and a brightening of the eyes, for only a moment. "Bed. Now," he whispered.

Grace gave him one more lethal look before she turned and headed for the stairs, and he watched her until she disappeared before closing the door amid a litany of curses. He grabbed the back of the chair Grace just vacated, and where she sat most of the day, where he could smell her tea and her perfume, and listen to her lilting voice, like a fucking lullaby in his ear.

The kiss had been a mistake. He'd never been so angry with anyone, least of all a beautiful woman like Grace Ashton Coolidge. She made his blood boil, and not just because of the nasty letters that fouled the desk drawer in front of him, or because of the accident that surely could have ended her life, had she been in that car. No, she made his blood boil because there was something about her, something special that he'd noticed for the first time the day he was assigned to the presidential detail. From that first day, he watched her, too. It took no thought when he scooped her up and carried her to safety when all appeared lost with her husband. And now he was here, in her home, watching her move, smelling her perfume, and wondering how he was going to get through this next two weeks without either fucking her until she couldn't walk, or spanking her until she couldn't sit.

GRACE SLIPPED off her robe and stared into the vanity mirror. Her nipples protruded through the thin chemise, and a delicious sting in the shape of Marin's hand bloomed on her bottom. She was falling for him. This man had always had an effect on her, and his mouth on hers, his hand in her hair, and his grip on her arms, and his sharp hand on her backside exacerbated already confused feelings. This wasn't the time for a new relationship; especially with a man who had been hired to protect her. Her upper arms were red, the shape of his fingers evident on her pale skin. They would bruise. His taste lingered on her tongue.

You need your goddamn ass spanked...

"Jesus," Grace muttered as she took her hairbrush to her blond mane. This very thing had been in her deepest, darkest, quietest fantasies for years, never uttered, never admitted to anyone, for they were hers and hers alone. Now that those fantasies could become a reality, she thought about the old adage of being careful what you wished for.

Marin was getting closer to the truth, and she wondered how she would keep him at bay until they arrived in Washington. Nothing would stop her now, not even John Marin.

Grace turned off the lights, slipped into bed and fell asleep with John Marin in her thoughts, and a throb in the shape of his fingers on her arms.

8

*G*race woke later than usual and didn't like the reason for it one bit. The larger than life man who currently occupied the room across the hall also occupied her thoughts throughout the night, waking her every couple of hours. Common decency and a woman's rebellious nature nudged her to toss him out on his ear today without further delay. *Ass spanked, indeed!* The practical side reminded her that she needed him, and it would take a small army to get him out of her way and out of her life now. It wasn't what she wanted in any event. It was clear now that only he could get her to her goals unscathed. She was safe with him, under him. She would do what she needed to do, and John Marin would see to it, whether he knew it or not.

She assessed her wardrobe in the full-length mirror—gray jeans, a long maroon sweater and black shoe-boots. The outfit exuded casual confidence, which she didn't feel in the least. It was neat but not overdone for a day around the house, or perhaps into town for some shopping.

All was quiet downstairs as she stood at the kitchen

window while the smell of freshly brewed coffee filled the room. Without Mathilda Whipple, Grace felt lost. How utterly ridiculous. She was perfectly capable of making coffee, or tea, or putting together a teatime, or making a full meal for dinner. But right now she needed the formidable woman around just because. At the very least she'd act as a buffer between herself and...*Himself*. She was at sea; she needed guidance, for she feared that without it, she would do something dreadful—like greet him for tea in the nude.

John Marin stood outside with his back to the house, and her view, in the middle of the circular driveway. She counted seven men surrounding him; who they were and where they came from, she hadn't a clue. She leaned her hip against the sink and held her coffee between her hands as she watched Marin address the group, his over-large hands cupped in front of him, as if he held every answer to every question

All the men who surrounded him were big, they all wore black, and all of them were armed. They stood as if at attention while Marin spoke. He stood balanced, legs apart, hands gesturing. His outfit of faded jeans, heavy dark blue sweater and black boots was no less formidable than what the others wore, yet it was clear he was the one in charge. Within minutes, the group came up the walk as a unit, and entered the kitchen. The room was suddenly filled with testosterone and the chill of an early morning fall in the English countryside.

Marin was different this morning. His countenance was one of indecipherable affect, reminding her of their encounter last night. She wondered if it kept him up all night like it did her.

"Good morning," she said. The men nodded and murmured the greeting in return.

"Good morning," Marin said. "Lady Grace Ashton Coolidge, guys." They each stepped forward and stuck their hands out for a shake. John introduced them: there was Dopey, Sleepy, Sneezy, Happy, Bashful, Grumpy and Doc. Only the one called Grumpy lingered, his blue-gray eyes holding hers, his overlarge hand engulfing her delicate one. He was overly familiar, with his flirty eyes and cocky smile; men like him were nothing new to her, nor was she all that impressed. Marin seemed unappreciative of his man's lingering attentions and didn't try to hide his annoyance with a sharp cough that broke the spell. A sly grin and a wink from this handsome ginger alpha-dog still clasping her hand communicated that he cared not a whit that his boss wished to move on.

"Are you Snow White, then?" she asked, glancing at Marin as Grumpy gave her hand a final squeeze and let go.

"No, sweetheart; you are." An icy chill swept over Grace as Marin turned to the men. "Thanks, guys. I'll be in touch. You know what to do." As each one nodded to her with a soft, "Ma'am" as they passed, Grace settled on one man, his almost black eyes meeting hers for a moment before he looked away. He was plain; nothing stood out, and in fact he was of average size, smaller than the other men, but equal in countenance. His head was shaved, and a shadow of growth circled the lower half of his head. His features were sharp and of little distinction. He looked to be the same age as the rest of the men—late thirties to mid-forties. He was like a hundred men who walked the London streets every day. He looked like the waiter at Dreswald's, the stock boy at Greene's, a taxi driver in London. In short, he was nothing special, yet he made her skin crawl. And, she'd seen him before, she was sure of it. It would come to her in time.

Grace shook it off as nothing more than the stress of the

prior day, and what Marin now knew. He'd brought in his big guns, and they were an overwhelming bunch. Marin closed the door behind him, and only the one called Doc remained. Grace soon forgot about the one who made her so uneasy.

Doc was enormous, yet he had been almost dwarfed by the one called Happy, a grim-faced Samoan who had to turn sideways to get out her kitchen door. Doc stood before her, his milk chocolate moon face open and intelligent, his grin wide and full of mischief, and his heavy square glasses gave him the look of a goofy nerd. But, Grace was not fooled. Underneath that sweet, kind exterior lived a warrior. His arms were the size of her thighs, and her hand disappeared into his when he shook it. His countenance was confident, and his eyes were direct—two traits she appreciated in a person. He wore a large sidearm on his hip.

"Grace, Doc will be traveling with us in the states, he'll secure any vehicles we need, and he'll do the driving. Doc spent ten years in Special Ops and he's a trained level-one trauma physician. He can also turn a stretch limo around on a dime."

"How do you do?" Grace nodded in his direction. "And the others?" she asked.

"They'll be helping us out in various capacities. You don't need to know more than that, for now. Know that there's no one I trust more than these guys, Grace. They've been briefed, and except for just now, you'll likely never see them again, except Doc here." Marin nodded at Doc, and with a slight bow and a murmured, "Ma'am", he left.

"Where is he going?"

"I'm sending an advance team to secure the first hotel in New York, as well as transportation. We're not leaving until Friday."

"No."

"Yes."

"John, that won't work. I told you we must leave Thursday. The Smythes are having twenty people for dinner Friday night, and I must shop, and, well..."

Marin shook his head. "I don't care. We're not ready to leave."

"Well, I am, and shouldn't that be all that counts?"

"Not while I'm in charge of your safety. You'll have to call them and send your regrets."

"I can't!"

Marin shrugged. "Then they'll wonder where you are come Friday night." He took a step closer. "I'm not arguing with you about this, Grace."

"Damn you! You have to be able to at least work with me here, John! I can't just cancel!"

John shrugged. "I don't know what to tell you. Maybe they can change the party to Saturday."

"Are you mad? The Levys are having a do Saturday that I must attend. And you can't just change nights—"

"I don't care."

"There are caterers, and...have you never done this before?"

Marin laughed. "You mean concern myself with someone else's bullshit? Can't say I have."

"Obviously this is quite easy for you. It isn't your reputation at stake."

"I'm sorry, but we are not ready for this trip because you didn't tell me about those letters or that banged up car out there. That changed everything, as I told you it would. This person got close enough to you to put a death threat in your purse, Duchess. What part of this don't you get? You're damn lucky I'm letting you go to the embassy dedication tomorrow."

"Letting me...!"

"Let me put it to you plain: I lead, you follow." Marin leaned against the kitchen counter, picked up *her* coffee, and took a sip. As if he were...*entitled*.

"You're being obnoxious."

"Then fire me."

"You seem to be pushing me in that direction."

"Then do it," he dared. "Stand for something, have some balls."

Grace shook her head. "I'm not going to do something detrimental to myself just to make a point."

"Smartest decision you've made yet." He took another sip of her coffee.

"You don't make it easy."

"Stop arguing and it'll get easier, believe me."

"You're punishing me for keeping those letters from you, and you know it. It doesn't have to be this way."

"Look at it however you want, but I'm telling you I'm not going into this trip across the pond without a whole lot of vetting and security."

"Please reconsider."

"No."

"You're impossible!" she shouted before stomping out of the kitchen.

And you're spoiled, Marin wanted to shout, but instead he laughed as she flounced out, her head high and her feet beating the ground.

Her fire should have been the last thing that excited him.

9

*T*he sun was setting over the valley and the sky was swirled in pinks and purples. Cole Porter played from hidden speakers in the ceiling of the kitchen, and on any other day, at any other time, Grace would have felt blissfully at peace. She wanted to kick John Marin in the ass for making her feel unhinged when it had nothing to do with the danger she was in from some unknown stranger. She felt in grave danger from him, and she feared it was the kind that would draw her like a moth to a flame. She'd go confidently into the good night of his arms and that would be the end of her—and him, if she had anything to bloody say about it.

Grace stood over a pot on the stove and took a tentative taste off the spoon. "It's good," she said into the phone.

"You've added the corn?" Mathilda Whipple said

"I have," Grace answered.

"And what does the soup look like? Is it thick? It's a chowder, you know."

"Yes, it's thick, and the color's a yellowy pink."

"And you've added the crab?"

"That's the pink, I do believe."

"Well, let that simmer for a few minutes—you don't want to overcook the crab. And then serve with that lovely bread I've left you."

"Right. Thank you, Mathilda. Oh, I'm so angry he sent you away. Bloody ape."

Mathilda Whipple tittered in her ear. "Oh, it's all right, darling. I'm sure he has his reasons. He's not responsible for us, is he, now?"

"Well, it's ridiculous. He's maddening."

"Men like John Marin usually are, love."

"Don't defend him."

"All right, darling."

"He was Matt's man, you know."

"I didn't, no."

"Head of his detail in the White house."

"No kidding! How lucky to have found him again...oh. Oh, dear, Gracie."

"Yeah. Strange, huh?"

"I'm sorry, love. Not good memories for either of you, then eh?"

"No."

"He's very handsome."

Grace bit a thumbnail. "Yes, well..." For some reason tears flooded Grace's eyes and her nose began to sting just a little.

"What is it, darling?"

"He..."

"He's what, love?"

"He's very angry with me." Her voice broke.

"Oh, he's not, surely...well," Mrs. Whipple amended. "He did seem in quite a state as we were leaving."

"Yes, indeed." Grace bit her nail and stirred the chowder. "He said I..."

"You what, dear?"

"Well, he finds me quite spoiled, actually." Emotion bled into Grace's words and she chided herself. *Bloody damn fool!*

"Oh, no."

"Yes." Grace's chin began to wobble, and this distressed her most of all. She sniffled, just a bit.

"Gracie? Love, are you crying?"

"Oh, we had a terrible row!"

"About what?"

"I'm sorry. I can't tell you. The less you know the better, and all that."

"I see. Oh, darling, don't fret." After a pause, Mrs. Whipple said, "You care what he thinks of you, don't you?"

Grace put her hand over her mouth to stifle a sob that came out of nowhere. "I do, dammit. Damn *him*! I can't believe this bothers me so. He's very cross with me, Mattie."

"He was quite lovely about it as he was kicking us out, but this is obviously very distressing for you. I should be there."

"Yes, you should. And yes, he can be very charming when he wants."

"Well, whatever you did, have you said you're sorry, love? That usually works."

"I have, yes."

"Well, he's a very stubborn man, then, isn't he?"

"Yes, he is," Grace said. "He said...he said...he said I needed a...needed a..."

"A what, dear?"

"A *spanking*." Grace whispered the last word, as if saying it aloud would etch the idea in stone. "Mathilda Whipple, you stop laughing this minute!"

And with that, Mrs. Whipple's titter turned into a throaty guffaw. A full minute passed before the woman got hold of herself.

"Are you quite finished?" Grace snapped as she wiped her eyes.

"Yes, oh I am sorry, darling, but…"

"Don't you dare say it!" That set the woman off again.

"I like this man," she said when she was sufficiently composed.

"You stop that snickering, or I shall speak to Jasper about you, I swear it."

"My husband is likely to agree with Mr. Marin, dear."

"Mathilda!"

"Oh, I am sorry, again, Grace, darling. Really. Indeed, the nerve of some men," she sniffed. "Most troubling. Most troubling, indeed."

"Yes, thank you."

"How does the chowder look?" Mrs. Whipple asked.

Grace gave it another stir. "I think it's done. And you've changed subjects."

"Needed changing."

"Mmmm," Grace admitted. "Well, let us just say he has every right in the world to be cross."

"Well, there you are, then."

Grace paused. "Wait…where am I?"

"I think you are right where you need to be."

"That's not very helpful." Grace huffed. "What am I supposed to do now for dinner? He'll have this pot gone in an hour. The man eats twelve times a day and he's been living on coffee and tea sandwiches since before you left."

"There are lamb chops in the freezer and some potatoes in the bin. You'll find the vegetables where they belong. You know what to do."

"I suppose."

"Chin up, ducky."

"Stop laughing. It's not funny."

"Yes, it is."

Grace sighed, and then laughed, too. "I'm a mess. I am so terribly sorry about this."

"I know. The good news is Jasper is making some necessary repairs to your flat and you'll be very pleased when you return."

"Oh, darling, thank him for me."

"I will. You could use some new sheets for your bed, and your guest towels are looking tattered. I'll go shopping."

"All right. Whatever you say."

"There's a girl. Do try to be good."

"Gah. What fun is that?"

"Indeed. After your trip you will stay at Shannonfield, and under my house rules of rest and plenty of sweets, you'll be tiptop straight away. I shall recommend it upon your return."

"I'll take you up on it. Thanks, old girl."

"You are most welcome. Call me later and tell me how Mr. Marin liked his meals. He's a lovely young man."

Grace turned at the sound of his footsteps. Upon entering a room, John Marin sucked the life right out of it. He exuded buckets of testosterone and alpha confidence. They didn't make men like John Marin anymore. His kind was either being phased out genetically, or by force thanks to a society that didn't know what to do with such a creature.

Oh, how desperately wrong were genetics and society.

"Yes, charming. Bye, darling." She had to stop this. She never pined after a man, ever. Why did she want to spend every moment of her time in this one's presence? Why did she want to spill her guts, tell him everything, ask him what she should do? Grace thought about all of it as she held a phone in her hand and stared at the formidable man in her doorway. She still hadn't packed, and she would spend the day doing just, even though she now had an extra day, thanks to her actions and the stick that made itself at home up the dratted man's ass. She also wanted to go over the speech she'd give at the new embassy dedication tomorrow. All of that, and all she could do was stare speechless at the beast's piercing blue eyes, and pray a booger wasn't hanging out her nose.

"Hello," she said.

Marin arched a questioning brow, and when nothing came flying at his head, his shoulders relaxed.

"Chowder? It will taste as if Mathilda Whipple herself made it, since she nursed me through it over the phone."

"Sure. Smells good."

Grace took down bowls and filled them. Marin took spoons out and met her at the table. "She's very protective," Grace said when she sat. "This forced exile is not sitting well —with anyone," he finished under her breath.

Marin simply nodded, when another man would have apologized, whether he was sorry or not.

"And you don't give one damn, do you?" she pushed.

"No."

"And despite that, she still thinks you're a 'lovely young man'."

"A lot she knows," he mumbled. "You okay?"

"Yes, of course."

"You've been crying."

"No." When Marin stared at her in reproach, she amended. "I...I'll be all right."

"Good," he said with a single, curt nod. "I looked into your security system."

"Yes? And?"

"You're being watched. There are cameras everywhere but they're on you, where you go, where you spend your time."

Grace gripped the edge of the table.

"A couple of my guys are taking care of it, and I'm having the house swept for bugs. Your flat in London, too. Want to tell me why the interest in you?"

"Whatever do you mean?"

"I understand stalkers. I've dealt with them before. I've never seen a stalker go this far. That's sophisticated equipment out there, not easy to manipulate. The cameras have been in place for a while. Some don't work anymore; others still do. I'm not taking any chances. I'm removing all of it. Any objections?"

"No."

"Anything you want to tell me?"

Grace shook her head. "Of course not. What would I know about this?"

"I'm hoping nothing. It's curious, though. Was all this done to watch your husband, whom you said never came here? Or was it to watch you? And if that's the case, why? And when did it start?"

"I don't know."

Marin scrutinized her. "I think you do. What I don't get is why you're not telling me. You hired me to protect you, came a long way to turn my 'no' into a 'yes', and now..." Marin shrugged. After staring at her for a moment and getting nothing, he sighed. "I'll let it go for now, and you'll deal with the consequences later."

"Meaning?"

He looked at the food sitting in front of her. "Don't just look at that; eat it. I haven't seen you eat a bite all day."

"You do the same." Grace stirred the soup. "Would you care to elaborate—?"

"Why, so we can argue over whether I will, or I won't? Sounds like a waste of time to me."

"Can we please...?"

Marin shook his head.

"You don't..."

"Understand?"

"Yes, that's right, you don't understand." Grace slammed her spoon into her bowl, splashing some onto the table. "You've sent my staff off without explanation, you've changed my itinerary...it's too much."

"Ah," he murmured when he saw she'd changed the subject. "I'm not being paid to protect Sterling Jarvis or the Whipples; I'm being paid to protect you."

"You're being paid to protect whomever I tell you to protect," she snapped.

"No, but nice try." He stood and went to the breadboard, cut a couple of thick slices of crusty bread and returned to the table, along with a plate of softened butter. He tossed the bread on the table, broke off a small piece and dragged it across the top of the stick of butter. "You're staying attached to my hip until this job is over, Duchess, and that's not negotiable."

Grace muttered and went to the cupboards and produced a small plate for the bread, as well as a butter knife, banged then down on the table, and sat again. Marin smirked and dragged his bread through the butter again.

"You've put me in a difficult position with the Smythes," she said, staring at the slowly disappearing stick.

"I don't give a shit about the Smythes."

"So, you've said. I, however, do."

"You put yourself in the difficult position, Duchess. It didn't need to happen this way."

"Would you have taken the job had I told you about those threats?"

"Of course. And then I'd have told you to cancel the embassy dedication and the trip to the U.S., you would have refused, and that would have been it—see ya." He took a bite of his bread. "And you knew it," he finished around the mouthful.

"*See ya*? That final?"

"Yup."

"Of course, I knew it. That's why I didn't tell you."

"It's what else you're not telling me that has me worried. I don't like being caught off guard."

"I'm not trying to be difficult, John."

"You're not trying not to be."

"What a dreadful thing to say."

"My patience is wearing thin. First, I'm getting pretty goddamn tired of arguing every point with you, lady. You're fighting me like I'm the enemy. Someone out there wants to kill you, somebody else—or the same person—fucked with your security system so you're on twenty-four-seven, and for some reason you're lying to me and digging your heels in about household staff. And then you want to traipse off to New York to attend 5th Avenue parties with Muffy and Randolph. You came to me; you pushed me into this. And now that I'm here, I'm going to do everything I can to ensure your safety, and I can't if I have to worry about other people, and about what you're not telling me. Is that clear enough?"

"Who the hell are Muffy and Randolph?" Grace shot up from the table and turned her back on him.

"An amalgam of all the shit I hate about your class of people."

That brought Grace around with a glare. The sharp pain that shot through her heart at his unfair assessment of her was swift and surprising. "Are you really that plebian, John? We've gone from arguing over a travel schedule to you insulting me, and people I hold great affection for. You know nothing about them, or me."

"I know enough. I spent four years in your White House."

"Yes, and what brilliant insights did you glean in that time? I'm dying to hear this." Grace folded her arms and stood off balance, a curvy hip jutting out defiantly.

"Never mind." Marin stood, too. "I'm sorry I offended you."

"Oh, no, you didn't offend me, John," Grace lied. "You sound like a clichéd, angry ninety-nine percenter who watches too much cable news, so I'd like to hear all of the astute observations you've culled in those four years you served my husband, four years that completely informed you about who *I* am." Grace watched Marin's jaw work as he held his temper. Unable to understand why he was so cross with her, she held her ground and waited for him to speak.

Marin gripped the back of the armless ladder chair he'd just left. The lady was angry and itching for a fight, and he'd led her there.

Walk away, he said to himself. *This will not go well.*

"Typical," she hissed, walking past the table. "Big mouth and nothing to back it up. Enjoy your meal."

Marin's hand shot out and gripped her upper arm before she reached the threshold into the hallway. Grace stopped but kept her eyes down, her arms folded across her middle. He was at her side, their clothes touching, and Marin felt her heat and her anger and her hurt, filling his senses with regret and anger.

Let her go.
Walk away.
Take her words and swallow them right down.
You do not want to do this.

He ignored it all. "I spent four years watching the people you call friends fuck your husband because he was young, and you were an outsider who didn't know she wasn't allowed to say no, or *think about it*, or have an opinion of her own. And I watched a man I admired blame his young wife for his inability to reach across the aisles to get things done because the status quo didn't quite know what to do with a man like him, or a woman like you. You were outsiders, but he was a man, and he was the president, so he got the pass; he had the buffers, you didn't. I watched him at first unable, and then unwilling, to guide you to help him, and then help yourself, and he spent the last three years of his presidency ignoring you while the Washington elite shunned you behind your back." Marin bent forward until his breath caressed her ear with every word he spoke.

"He blamed you for his deficiencies and allowed the people who put him in the White House to lead him farther away from you and your God-given talents. I watched him hurt your feelings more times than I can count—call you spoiled and ungrateful and a prima donna. And the tears I've seen swimming in your eyes in the last handful of days were more than I saw in that entire four years, because you pushed your shoulders back and you soldiered on, because that's who you are. You are tough as nails, and those fucking people didn't know what they had with you. You were a twenty-nine-year-old first lady, and they all underestimated you. You scared them. You were actually naïve enough to think they'd see you for what you really were: a brilliant, beautiful, thoughtful, caring woman who had the world in

her hands without working too hard at it, because sometimes life rewards beauty and goodness, and heart, because
that's a hell of a lot of work right there."

Grace brought a hand to her mouth as emotion threatened to topple her.

"You think senator's wives wanted to get next to that?"
Marin went on. "You were where they wanted to be at half
their age, and they weren't going to help you be more
successful. So, yes, when I have to sit here and listen to you
sing the praises of Muffy and Randolph, I want to slug
something." He turned her so she was facing him.

"Those days weren't your failures, Duchess; they were
your husband's, and all those other people who couldn't be
kind, when it took so little effort to be just that. You are an
incredible woman who could have done so much had she
been allowed. My comment wasn't about you; it was about
those people you admire so much. So forgive me if I'm not
in a rush to hop a plane before we fully vet this trip so you
can rub elbows with people who don't value you."

With his hand on her arm it wasn't easy to pull away, and
when Grace tried, Marin tightened his hold, just enough to
keep her there, in front of him.

"Let me go," she whispered. "Please."

"Grace." He watched her war with her emotions and all
he wanted to do was take those quivering lips between his,
run his tongue over them until they stilled, until the fear in
her eyes disappeared.

"Please."

Marin released her, while his own mouth ached, and
watched her disappear down the dark hall. When the
clicking of her shoes ceased, he sat heavily in the chair.

"Good work, jerkoff." He picked up the remaining hunk

of bread he'd been working on and tossed it back on the plate.

"Fuck."

10

*M*arin gave Grace ample time to cool off, and when it was up, he sought her out. He found her in a cozy sitting room across from the library. Her face was lit by a fire and nothing more, her thoughts so far away she didn't see him watching from the shadows. When alone, when she thought she wasn't being watched, she looked older than she was. The stress of four years in the White House, the assassination, and now her current troubles beginning, Marin was certain, with the shooting in May, took a toll. It took root in the deep creases between her eyes, and in the hard set of her angular jaw, and in the slump of her slender shoulders.

At other times she looked like a little girl. He pictured her in a pair of overalls with holes in the knees and twigs in her hair, looking like she knew she had a good scolding coming, and daring someone to give it to her. The regal air, the strong, sophisticated lady she was all the other times, the woman he so admired, was nowhere to be found at this moment. He wanted to learn the subtle nuances of all these women, all these faces of Grace; he wanted to learn her so thoroughly that he'd know what to do for her in an instant, with just the slightest variance in her look, or tone. And he would learn how to handle her so adroitly that she'd never look at another man again.

Never look at another man again? What was he thinking? Once this gig was over, he was gone, off again to another job, or back to St. John. Or maybe home to Cody, finally. Marin thought about Grace with another man, someone who occupied her thoughts, someone she thought about, smiled about when she thought no one was looking. And the very idea made his heart beat faster and his hands clench into fists. He'd been in the woman's presence for five days, and in those five days he'd scolded her, planned an itinerary with her, kissed her, swatted her shapely backside, and argued with her ad nauseum. He shouldn't, and of course *didn't*, give one damn who she looked at or thought of. While smiling.

Ignoring his throbbing cock and an almost uncontrollable need to bury it so deep in this woman he'd disappear forever, Marin shook free of such thoughts and went back to the kitchen. He returned with a tray, laden with the supper he was determined she would eat.

"Oh, you startled me," she said when he walked in the room. He set the tray down on a table in front of two 1920s French leather club chairs. High-backed and deep-seated, Grace looked eaten up by the one she sat in, with her legs pulled up and her feet tucked under, her beautiful face lit only by the light of the fire.

"You didn't eat," he said, sitting in the other chair and turning on the lamp atop an antique Louis XVI side table. A bowl of fragrant, steaming chowder, a plate with a hunk of bread and a slab of butter scraped on the edge, and a pot of tea with sugar, cream, and two cups sat on the overburdened tray.

Grace waved her hand in the air. "I don't think..."

"Unless you want me to take you in my lap and hand feed you like a bird, I advise you to dig in."

"You wouldn't dare," she huffed in mock surprise, light shining in her eyes.

"Try me, lady."

"I do believe that falls way outside your job description, John, although I would not put it past you to try."

"My job description is fluid at the moment, Duchess, so don't test me."

She eyed him warily. "What about you?"

"I had something already."

"Besides Mathilda's good bread dragged through butter?"

One corner of his mouth turned up and he had the good manners to keep quiet. Marin stared into his lap as she picked at the piece of bread. "I'm sorry, Grace."

"Don't. You were spot on."

"I know I was, but I started off wrong. I didn't mean to put you in a category with those people. You're nothing like them. You're stratospheres above them."

Grace held her hand up again. "Don't get carried away, please. We did, and do have friends in politics, people who guided a very young, but extremely smart president—and his wife—straight to the White House. But the things you saw between Matt and me? You only saw one side. I was young, to be sure, and very insecure. I sought his guidance; I sought *him*. But I don't think either of us realized the work and the time it would take to do such a job. My God, if everyone knew what that job does to a person, why...only a fool would pursue it."

"When it comes to you, I'm not sure he deserves the break you're giving him."

"You judge too harshly, then. Matt did his best. He was charged with running a country. He didn't need to run me, too. Were we perfect? No. Did I get what I needed from him? Sometimes. Sometimes, I did. But I believed we had time to make it right again; that after four—or eight years, if we were lucky—we'd have the time back. We thought it would be lovely to have a child while in the White House. A child, perhaps, would give the country hope." Grace shook her head. "But it wasn't meant to be."

"I'm sorry."

"Truly, there is nothing to be sorry for. It just...was. I have grown leaps and bounds since then—despite what you think of me at the moment."

"It so happens I admire you quite a bit *at the moment*. You were the first lady, but you were a lady first, always. And you still are."

Warmth the likes of which Grace was most unfamiliar spread across her chest. In her life she desired admiration from only a handful of people, but all of those accolades did not compare to the one she just received from this rugged protector, who had her in tears not half an hour ago.

"Matt had a mistress." Out it came; Grace hadn't thought it through, hadn't considered what admitting it out loud would do to her, or what John Marin's reaction would be.

When Marin simply stared at her, she looked down at her hands. "But, of course, you already knew that."

Now that she'd said it, Grace found that the only feelings she had on the declaration was what John Marin thought. Did he think her a fool for not knowing, or for knowing and not leaving?

"That's on him, not on you," he said. "And for the record, I had no idea." Marin looked down at her untouched soup.

"Grace, I swear to God, if that soup gets cold before you eat it, I'll…"

"I'm eating," she said, lifting the bowl and taking a bite. "Lovely, just delicious."

"Every bite."

"And you use a bloody knife for the butter," she mumbled, happy to change the subject—again.

"One has nothing to do with the other. Tea?"

"Please."

Marin poured her a cup, then creamed and sugared it without asking. He knew her at least this much. He'd been watching her for almost a week. He poured one for himself and set it down on the Louis XVI table. Grace huffed and set his cup in the saucer. It brought the slightest crook to his mouth.

"Cheers, Duchess."

"Why do you call me that? Are you making fun of me?"

Marin glanced at her over the rim of the dainty pink bone china cup and arched a brow. "Not at all. You've earned it, I'm guessing."

"Only if I'd married a duke or been given the title outright. The correct title for me, if I were to insist, would be Lady."

"Lady," he pondered. "I like Duchess better."

I do, too, Grace thought as took a first sip.

"You going to be okay? I mean with…Muffy and Randolph."

"The Smythes?"

"Whatever."

"I believe I will survive the social misstep your dictates have caused."

"Your own doing," he reminded.

"I suppose I thought that if you saw this as an easy two weeks, you'd be more inclined to agree to the job."

"And now that I'm here it's harder for me to walk away?"

"I suppose."

"You get away with this kind of manipulation all the time, I bet."

"Perhaps that's why I'm alone."

He wanted to tell her that a certain kind of man would find the challenge of taming her very attractive. Instead, he said, "Poor you. Don't lie to me again, about anything."

"I'll do my best."

"Do better than that." After a pause, he said, "I think you're scared."

"Hmmm."

"Tell me how Inspector Devon is involved. He called yesterday, which prompted me to look in that envelope."

"Snooping, were you?"

"I was looking for a pad of paper and it was there in plain sight. For someone who likes to keep secrets, you don't know the first thing about camouflage. Unless you wanted me to find it."

"That's it; you've caught me, red handed."

"Devon?"

"We were trading calls about the accident."

"I'm not sure how I want to deal with him yet."

"Whatever you say."

"I should write that down."

Grace set her bowl on the tray and took up her tea. "Are you close with your family?"

"We're changing the subject."

"If you please."

"Yes."

"Yet you haven't been home in a year."

"No."

"Why?"

Marin was quiet for a long time. "Hard to go back to life after failing at the one job you had—protecting a life."

"It wasn't your fault, John."

"Then who's was it?"

"It wasn't yours. And you saved me. I don't know what I would have done had you not acted."

"Thank you for that."

"Will you go home after you're finished with me?"

"I don't know." Marin leaned forward and pressed his fingers together, wondering if he'd ever be finished with this woman. "When someone has been through something life changing—a kidnapping, a crime, something traumatic— they often find it hard to go home—or at least stay home— after. There are a couple of reasons for that. Shame is one; feeling tainted, or dirty, or unworthy, like in the case of a violent crime, or if someone has been kept in captivity for a period of time. Through no fault of their own, they feel unworthy of normal."

"How incredibly sad. Is that why you went to St. John?"

"Yes."

"You felt tainted, unworthy somehow."

"Yes. And I didn't want to talk about it. I didn't want to hear, among other things, that it wasn't my fault."

"Which you still cannot seem to hear."

"It's easier to be alone. It's better if I don't get too close; it's better if I keep my distance. I work better that way. I always have."

"I'll bet your family disagrees. I'm sure they love you very much."

Marin sighed. "It just is, Grace."

"What types of people did you protect when you had your security firm?"

"Me personally? Rich businessmen, elite military, an actor once in a while."

"No women?"

"My people did. For me, a woman by herself? Never. Why?"

"I don't know," she sighed. "You're certainly not squeamish. You seem to know perfectly well how to handle a woman."

"There are a few who'd disagree."

"And what about a woman in your life?"

"No one important."

"Have you ever been in love?"

Marin stared at Grace for a long time before he answered. "I probably thought so a time or two."

"So, you haven't been home in a long while, and you're not terribly bullish on love. You believe you do your best work when you're free of emotion, is that it?" she pressed.

"Basically."

"Yet you seem to show great emotion with me."

"That's anger, Duchess. And frustration."

"I don't think so."

Marin met her eyes. "Drink your tea, Mrs. Coolidge. It's getting cold."

"And you're avoiding the subject."

"The subject is closed. Drink your tea," Marin ordered, "and tell me about Sterling Jarvis."

"Why the interest in Sterling?"

"I need to know about everyone you're close to. Start with him."

The beginnings of a smile crossed Grace's mouth. "He's been with the family in one capacity or another for years."

"How many years?"

"Over ten. I took him on as my personal secretary after the assassination, after returning home. Why?"

"I'm wondering why he didn't go to anyone about what was going on."

"I forbade it."

"If he cares for you like he says it wouldn't have mattered."

"Have you ever had servants?"

"Do I look like I've ever had servants?"

Grace looked down at her hands, suddenly embarrassed at how she must sound to him.

"Does it bother you at all that when he had a chance to protect you, he couldn't, because you *forbade* it?" Marin continued.

"Yes, it does, believe it or not. Sterling is more than my secretary; he is a friend, and in fact I don't think of him, or the Whipples, in any other way. I have my American-born mother to thank for that." Grace stared into her tea. "Are you sorry you took this job?"

"No."

Grace met his eyes. "Really?"

"Really. I think the president would have wanted me here, to protect you."

"He would have." Grace looked around the room. "He hated all this, hated my father's title, hated the pretension, hated England. Part of his eventual resentment of me was that I refused to give it up, refused to become wholly American. I am both an American citizen and a British subject, and he hated it. He didn't believe you could love two countries the same. But I did, and I do."

"That must have been hard to take."

"I'm more resilient than you think, especially when it comes to loyalty."

"I know the president wasn't perfect, but I admired him; I admire you as well, and you seem to need me here, despite your attempts to either drive me away or anger me into killing you myself."

"So, it's my charm that keeps you glued to my side. How lovely," Grace smirked. "Is that all?"

"You know it isn't, which brings me to the next subject."

"Oh?"

"Kissing you last night was a mistake."

Grace felt herself jerk in response, as if she'd been slapped. Tears pricked her eyes so suddenly that she blinked them back into oblivion before, she hoped, he took notice in the dim light. "And why is that?"

"I think you know why."

She straightened her back. "Are you afraid I'll demand marriage?"

"No. But right now neither of us can afford to get personally involved. Emotional attachments are dangerous under these conditions."

"And, God forbid you should form an attachment." Grace looked down at her hands, folded in her lap. "I'm sorry; that was rude."

"Yes, it was," he said with a controlled authority that caused the butterflies in her stomach to take flight.

"There is something between us," she said, looking him straight in the eye.

"There can't be."

"*Can't* and *is* are incompatible."

"It can't happen again, Grace."

"If you say so."

"I say so. I'm here to protect you, make sure you get

through this trip and back home safely. I'm nothing to you, except a protector."

"You are far more to me than that," she whispered.

"Sweetheart. Please don't make this hard."

"Then stop calling me sweetheart."

Marin sighed. "Don't take anything I do or say personally. Just follow the rules I've laid out and do as I say." Marin stood. "This will be over soon."

"I know." And as she took another sip of tea, she wondered how in hell she was supposed to not take things personally from a man who kissed the way he did.

11

*G*race and Marin sat in mostly companionable silence the next day, she going over her itinerary, and he making corrections and adjustments.

"The smaller the hotel, the better I can control security," Marin told her, after she insisted on staying in a certain large and high-profile hotel in New York. "This one's been vetted, and the two-bedroom suite has been secured already."

"And all this without consulting with me," she snapped.

"I did consult with you, but what I'm learning about you is that if you don't agree, it's as if we never discussed it, like the conversation never took place."

"That's absurd," she argued.

"Yeah, it is. This shouldn't be up for argument, Grace, but of course it is, as is everything. Let me do my job. I know what's best."

Grace stood. "That leaves little else for the rest of us to do, except blindly follow."

As she stormed out of the library, she couldn't help but hear him mumble, "Works for me."

Marin sat back and kicked his foot up to rest across his knee. He was falling for her, dammit. Despite his valiant attempts not to, the warmth that sat in his chest simply wouldn't go away. She brightened every room she walked into; she was funny, intelligent, beautiful inside and out, and that accent! He found he could listen to her all day. But lord was she stubborn. Trust. It was a hard thing to do; he knew that. He ran into it with every client. Eventually they all came around, and Grace would, too.

He couldn't help but notice the stress she held in her back and shoulders, the sadness in her eyes, and the reluctance to do this memorial, this tribute to her husband. It was like going back to the scene of the crime, even though the memorial was in D.C. and the assassination happened in New Orleans. Trauma did not let go, and it reared its ugly head often and when you least expected it.

Marin looked down at the copy of the itinerary he'd given her earlier. Her handwriting was artistic and feminine. Taught well in the finest schools, he mused, schools known for cracking knuckles with rulers for incorrect form and misspellings. He found himself growing angry at the thought of anyone taking a stick to those beautiful hands, or in any way making her cry or making her fearful. That he wanted to paddle her backside into submission at times was entirely beside the point. He was allowed to feel that way, no one else.

Grace had made notes, added addresses and provided guest lists for the two parties given in her honor they would attend Friday and Saturday evening, and an art exhibit at the Met Sunday night. The Friday night party, of course, was out of the question. She'd already made that call, and to put punctuation to it, Marin crossed it off the list.

The following week would be filled with lunches and

intimate dinners with friends and political associates in small restaurants. Those were easy. Marin told her to stick with small restaurants and private rooms, and he was pleased to see she had complied. Grace wanted a day or two to shop; that would be easy as well.

He was about to compare what he had to the list Grace had come up with when the doorbell rang. He met Grace coming out of the kitchen and held his hand up, stopping her. Grumpy and Bashful stood in the doorway.

"Come in," Marin said. "Whaddya got."

———

GRACE SAT in one of the chairs by the fire while the three men stood hunched over the desk, all the missives Grace had received spread out, and several photographs lying next to it all in a pile. Marin did his best to shield her from the harsh words and threats that screamed out from the pages, but both knew that wasn't necessary. She'd seen it all. The pictures, however, were new.

"Where did these come from?" she asked.

"When was the last time you checked your emails? Grace?" Marin prodded when she looked down at the desk and didn't answer.

"I don't know."

"Yes, you do," he said. "I had a hunch that there was more going on than the letters, so I had Grumpy here look into your laptop. But you knew what was there, didn't you?"

"Yes."

"Where was this?" Marin asked her, pointing to the first photo, printed on plain paper, matte rather than glossy like a photograph, but clear as glass, the detail impressive.

Grace stared at the photo. "I was...at the market, about ten days ago."

"Around the time you found the threat in your purse."

Grace nodded. "Perhaps."

"And this?"

A lump formed in her throat like a rock. She knew the somewhat shadowy figure, taken through the window of her bedroom of her London flat to be her. "My Hyde Park flat. I'm...I'm in my bedroom."

"How about this one?"

"I'm...driving down the road toward Shannonfield Manor—here."

"On a deserted road," Marin added. "You never looked at these, did you?"

Grace shook her head.

"Why?" he asked.

Grace looked up, remembering for the first time that Marin's men also stood in the library as he scolded her, and she searched in vain for excuses.

"I...I've been schooled, I'm afraid, to not open attachments."

"But you saw the emails, you read them."

"Yes."

"He knows where you shop, where you live, and the places you go to relax." His tone was harsh. "This isn't a game."

"I know," she whispered.

"The security system has been dismantled. Maybe we can use it the way it was intended. I'll have someone I trust on it while were gone. I've had the house swept for listening devices and cameras."

"And?"

Marin hesitated. "Do you really want to know?"

Did she? Did she want to know if a camera had been installed in her bedroom, and someone watched her undress every night—or the many other things she felt comfortable doing in the privacy of her own bedroom?

"Not now," she whispered. She jumped when Marin addressed the men with a sweep of his hand over the desk and a curt, "Figure this shit out and get back to me." He never asked them to leave; they just went.

Marin stood straight, folded his arms, and pierced her with a stern look.

"What now?" she asked. "Dungeon or whipping post?"

"I'm not opposed to either one."

"Charming."

"When I say, 'what else', or 'is there anything else you have to tell me'," he shouted, "what is it you hear? Is it little birds chirping, dolphin squeaks? Or maybe a choir?"

"Oh, stop it!" Grace stood and turned toward the fireplace, her back to him.

"Turn around," he ordered. A knot formed in her stomach and warm liquid coursed through her. "*Grace!*" Slowly she did as commanded.

"Did it ever occur to you that this stuff can be traced, and that time might be important? I've got one of the best computer forensics experts in the world in Grumpy, and he could have been on this a week ago!" At his raised voice, Marin watched her shrink, and he knew that his frustration meant little compared to what she was doing to herself. He stepped forward and took her hands in his. A single tear fell from her left eye and landed on his wrist. Without a thought, he set his thumb on her cheek whisper soft, and wiped a second one away

"I know you're scared. I know that admitting all of this, facing it, makes it real. I get it. But I'm trying to help you,

Grace, and in order to do that in a way that will satisfy me, I have to know everything. That includes emails or letters, or phone calls from someone you don't know, or a fucking conversation with a waiter at the café that made your hair stand on end. I need to know all of it. Do you understand?"

"Yes."

"Look at me." When she did, he said, "*What else*?"

"Nothing else."

"Swear it."

"I swear it."

"If you're lying to me, lady, we're going to have a problem, and that's a promise."

"What the devil does that mean?"

"You want details?"

"Not really."

Marin sighed and squeezed her hands. "What is going on inside that head of yours?"

"I feel like a victim, I feel weak," she whispered.

"And that's what this asshole wants. You lose your power, and he wins—he wins before he causes you a second of physical pain. Do you understand? Killing you is a period at the end of a long sentence if he's paralyzed you now. You want him to win?"

"No."

"Me, either. Look at me. You're stronger than this. Stop telling yourself you're not. And you're smarter than this, too. You know that ignoring this isn't going to make it go away, but the more information we have, maybe, will. You see that, right?"

"Yes, when you put it like that."

He took a deep breath. "You're not to touch the mail, in case there are any fingerprints. Besides, you've been through enough and you don't need to see this kind of thing anymore."

Grace nodded.

"And please don't look at your emails unless I'm with you."

"All right."

"I want to respect your privacy, but you don't need to put yourself through that alone."

Grace nodded.

"You don't answer the phone, I'll do it."

She nodded in agreement. "I'm sorry, John."

And without thinking, Marin brought her hands to his lips and kissed the backs. "I know."

———

LATER, after Grace got herself ready for bed, she stood in front of the door to Marin's bedroom. The bed was neatly made, his bags were put away, and the only thing that gave away his presence was a holstered pistol sitting on top of the low dresser against the wall, and a stack of papers with a pair of reading glasses on top, sitting on his night stand.

She wanted to tell him, spill it all. Lives were at stake and telling him—telling anyone—could compromise all they had worked for. The sound of running water pierced the silence of the room. She didn't want to intrude, but already his essence, a scent so unique to him, had permeated the room, the walls, the furniture. She wanted more of it. She was put out, restless, nervous about the trip and about the embassy dedication. She was ready, but she didn't know what to expect, and it unsettled her. Would something happen at the embassy? Would that be the day? Or would it all look better if it happened on American soil?

Grace entered his bedroom and strolled casually over to the dresser. She ran her finger along the leather holster that held his gun, a gun he wore even in the house. It was ever-present, and she was so used to it now that she stopped noticing it secured under his left arm. Sitting here on the dresser, it was out of context, it was new. It excited her.

John, I came to tell you that there is more, so much more, so much that I'm hip deep...

She closed her hand around the soft, firm leather, finding that caressing it simply wasn't enough. Maybe she should start carrying one of these. How hard could it be to squeeze the trigger and stop the madness?

"Grace."

Grace jumped and spun around to see Marin standing in the bathroom doorway. He was bare from the waist up, fresh from a shower. Water glistened off a thatch of light hair that covered his chest, then thinned out to a narrow line that disappeared inside the waistband of a pair of thin black lounging pants that sat low on his broad hips. Her tongue moistened her dry lower lip as she stood, caught uninvited and red-handed, in his room.

"I'm..."

"Are you okay? Is anything wrong?"

She hesitated. Now, of course, was the time, the moment, the opportunity. "No...no, of course not. I'm fine." She turned her head toward the gun. "I just...I'm so sorry. I've intruded."

Marin walked over to her, and without taking his eyes off hers, he picked up the holstered weapon and slipped it into a drawer. "Yes, you have," he drawled. "What do you need, Grace?"

"I..." The fingers of her right hand fiddled at her throat

as she glanced behind her at the now-closed drawer. "May I look?"

Marin shook his head. "That's not for you," he said in an octave lower than he normally spoke. "You don't touch that."

Her heart lurched, and an ache sat in her stomach. Tears pricked her eyes. "I...yes, I..."

Marin placed his finger at the side of her chin and turned her to face him. He didn't speak until she looked up and met his eyes "You do not touch that, not ever. Do you understand me?"

Chastised once again, Grace only nodded.

"Promise me."

"I...I promise." Damn those traitorous tears, making themselves at home in her lashes.

"What's wrong?"

Grace swallowed hard. "I...I..." *No. Not yet.* "I wanted to attempt, once again, to talk to you about the hotel in New York. They know me, they are used to high-profile guests, and I think you'll find that I'll be much safer at the Palace." She paused. "It's where I'm most comfortable."

Marin stared at her for a long moment before he spoke. "And you needed to pick up my gun while you communicated that to me?"

Sudden anger heated her face. Eyes blazing, Grace jerked out of the grip he still had on her chin and walked out.

"Duchess." He was standing in the doorway when she turned.

"It won't happen again," she said, and disappeared behind the door to her room.

Marin watched that door close with a definitive bang, knowing her visit had nothing whatsoever to do with hotels. He growled and stared at the ceiling. Every time he snapped at her and she got that look on her face, when moisture filled her beautiful eyes, he wanted to rip his own heart out, hand it to her and say, 'Here. See what you can do with this thing'. He opened the dresser drawer and removed the leather holster. It creaked in his hand, the smell a familiar one.

He slipped on a t-shirt and walked across the hall. Hesitating at her door, he questioned the wisdom of rewarding her intrusion with a lesson in gun safety. That he wanted another ten minutes in the same room with her was beside the point. He tapped on her bedroom door. When she didn't answer, he tapped again. "Grace?"

She stood in the open doorway in a platinum open kimono and indigo silk pajamas underneath. She looked at him, then down at his hands.

"I'm sorry. You have a right to know what I bring into your home. I didn't mean to be harsh."

"I shouldn't have touched it."

"No, you shouldn't have," he said with stern reproach.

The robe slipped down, revealing the top of her camisole and the delicate bare skin of her shoulder. He instinctively reached up to replace it, but she got there first, giving no hint that she'd seen him move. "Would you like to discuss it?" he choked out.

"If you don't mind." She rested her hand against the edge of the heavy wooden door. The contrast of feather light against dark and heavy, while in that robe, made his mouth go dry. "Come in." With a wave of her hand, she invited him to sit. The piece of furniture was an ornate thing in deep blue velvet, a sofa with half a back that wrapped higher around one side. Grace sat, and Marin joined her. He unsnapped the holster and withdrew the gun.

"It's loaded—all the time," he said, "which is why you don't touch it."

"Yes," she whispered. "I've got it."

"This is a Glock 19, nine-millimeter pistol, and this," he said, removing something from the grip of the gun, "is the magazine. It holds the bullets." He opened the rectangular device and several shiny bullets fell into his hand. He checked the chamber again before handing her the gun. "It's not loaded anymore. Now you can hold it."

Grace hefted it in her hand. "It's heavy."

"One the right size for you wouldn't be so bad. This one fits my hand perfectly."

"I see that," she muttered, observing his overlarge hand dominating a weapon of death like it was a small, harmless puppy.

"You hold it like this." Marin covered her hands with his and raised the gun. "You set your sight there and squeeze the trigger." The snap made her jump. "You've never handled a gun before?"

"My father hunts; he has rifles. I've fired them before, but for some reason..."

"A pistol's personal." Marin ran his hand over hers and held it, felt it quiver beneath his. He grew hard. He'd teach her so much if she were his. She'd never fear anything if she belonged to him.

"I have a clip that attaches to the weapon," he continued, "so I can slip it in my waistband. The clip holds it here, like this." Separating from her, he demonstrated.

"I also have something I wear over my shoulder so I can just reach in like this. And I wear something here." He lifted his pant leg. A gun was secured in a black holster attached to his calf. "This holster I wear at my hip. I just slip my belt through here and it's secure."

Grace nodded. Marin placed the bullets back in the magazine and loaded the pistol. "You have any questions?"

"No, not at the moment."

"We're in the right place if you feel yourself start to go." His mouth twitched up in amusement as he scanned the piece of furniture they sat upon.

"It's called a fainting couch."

"I know. I've seen Masterpiece Theater once or twice."

"Well, this one's very old. It served a purpose once. Women of my generation don't faint."

"No?" he asked, gifting her with one of his rare and winning smiles. "What do they do?"

"They carry on. They throw their shoulders back and they carry on. Gin helps, as does a strong cup of tea."

He stood and looked down at her. "You're safe."

"I know."

"You want to learn to shoot, I'll teach you, but until that happens you don't touch these."

Grace nodded.

Marin ran his finger along her jawline and she looked up into his eyes. "This isn't a game," he whispered, knowing there was so much more to that statement than he'd ever admit. If she only knew. God, how he wanted her. He could smell her, the clean fresh scent of soap and her woman's musk. How he wanted to pull her to her feet, run his hands all over her silk-covered body, and then kiss every inch of her until she forgot about everything, except him. He'd work to keep her in that blissful state until life for her was good again. Instead, he stroked her cheek.

"Goodnight."

He turned and walked out before she could answer.

og sat low on the grounds when Grace awoke at five a.m. the next morning. She dressed in the semi-darkness of her room in tan jodhpurs, a black tank, and a forest green sweater. She slipped on her high black riding boots and went out to the stables. She missed Jasper —their banter, his care for her and her stallion, Shane. She needed a ride, some quiet time alone, away from the house and John Marin's scrutinizing glare and admonishments, and the sexual tension he refused to acknowledge, and she couldn't stop thinking about.

She heard a noise, something scratching in the dark corner of the stables. She knew rodents often made themselves at home in the warmth of the hay, dark corners the perfect place in which to hide. Shane jerked his head away as Grace fitted him with a simple rope bridal and secured a suede riding pad with stirrups over his back. He heard it, too.

"Hello?" Perhaps one of Marin's men was wandering around. Of course, he, or they, would make themselves known. "*Hello?*" she called again, a bit louder. Part of her didn't want to know, didn't want the source of the noise revealed. She didn't want to be thwarted; she wanted a nice, quiet ride before the day set in and she became too busy.

The previous day had been trying, and her emotions had taken a rollercoaster ride since. John Marin was a difficult man to understand. One minute he was treating her like he owned her, and the next he was holding her at arm's length. She should not care, of course, about any of this; his only job was to keep her safe until after the U.S. trip. Yet, she seemed to seek his approval over the least little thing. And the idea that their time together would end sooner than she liked flayed her.

She'd spent the night, in sleep and awake, imagining herself naked and spread out on that blue velvet couch while John Marin tended to her with that sensuous mouth, and those large, strong hands—on her breasts, on her ass, between her legs. She imagined what his cock would feel like buried deep inside her, if he would take her hard, or if he'd be tender with her. Her core ached at the thought. She'd never wanted a man more, and it physically hurt her now swollen lady parts to know she'd never have him, except in her own fantasies.

It was bloody unfair!

He'd awakened something in her long buried. She felt giddy in his presence. He gave her a hard time at every opportunity, and she had to admit she gave him plenty of reason. At other times he was tender, showing great emotion where she was concerned. And he teased her. When was the last time she'd been teased by a man? The early days, before the White House, Matt was easy-going. They laughed easily together, but that changed once political responsibilities mounted. And she had to ask herself what happened to drive him into another woman's arms—especially *that* woman. But all of that was in the past, in another lifetime. She had to live this life now—and she was determined to survive it.

Grace mounted Shane and led him down the narrow path that circled the property. The sun was rising over the village of Plaistow as she followed the river along meadows that bloomed with wildflowers in the spring and summer and frosted over in the winter. She looked behind her a few times to make sure nothing nefarious followed. On this early October morning, a chilly fog blanketed the rolling expanse she loved so much. The embassy dedication was in a few hours, and Grace reviewed the speech in her head as she led Shane down the trail away from the house.

The trip to the states was also very much on her mind, and Grace thought about all the people she would see. For the most part, she was looking forward to all of it, now that it was planned; now that she would have John Marin at her side. At least until the end.

As she rode along the river, with its gentle rush and the smell and sounds of the damp earth under Shane's hooves easing her mind, she thought about how the parties, the get-togethers with friends, and seeing her mum and dad before the memorial would give her just the boost she'd need to endure the rest of the trip. And then a dark foreboding over-took her. It was all threatening to unravel her now, and had Marin not come on the scene, Grace would still have her head buried in the sand, pretending that none of it was happening or mattered. He changed all of that, and she felt no better for it.

"Damn, blasted man," she growled, and Shane nickered in agreement. She lost track of the time in her musings and daydreams as the morning unfolded, and she felt Shane growing restless. She hadn't taken him on a full run yet, and realized it was something he needed, as did she. She crested the hill, the view of the village below, and she felt Shane's anticipation.

"All right then, old bean. Let's have a go, shall we?" With a firm squeeze of her knees, Shane started down the path, gaining speed as the meadows opened up in front of them. The animal kicked up a grand froth as he opened up and ran full throttle. He took her across the meadow at lightning speed, his breath coming in great huffs, while dirt, wild-flowers and the last of the fall grasses kicked up behind. When they came to a fence, he jumped over; when they came to a hill, he climbed up. A flock of geese took flight in the distance. Hunting season would come soon, and Grace was looking forward to the honks of geese and the faint sounds of gunfire in the distance. It meant the holidays were near; it meant family, and good food and warmth and long walks. The chill of the morning was bracing across her face. She would return red-faced and a bit chapped, and she knew she would spend the remainder of the morning getting her normally porcelain skin under control via green-tinted creams and essential oils before the embassy dedication.

Grace slowed him down as they came to a spread of still-green rolling hills and they veered off through a copse of trees until she spotted the small, worn wood building where the manor cooks would smoke fish and game when she was a child, and generations before then. The faint smell of woodsmoke still permeated the area, and Grace loved coming up here to imagine the work, the camaraderie, and the pride that went into feeding a working manor house full of family and employees. As American as she felt, her English blood roared through her when she was at Shan-nonfield Manor. She would return, after all was said and done, and find herself again, as Mathilda Whipple suggested. She would need it; she had a man to get over.

Grace led Shane under an old English Oak, its trunk covered in moss. She slid off his back and he found a patch of cocksfoot and timothy to chomp on. Leaves crunched and squished under her boots as she made way down a slight hill to the edge of the river. She looked over her shoulder at Shannonfield Manor on the hill opposite from where she stood, and hidden from view from most every other vantage point on the property. She loved this spot for that reason: she always knew the way back home from here, yet she could not be seen.

On the other side of the river something moved, and Grace held her breath as a red Caspian stag came into view, autumn's yellow leaves serving as an artist's perfect background behind the grand creature. The stag sported a thick neck mane and a grand set of antlers. Rutting season was in full swing, and by the deep-bellied roar of the animal, he was searching for a darling to call his own while he grazed at the riverbank.

Grace squatted and watched him move through the trees as he bellowed for his ladylove. The mating call from this grand male was aching and deeply erotic, and it hit Grace on a visceral level. There was nothing weak or ambivalent about this animal's desires. He was on the hunt, and it was only a matter of time before he captured his prey. Oh, his lady would demure—they always did if they were smart. But she'd find herself unable to resist him. He was strong, virile, and he would be persistent. And for the time that he was buried deep inside of her, she would know peace; she would know freedom—freedom from thought, freedom from pain, freedom from responsibility.

She tried to tamp down a deep ache of her own, the

cramping between her legs close to painful. Despite the chill in the air, a thin layer of dew covered her forehead and upper lip. A pair of Black-Throated Drivers floated past, dipping their long necks into the water for an early breakfast. The stag raised his head and met her eye, holding it for a few seconds before dashing through the trees in a great rustling.

Something moved behind her, and Grace gave a startled yip as a man appeared through the trees.

"Why, Gerry!" she gasped

"Don't you fucking move."

Grace jerked her head to the gruff sound of that familiar voice; John, Grumpy and Bashful had guns raised and pointed at Gerry, her now-white-as-a-ghost landscaper.

"Wait, he's my—oomph!" and as Marin turned to meet Grace's eyes, she lost her footing and fell straight back into the easy flowing river, her bum landing on hard river rock and flats of mud.

"Lady Grace...oh, dear, oh dear," fussed Gerry as he rushed to her aid.

"I said don't you move!" shouted Marin.

"Oh, Christ, John, Gerry is my gardener."

"Grab him!" Marin ordered, and as he went for Grace, Bashful held poor Gerry back.

"I certainly didn't mean to frighten you," Gerry said as Bashful stretched an arm across the tall, slender man's chest.

"Who the hell are you?" Grumpy barked as Marin held a hand out to Grace, who took it and was pulled unceremoniously from the river. The seat of her jodhpurs was wet, as was the bottom half of her sweater.

"Oh, do put those things away, gentlemen. It's just Gerry."

If a look could end a life, Grace would be six feet under, for Marin pierced her with such rage, she believed planning her funeral now as opposed to years from now might be in order.

"I, well, I'm the manor gardener, surely, as Lady Grace said. Dear, I didn't mean to frighten. I saw the lady and Shane up on the ridge, and well, I hadn't seen…" Gerry turned his ashen gaze from Bashful to Grace. "I hadn't seen you in weeks, and well…oh, dear. I have made a mess, haven't I?"

"Please let him go immediately," Grace ordered, and before checking with his boss, Bashful lowered his arm. Gerry was too afraid to move, so he stood like the dead, wide-eyed and staring around as if he'd just noticed the other men, with their guns still drawn. Was it Gerry she heard at the stables? He was a bit hard of hearing, so it wouldn't surprise her if he simply didn't hear her call out.

"Handle this," Marin said to his two men as he lifted a pant leg and slipped his gun back into a holster attached to his left ankle. Then he grabbed Grace by the arm, hauled her up the riverbank and dragged her behind him, snatching up the dangling reins of the horse. He led both horse and woman down the path out of the copse of trees to the wide meadow.

"Let go," she demanded as her boots tap-tap-tapped the soft ground behind him, her attempts to halt his progress down the narrow path proving impossible. "Dammit, John, stop!" She dug her hand around the one attached to her upper arm, but he was latched onto her like a shark. Marin let the reins fall to the ground, and then he turned, hooked an arm around Grace's back, and lifted her off the ground. What happened next was swift and shocking: with Grace staring at the ground, Marin took a deep breath and brought the flat of his hand down once, then twice, then a third time in lightning-quick succession, the sound like a series of thunderclaps echoing through the quiet morning as, with each connection of his hand, water flew off the wet seat of her padded jodhpurs. Shane, sensing something was amiss, nickered and sidestepped. She was placed back on her feet as quickly as she was taken off them. She grabbed her offended hind parts and glared at him wide-eyed, her ashen lashes holding tears she had no intention of allowing to fall. Her bottom tingled and her core ached, and then her face erupted into humiliated flames.

"How dare you strike me!" Grace snapped.

"It wasn't hard," Marin breathed, and Grace caught the double meaning. He paced in front of her, his breath coming in huffs as if he'd run a mile. The distant rumble of the four-seat off-road tracker the men had arrived on reminded Grace they hadn't been alone just now and made her wonder why she hadn't heard its arrival moments ago. Never mind that Marin's men—and Gerry, of all people— quite possibly saw what just happened.

"I'll have you arrested!"

"You can try." Grace wound herself up, prepared to blast him until his ears bled. Marin lifted a finger to stop her, his eyes deadly. "Mouth off again and you won't sit for a week. *Shut. Up.*"

Her mouth flopped a number of times in search of an insult or some kind of protest, despite his threat. Nothing came. Finally, Marin rolled his eyes. "Ah, hell." He snatched up her arm and dragged her against him, laced his hand in her hair, clasped her jaw with his right hand, and covered her parted, stunned lips with his own.

She tasted sweet, like cherries and early morning chill. He pulled her lips between his and plundered her mouth.

He did it slow, with care, as if he had all day. Grace latched onto his heavy sweater and drew him to her.

What happened to *kissing you was a mistake,* and *this can never happen again*? Grace wondered. How did a bad idea from two nights ago turn into a good one now? She did not care. This man was delicious, and she would handle whatever fall-out there would be once she'd been thoroughly kissed.

Grace Ashton Coolidge wasn't close enough, by Marin's standards. He slipped an arm under her wet bottom, lifted her, and pulled her hips against his. Their chests rose and fell in unison. Even through the heavy sweaters they both wore, Marin could feel her rounded breasts, soft and delicious, against him.

Soft and delicious. What the hell was he doing? He shouldn't be kissing her. He should be reddening her ass for pulling such a foolish stunt. And yet, here he was, with the former first lady in his arms, and he was kissing her like he'd kissed no other woman, ever. With stark realization that he'd gone against every rule of protection, and his own mandate of a few nights ago, he pulled off her with a firm pop and raked her with a righteous, authoritarian glare.

"Do you need more, young lady?" he growled.

Grace searched his indigo eyes as the chilled October morning caressed all the places she was damp. "Yes?"

Now both brows shot up. "Careful, Grace," he whispered. "Next time I'll spank you properly."

"Prop...properly?"

"I'll bare your ass. You didn't feel a goddamn thing just now."

Grace felt herself spiraling down and down and down, and she chalked it up to being so rudely upended and then being so delightfully kissed. Indeed, she hadn't felt a thing, yet every connection of his hand set her aflame like a lightning strike to dry timber. And the thought of him baring her did things to her body she'd forever be too ashamed to admit. The whole of her feelings confused her and all she could do was stare at him with her mouth wide open.

Yes, Daddy.

She was losing her bloody mind.

"Good God," Grace gasped, and attempted to right herself from her off-balance position in his arms. Marin held her firm. "I thought you meant...meant kissing," she hissed.

Marin's eyes widened, and he had the good grace to blush. It was not the first time he'd taken a recalcitrant female across his broad lap for a spanking. He was who he was; it was how he was wired. He liked control, and he liked women who gave it to him. At the moment, however, he was torn as to what, exactly, would do this woman the most good.

"Ah, well then..." And he kissed her again. It was as if he no longer had a mind of his own. Jesus Christ, she tasted good. Her wet bottom, from having fallen into the river, soaked into the arm of his sweater as he held her against him.

Tentative at first, Grace allowed him to move freely over her mouth, her chin, her cheeks, her neck, before she took his face in her hands and kissed him properly. Her breasts ached for his touch, her core pulsed to feel him deep inside her. He tasted like coffee and musk, lime and cedar. She wanted to stay in his arms like this and just kiss him, have him hold her, like this, and tell her it would be all right; it would all be just fine.

He pulled off her and dropped a gentle kiss on her forehead. "What am I going to do with you?" he muttered.

A smile crept across her mouth. "Dear of you to ask my opinion," she sassed.

Marin raised a stern finger. "Don't move." Grabbing the reins that had fallen on the ground while Shane grazed, Marin swung up onto the horses back and held out a hand to Grace.

"Let's go."

It was a command, nothing less; and when she was hoisted up she let out a squeal when Marin pitched her onto her side across the lower portion of the horse's neck—and his broad lap. Her left arm was imprisoned between his body and hers, her right hand rested flat against his chest, and once again they were inches from each other.

"You're taking liberties you're not being paid to take, Marin. That I'm allowing it goes to my current state of mind."

"Which is what?" His mouth twitched in amusement.

"Nerves mingled with something inadmissible, I'm afraid." The heat of his hand at her waist had her pressing herself into him, and when he moved that hand under her sweater and pulled the tank top from the waistband of her wet jodhpurs, the chill that caressed her skin was warmed instantly by his palm, his roughed fingers dappling against her ribs.

"Touch me," she whispered against his mouth.

"Just so we're on the same page, Duchess, I'm assuming you're not asking me to take my hand to your ass."

Now it was Grace's turn to arch her shapely brow. "Hardly."

Marin's eyes were hooded, his breath coming in huffs. "Bare them, Grace," he whispered. "Now."

Grace's body convulsed at the order. His hand, white hot on her waist, never moved as she reached up under her

sweater and tank and unfastened the closure at the front of
her bra. Her nipples ached at his command, and her whole
body felt on fire, white electric-hot fire. She raised both
garments, baring her porcelain skin by inches to the cold
morning air. Her lacy lilac bra was open in front but still
covered her breasts, and Marin held her eyes until she separated the sides and exposed her alabaster globes to his eyes.

Her breasts sat firm, their tips mauve and curved
upwards in offering. Her areolas were pebbled; her nipples
were taut—no doubt caused in part by the bracing weather
and the chill of the cold river. Marin liked to think he had
something to do with the way they sat high and tight, and
quivered of their own volition under his lustful scrutiny.

Mine.

"Christ," he hissed. He latched his fingertips over an
already diamond-hard nipple and caressed outward. They
responded by jutting from the center of a dusky areola,
peaking and darkening with every gentle tug of his fingers.

Mine.

Grace grabbed his wrist and arched her back, pushing
her breasts toward him while seemingly holding him back.

Ah, the war between want and need. Marin's hand
stilled, her grip slowing him down. Sensitive—yes. Marin
wondered how long it had been since this beautiful woman
had been touched. He turned his hand over and caressed
her whisper-soft, her nipple hard against the backs of his
fingers.

Mine.

The lump in her throat bobbed and disappeared, and
then her ice blue eyes closed. And when they met his again,
they begged him to continue. He caressed, he gently
plucked, and all of his attentions sent delicious zings of
pleasure coursing through her body. When he bent down

and curled his tongue around one protruding nubbin, Grace almost came undone.

"Oh, John...God...!" she gasped as he laved and suckled, pulling her sensitive buds free of their imbedded comfort. Grace held his head, ran her fingers through his hair, and allowed him to suckle. Grace wondered if it was possible to orgasm by breast stimulation alone. There was no doubt that if anyone could make her go there, it was John Marin.

He caressed her pebbled peaks with the flat of his tongue, then his mouth turned rigid and he pulled and flicked her nipples with the stiff tip until she thought she would scream. Marin lifted his head and looked into her eyes with hooded lids.

"Jesus Christ, Grace." His mouth crashed against hers, all thoughts of tenderness gone. He wanted this woman like he'd wanted no other. And by her reaction to him, to his kisses, to his touch, she wanted him, too. Marin knew this was not a good idea, but he could no longer help himself. He prided himself on self-control, but he found little sound reason to exercise it now.

As he swept lustily though her mouth, he slid his hand down her body to the V between her slightly parted thighs. She was wet there from her fall, yet her heat burned his hand, and her musky woman scent drifted across his nose. He suspected there was nothing between her and her cotton-lycra riding breeches; she'd felt firm, yet loose, under his descending hand a moment ago.

All mine.

Grace arched her hips and pressed into his hand. Marin needed her, needed to feel her, bare beneath his hand. Against his better judgment, he reached for the fastenings at the front of her jodhpurs, and then jumped as something crackled in his ear; and then he heard an intake of breath, and the too-loud voice of Grumpy.

"You two okay?"

"Fuck," Marin muttered, yanking the earpiece out of his ear. It hung limp against his shoulder. Grace attempted to rise, having no idea why Marin had ceased what she was certain would be a most incredible round of lovemaking, replacing the lust in his eyes with a scowl and muttered expletives.

"What is it?" she asked.

Marin pulled her close and placed a tender kiss at her temple. Then he spoke into an inconspicuous piece of jewelry around his wrist.

"Fine," he snapped. "We're..." He looked down into the hooded eyes of his charge. "Having words."

Grace buried her face in the hollow of his neck with a contented smile. *Indeed, we are,* she wanted to say. As if she'd spoken aloud, Marin scowled. Then he pulled her up to his chest and rested his forehead against hers.

"I'm sorry," he whispered.

"So am I," she conceded. "I've never made love on a horse before."

Marin pulled her sweater and tank down. "Not what I meant," he said.

"Oh."

"We talked about this."

"Yes, and it appears at least one of us changed his mind."

"Yeah. At least one." Marin sat her up fully and turned her to ride astride in front of him. He adjusted, sliding back on Shane's flanks to give her room.

"Shit," he muttered. His steel-hard cock had no place to go—in the jeans he wore and the position he was in. He slid off Shane and walked a few feet away, adjusting himself. He slammed his hands on his hips and stared up at the gray sky. He'd done it now. Like a wild animal who'd tasted human flesh for the first time, he knew he'd never get enough of her.

"Would you like some help?" Grace asked coyly.

Marin turned to her and lifted a warning finger. "Knock it off."

"If it's any consolation, I'm not terribly comfortable either."

"Good."

Throwing him a wicked glare, Grace got down off Shane and started toward him, but he turned and went around her, took up the reins and led Shane back into the copse of timothy the beast enjoyed earlier. Then he returned to Grace, took her by the arm, and led her to a large rock next to the river.

"Sit."

Marin paced in front of her and then walked a few feet away and stared at the village below. "That, uh...that was..."

"A mistake, yes, I know," she quipped.

Marin turned to face her. From several yards away, she could still see that he was unsettled. "You came out here without a coat on," he scolded.

"As did you. Is that really why you're angry?"

"You took off without telling anyone."

"Ah, there it is. Yes. I wished to be alone."

"Not an option, under these circumstances. But I've only said that to you about a hundred times."

"You spanked me."

"Yes, I did." Hands on his hips, he drew closer. "Now that we've recapped the morning, what's it going to take for you to hear me?" His voice was quiet, formidable and alpha-dominant. Laying against his chest moments ago, Grace felt cocooned against the hard-soft wall of him, and she could have gone to sleep for hours against him. She felt safe. Now he looked ten feet tall, anger and frustration coming off him like steam in an ice storm.

"So, it's time for the lecture, I see. One moment while I put my breasts away." She folded her arms over her chest. Her bra was still open and hanging off her shoulders underneath her sweater, her sensitive nipples chafing against the soft wool, causing them further ache instead of blessed relief.

"A lecture should be the least of your worries."

"Should it now?" she sassed with a naughty arch of her brow.

"Yes, and I said I was sorry."

"For what?"

"The...stuff after the..."

"Hmmm. I'm not. But if you don't mind, I'd like to settle from the other before you begin scolding me for my wanderings."

"How long do you think that will take?" he growled.

"How long will it take you?" she countered, glancing down at his crotch.

Marin turned his back and laughed. "Fuck."

"My sentiments exactly." Grace reached under her sweater and attempted to herd the ladies back into containment, and after several tries, she reached into her sleeves, pulled the offending straps down, and tossed the lilac undergarment into the heather with an indelicate swear. Marin looked over his shoulder, first at the tossed intimate, and then at her.

Marin chuckled. "God, woman, if you were mine...."

"As if that caveat mattered," she sniffed, straightening what attire remained.

Marin bent down and picked up the delicate undergarment she'd tossed away. He stared at it for a moment and brought it to his nose, inhaling deeply before folding it with reverence and slipping it into the front pocket of his jeans.

"Give me that."

"No."

"Marin!" When all he did was stare her down, she scoffed, "How childish."

"Yes, I agree." Marin sighed. "I'm not leaving you, Grace."

"Well, that's a rel…"

"Sit down."

"Why, so you can loom over me like a caveman?"

"That's right. That's me. Sit your ass down."

Grace stomped one booted foot on a bed of dry leaves. "I am the former first lady of the United-bloody-States, and I will not…"

Marin put a finger over her lips and arched those masculine brows. "Sit. Down." He pierced her with fiery eyes until she sat once again. "I'm not walking away from you, Duchess. Do you understand?"

Grace blinked several times before she whispered, "I know that. God knows I've done enough to drive you to it."

Marin crouched down in front of her and stared at the fog as it rose off the meadow and faded. "Why do you think that is?" When she turned away, her eyes filling, he chuckled, but amusement was the last thing he felt. "Something's going on. And I honestly believe you'd tell me if you could." When Grace pressed her fist against her mouth as tears rolled down her cheeks, he knew he was right. "You want to tell me; that's why you're acting this way." Marin picked up a stone and threw it against a tree. It ricocheted off and hit the spiky flowered tips of a wild ramson, sending the petals skittering to the ground. "I've done enough of this kind of work to recognize when someone's been backed into a corner. They look like you do right now: fucking terrified. So," he sighed, throwing another stone, which missed the tree altogether. "How do we work going forward?"

"Go, now." It came out of her as a desperate whisper. "Go back to your island, to your life."

That stuck feeling, like a plastic film over his being that formed immediately after the assassination, started to shift. He'd boxed it all away, believing he no longer had the right to such dominance, such hubris, such boldness. They had failed him, those traits that made a man good at serving and protecting. He stared at his charge now, and he felt the subtle shift again, the delicate but well-constructed shell he'd built around himself cracking.

"You didn't come all the way to the Virgin Islands and nag me to death to take this job, only to let me go before we get to the states, Grace." Marin stood. "I thought they were forcing you to take security. Are you saying you're willing to pass on the embassy dedication later, and the trip to the states, and the memorial?" Grace stared at him wide-eyed, and in that moment, Marin saw that she couldn't, even if she'd wanted to. But why?

"You know," he continued. "It's not lost on me that I'm here because someone in charge is allowing it, not because you made a few demands. And what that tells me is my presence here, with you, is furthering someone else's agenda and not yours. I don't like that. I don't like being used. That being said, your agenda is the only one that matters to me." Marin stared down at her, his silence deafening. "Stand up."

Grace peered into his hooded eyes, anger etched on his face, and mixed in with that anger was staunch determination—to do what, she was not yet sure. A chill ran down her arms as she stood, and his hand shot out and grabbed her forearm when she staggered.

"Look at me." The order was given with no thought that she'd disobey him; it was how he thought, how he seemed wired, yet Grace could see a sudden shift in him, and it scared her, just a little. It turned her on quite a lot.

"I'm a different man than any you might be used to. We've played nice since you showed up on my island—please believe me on that. You tell me you need to go do these things, I'll get you there, and I don't even need to know why, yet. You'll damn well tell me at some point, though, I promise you that." Marin cupped her chin and lifted until their eyes met. "You had no idea what you got with me when you came calling. You'll learn now. I'll be your dark knight, and in return, you'll obey me, and you'll do it to the letter, one-hundred-percent of the time, every time, every second that we're together. I told you on the boat that I was in charge, that I lead and you follow. You will learn, in all the ways a person can learn, that I was not kidding. You will obey me, Duchess, because you hired me to do a job, and I'm going to see it through. You'll obey me, and I'll get you where you need to go, you'll accomplish what you need to accomplish, and you'll succeed, because you will not die on my watch. You'll obey me because I am the only one who can do this for you. And you'll obey me because, deep down, you want to.

"You want to know what will happen if you disobey me; you've pushed so close to that moment so many times that you're looking forward to pushing to see how far I'll take it. I warn you now, make the mistake of tripping me up or disobeying me, and I will punish you. It will be painful and it will be humiliating, and then you'll know, and hopefully you won't make the same mistake twice; if you do, it will only be because you want more of the same." Marin shook his head. "You have no idea what you have with me. But you will learn."

Grace stood before him slack jawed while her stomach plummeted to her feet. She dug deep for an indignant comeback, a retort that would put him in his place. But all she felt was a deep sense of relief that now, finally, she'd be safe. That with John Marin with her, next to her, *on* her, she would be safe from outside harm. Safe from him was an entirely different story.

"You'll listen to me. No more threats, no more warnings. Agreed?" When Grace only stared at him, one corner of his mouth turned up. "Do you trust me?"

"Yes," she whispered. "With my entire life."

"Then agree." He still had a hold on her arm, and when she cast her eyes down and gave a nod of agreement, his cock stirred. The world felt right again. He let go of her arm and took half a step back. "Take my hand." She would come to him now. It was all on her. He gathered up the horse's reins and John Marin walked both lady and beast home, the tides having shifted, finally, in his favor. He would save her, and he would come alive again, like Phoenix, rising from the ashes.

13

*G*race had her bags by the door early. A large, black SUV had arrived, driven by Bashful, and while he, Grumpy and John loaded their bags, she enjoyed a cup of tea and a biscuit as she held a phone to her ear.

"We'll miss ya, lovey," Mathilda Whipple said. "How are things with our Mr. Marin?"

"I continue to infuriate him, I'm afraid."

"There's a girl. Have you decided you'll stay at Shannon-field for a bit once you're back, then?"

"I think so. I feel better here, and I know that once I get through the memorial, I'll be all right."

"That's fine. How did the embassy dedication go?"

"Oh, splendid, I suppose. The annoying ambassador forgot himself for a moment and got a bit handsy. I think my keeper slapped his hand off the small of my back, but I can't be sure."

"Good show. I knew I liked that man."

"Yes. He covets what's his, and for the moment that appears to be me."

"Jolly good." Mathilda Whipple paused for a moment. "Do you miss him, love—the president?"

"That's an odd question."

Mathilda Whipple paused. "I s'pose it is." Grace could never fool Mrs. Whipple, and there was no upside to starting now.

"I miss the president. He was a good one."

"That he was."

"I don't miss my husband." Grace glanced out the kitchen window. "But you knew that, hence the question."

"He was never right for you, lovey. You were too much for him, and he wasn't enough for you."

"You've discussed this with my mother."

"Not since the wedding, no."

Grace laughed and set her teacup down. As she looked out into the foggy morning, she saw Marin, Bashful and Grumpy disappearing inside the stables. Then Marin rushed out and went back in again.

"Take care while I'm gone, Mathilda." Grace craned her neck but saw nothing further. Something was up. "You'll have two men here to feed, in addition to Jasper—Grumpy and Bashful, they're called."

"Charming."

"Maybe you can get their real names out of them while they're eating. They're John Marin clones. Don't spoil them too much; I don't want to be stuck with them when I return."

"How very exciting," Mrs. Whipple said dryly. "We'll arrive around noon today. Everything will be in tip-top for your return."

"Bye, darling."

"Safe flight, love. And be kind to Mr. Marin. He likes you."

"Yes, well...I like him," she confessed.

"I know."

"I'll call when we land." Grace hung up and went out the back door and down the steps as Marin came out of the stables. He started toward her; Bashful came out of the shadows behind him.

"Grace," Marin said with some force. "Go to the car."

"What is it?"

"Do as I say."

"John..."

"Stay where you are," he said with more force as she followed the path toward the stables. *Stay where you are. Go to the car.*

"What's going on?" And as she got close to the men, she looked down at Bashful's shoes. They were covered in what was obviously blood, and lots of it.

"Oh, God!" She raced to the rough-hewn building, dodging Marin as he reached for her. He caught her around the middle and Grace left her feet.

"Stay here," he growled in her ear. "Stay with me."

"Let go! Let go, damn you!" She managed to escape his hold, but only because he allowed it. As she entered the dark of the stables the pungent odor could not be ignored. Marin came up behind her and wrapped an arm around her middle as Grace looked down. The dirt floor was dark and wet, and Marin stopped her just before she set her boot into a puddle of blood. Ahead of her lay dear Shane, his eyes open, his regal body unmoving. She knew then what she was smelling: the coppery odor of something foreign mingled with horse dung, but it was not the sweet grassy smell she was so familiar with. This smell was primitive, acrid, fear-filled. The sound of flies buzzing around was almost deafening, until they landed in the open gash across the horse's throat. And then there was silence, eerie silence. Grumpy appeared out of the shadows, his shoes dark, too, as if he'd stepped in mud. Marin held Grace tight as she sagged in his arms. And then she screamed.

"No! *No!*" She fought him as he tried to pull her out of the stables. Finally, he picked her up and carried her out.

"No! Put me down! No! *No!*" Grace threw her head back and came into contact with something hard. Marin growled a string of curses and tightened his hold.

"Grace! Stop it! Stop it now!"

Grace struggled in his arms, and looked up, her face a blanket of sorrow, her eyes filled with pain and shock. "John..." Blood dripped from a gash along his left eyebrow.

"I got you. I got you, sweetheart."

"Get her the hell out of here," Grumpy ordered from behind them. "Now."

Marin hesitated a brief moment and looked down at her. Grace stilled in defeat as Marin carried her to the car, and Bashful raced up ahead and got behind the wheel of the SUV and started it up. Marin deposited Grace in the back of the vehicle and got in beside her.

"Go!" Marin shouted, and before he had the back door closed, Bashful peeled out and raced down the drive.

———

MARIN HAD to drag the visibly upset former first lady onto the private jet while Bashful explained to the pilots that the woman had just experienced a trauma and she was in no danger. The golden tan interior of the plane was soothing, but it didn't seem to be working for Grace. She paced the aisles like a caged animal, her eyes swollen and red, and the look of utter devastation etched her face. And all John Marin could do was watch.

"Folks?"

Marin turned in the direction of the co-pilot, who was making his second appearance to ask them to sit for take-off. He had seen to Marin the moment they boarded, cleaning the wound on his head and dressing it with two butterfly bandages. All of that was forgotten as Marin stalked over to him with a scowl.

"I need you to get this fucking thing in the air while I take care of her. I'll have her in her seat before wheels up, and then you can come out and tell us all about this plane. But right now, I need you to be elsewhere. Does that work for you?"

"Yes, sir, of course."

"Thank you." And when the man returned to the cockpit, Marin turned to Grace. He set his hands on her shoulders, halting her pacing.

"We're about to take off, sweetheart. I need you to sit down."

"Don't handle me."

Marin stood before her with a glare that pulled Grace from her rage and fear and sorrow long enough to remember his words from the day before: *you will obey me.*

Grace sagged and Marin caught her before she fell. He sat her down and pulled the jump-seat style restraints over her shoulders and connected it all at her waist. He sat across from her and did the same for himself. She didn't speak again until they were in the air.

"How could you?" she whispered through tears.

"Staying at Shannonfield wasn't an option."

"He...*it*...was on my...my prop...property. What kind of a monster would...would do this?"

"I don't know, sweetheart." Marin removed his restraints

and crouched in front of her. "You understand why we had to go?"

Her chin wobbled but she nodded. "I'm sorry I...the way I behaved in the car." Marin reached for her hands, but she put them up to her face before he could and sobbed. He removed her restraints and had her in his arms as the plane leveled off. Rules be damned, Marin carried Grace into a room at the rear of the plane, separated from the main cabin by a set of accordion doors. He sat on one of the large reclining chairs, bringing Grace into his lap. She curled into him, buried her face in his neck, and Marin held her as she cried angry, bitter tears.

Given a moment to think, Grace moved to get up. "You don't...don't have to ...to do this."

Marin pulled her against him. "Stay still."

"John..."

"It's okay." He held her across his lap, her hip settled between his legs, her body curled in tight. Grace wrapped her arms tight around him and sobbed. "That's it. Let it go, sweetheart."

A long time passed before Grace settled, and a while after that before Marin realized she'd fallen asleep. He carried her to the sofa, laid her down, removed her shoes and covered her with a blanket. Now he paced the main cabin, a scotch in his hand at eight a.m. Hoping they were still under 10,000 feet and still over London, Marin snatched up his cell and dialed.

"Hey. How is she?" greeted Grumpy.

"Out of her mind," answered Marin. "What's going on there?"

"Inspector Devon and his people are here, and they've called in a forensic veterinarian. Ever heard of that?"

"Nope."

"Yeah, me either. Big amongst the horsey set. The upper crust wants to know what kills their prize studs, apparently. Anyway, I'm learning something new."

"Good."

"What's she doing now?"

For a moment, Marin felt his hackles rise. He found himself suddenly protective of her, especially when another man—this particular man—was asking. And then he remembered that they were all on the same team, and that Brian Dean was his best friend.

"She's sleeping," Marin said.

"It was right to get her out of here."

"I know. Thanks for insisting. I had a different perspective."

"You wanted to stay and hunt the fucker down; I know."

"Yeah, something like that."

"That shit's why you have us."

"Yeah."

"How's your noggin?" Grumpy teased.

"Throbbing in time with my beating heart."

"She clipped you good."

"Yeah."

"Leave a scar."

"Yeah."

"Chicks dig that."

"Yeah, especially when it's their doing," grumbled Marin.

"I've found it doesn't matter."

"You'd know better than I."

"That's true." Grumpy paused for a moment, then continued. "There'll come a time, after these people are done with the horse, when she'll have to decide what to do...with it."

"Yeah, okay." Marin sighed. "That'll be a fun conversation."

"Go gentle. Not your strong suit."

"Fuck you, Brian."

Grumpy laughed. "Later, buddy."

Marin sat for a long time and stared out at the gray clouds below and the crystal blue sky above. What a hell of a thing. He'd not seen pain like that on anyone's face for a long time, and then realized the last time he had, it had been on hers, as he carried her away from the carnage left in the wake of her husband's assassination. He wanted, now, as he'd wanted then, to take it away for her, make things right, make things good for her again. But he knew he couldn't unring a bell or pull back a breath that had already been expelled. All he could do was lead her out of it and onto the next thing, and hope the sun came up for her again soon.

When had he become so closed off? Was it his time in the Middle East, or was it losing his most important client that sent him running in search of a simpler life? Was it the nightmare that happened after, the draw into the viper's nest that caused him to sell everything and flee to a place they'd never find him? Marin chuckled at that. They could have easily found him; Grace Coolidge certainly had. He was out of the way and he hadn't breathed a word of their 'offer' to him after the president was assassinated. That he'd hesitated a second when Grace came asking for his help was hard to fathom, but he had. At the end of the day, he had far more to make up for than failing to protect the Commander-in-Chief.

And his family—what had they done to deserve his silence, his distance from them? He'd always been close to his parents, and to his four younger sisters. He'd spoken to them a handful of times since the assassination and hadn't been home since before the Coolidges entered the White House. His family deserved better. After this was over, maybe he'd go home, to Cody. That he was considering such a thing had a lot to do with the lady in the adjoining cabin, of that he was certain. She'd opened something inside him that had been closed tight and long dormant. He vowed he'd never shut it away again.

He took his drink into the back room where Grace slept. It was dark; he'd drawn the shades and turned out the lights when he left earlier. Now he sat in the lounge chair, where he'd held Grace in his lap, and switched on an overhead light. It cast a soft, pink glow across the aisle, caressing the angles of her face. Her cheekbones were higher than they'd been a week ago. The collar of her loose-fitting copper sweater fell across the top of her right shoulder, revealing a long neck and a collarbone that looked delicate, breakable. He realized that this was one of the few times he'd seen her completely serene. Even in her calmest moments, he still saw the stress of the past in her eyes, in the way her face set, in the way she carried her shoulders, a huge weight piled there with no relief in sight. How he wanted to take those burdens from her. He hadn't known it until now—or maybe he had and was finally ready to admit it.

In his lap earlier, Grace had been soft, fragile, and she had every right to be just that, only that. She'd let herself go for a moment and allowed him to care for her. The truth was, he *wanted* to care for her, and he'd done it. He'd picked her up, carried her to the back of the plane, and held her, without really giving her a choice. When Grace tried to brush him off, Marin didn't allow it. Another truth was he'd wanted to take care of her since she'd shown up on his boat. One moment on the dock, something she'd said in response to an off-handed comment.

You don't belong here, Mrs. Coolidge, you or your goon, he'd said

Well, that's certainly not the first time I've heard that. In fact, Senator David Howell said the very same in my ear after asking me to dance at the inauguration.

It affected him at the time on a visceral level, and it had angered him. That he was thinking about it still, angered him more. He remembered that inaugural ball; he'd been there. Grace Coolidge looked stunning, in a platinum gown that flowed over her like water. She had the eye of every man in the room, and every woman paled in comparison. Marin didn't remember that one dance in particular, but he pictured this beautiful woman, vulnerable in the arms of a man not her husband, as she was lead onto the dance floor in front of millions of people. And what she must have felt as Senator David Howell whispered those few words that spoke volumes into her ear. Escaping the man had not been an option, so she'd been forced to endure the rest of the dance that must have felt endless, in the arms of a man who held her and her husband, the new president, in such distain.

"What are you thinking?" came a voice, weak, unsure, and it tugged at his heart. He could just make out her face in the dim glow of the pink lighting, and in this moment she looked like a confused little girl.

"How do you feel?"

"Better," Grace said, sitting up and pulling her legs underneath her. "I needed a lie-down, as Mrs. Whipple is fond of saying. How long did I sleep?"

"Half-hour or so."

"What were you thinking just now? You looked cross. I haven't given you the easiest of mornings."

"You haven't had the easiest of mornings, Duchess."

"I've been more trouble to you than I'm paying for, I'm afraid."

Marin shook his head. "Let me be the judge of that."

"So what has you with your brows drawn together like a fuzzy blond caterpillar?" Despite the morning she had, she managed a sassy, teasing smirk that cheered him up, when it was the lady herself who needed the cheering. Marin paused for a long time, wondering what the upside would be in telling her what he was thinking.

"I was thinking about the inauguration, and what you told me the senator said to you on the dance floor," he said.

Grace's heart thumped in her chest, to the point where she worried Marin might hear. "For heaven's sake, why?"

"I don't like it."

"I'm sorry. His comment certainly wasn't the worst thing uttered in my ear during my four years as first lady."

"The man bullied you on a dance floor in front of millions of people, and no one saw him do it."

"He had to bang his willie against someone. I happened to be there. I haven't given it another thought."

"Tell me about Howell."

"About him? Well, he's an Ohio democrat, Yale educated, career politician, under 'Term Limits' in the dictionary there's an arrow pointing to him as the reason why the law is necessary. Shame, too, because he's very smart. Is that all?"

"I don't know. I'm trying to figure out the vitriol."

"As you pointed out so correctly the other day, Matt and I weren't short of detractors. Howell's party lost the election to a third-party outsider because their candidate was so horrid. He was angry. And, to a degree, scared. Still is, I'm sure, since he lost to Bannish after the assassination."

"Okay."

Grace rested her chin on her bent knee. "Did I, by

chance, make you any grandiose promises when I hired you that this would be easy?"

"You didn't, no."

"Wishful thinking on my part, perhaps."

"Not a bad thing, as long as reality's there somewhere," he said with a sardonic quirk of his mouth.

"So you've pointed out more than once. Your eye," Grace noted.

"It's fine."

"You'll need a stich or two."

"Don't worry about it."

"I'm sorry."

"I know. It's okay."

"It isn't."

"You're arguing with me again."

Grace smiled. She adored their banter. Matt wasn't a banterer. He wasn't much of a teaser. She found she loved it; she needed it. It made her feel noticed, important. Sexy. What in the world would she do when their time together was up?

"Our steward-slash-co-pilot wants to serve a meal," he said. "Are you up to it?"

"I'm probably not, but I should give it a go." Grace stood, eyed her shoes and waved a weary hand. As Marin drew next to her, she turned to him.

"I warn you, I am about to disobey one of your rules again. Hard to say, honestly, since your rules seem to be fluid lately."

"Think it through, lady," he warned.

"I have, and I apologize in advance." She placed her hands on his rough cheeks, pulled his head down, and placed a lingering but very chaste kiss upon his lips. "Thank you for handling me with such kindness, and I am very sorry about your eye." She dropped her hands. "Now, shall I put myself across your lap before we dine?"

Marin looked down at her and tried not to smile as his cock gave an involuntary jerk. He placed the length of his index finger under her delicate chin and tipped her face up. "It can wait. I'm keeping track."

"Oh, isn't that lovely," she returned.

"Do you think he suffered, John?" Marin arched a brow. "Shane?"

"No," he said right away.

"That is at least the second time since we've met that you've told me exactly what I wanted to hear."

"The truth is refreshing."

Grace did not miss the dig, however unintentional. "How do you know...that he didn't suffer?" When Marin hesitated, she said, "Please. I can talk about it without falling apart. I've done that already." After another pause, Grace put her hand over his. "Tell me."

"He fell where it happened. The blood was all in one place. Had he thrashed around, blood would have been scattered, but it wasn't. It was quick."

"He was out of his stall."

Marin nodded.

Tears suddenly bloomed in her eyes. "Thank you."

"I'm sorry, Duchess, I really am."

"I am, too. Shane was a dear old fellow."

"He was. He let me get on him without any problem at all. He knew who was in charge."

"Indeed—one alpha to another." Grace blushed and

then looked Marin in the eyes. "He saw you as a friend. As do I."

Marin tapped his spoon against the saucer on which his coffee cup lay, their meals finished but not yet cleared by the over eager co-pilot-slash-steward. He wanted to say the same; he wanted to tell her what an honor it was to serve her again.

"What happens now?"

"I spoke to Grumpy while you were asleep. They've got a forensic vet on the case, and Shane's being looked over now."

"A forensic...? I don't even have the energy to ask."

"They figure manner of death, time of death, and if there's any evidence, they'll find it."

"I see."

"You don't have to think about it right now, but eventually you're going to have to decide what to do with him."

Grace nodded. "Thank you."

"You're thanking me for a lot of things I'm not responsible for, sweetheart."

"You are responsible right now for my mental and physical well-being. You deserve every ounce of thanks I can muster."

"We were isolated at Shannonfield; things will be different once we land in New York."

"I know."

Marin paused. "Grace?"

"Yes?" When Marin simply stared into his coffee cup, Grace sat back in her chair and folded her arms. "Uh oh. My keeper has something to say." She had the nerve, or the good grace—Marin wasn't sure—to smirk.

"This might seem out of line, but I'm going to say it anyway."

"You mean more out of line than kissing me and my proffered tits, or swatting my arse?"

Marin chuckled, flushing at the memory. "Probably not."

"Well, I'm intrigued, then. Do go on."

"You've been through a lot—the assassination, the shooting in May, and now carrying the burden of these threats all by yourself. You've committed to this upcoming memorial, which I know you're concerned about. Have you...talked to someone?"

"You mean have I sought professional help?"

"Yes."

"Have you?"

Marin laughed. "No. I sold everything, bought a boat and filled my galley with a lot of good rum."

"And how has that worked for you?"

"It hasn't *not* worked." Marin leaned forward. "But we're discussing you, Duchess. You've been through a lot and I can tell you from experience that it will catch up with you. It's not if, it's when."

"I'm good for now," she managed with a whisper.

"You're not."

"I said for now. You have helped."

"Really?" His brows flew up. "Good to know." Marin looked out the window. Grace had taken his words better than he thought she would, and he'd already made up his mind that he'd revisit it with her again, as many times as it took. He was no psychologist, but he believed that none of this was Grace's normal behavior. Nothing that had happened to this woman was normal. And she was still young.

"It bothered you, didn't it?" he finally said.

"What?"

"Our discussion the other morning."

"There are different degrees of *bothered*. What do you mean?"

When Marin only stared, Grace sighed. "I don't know what to say. Obviously, it didn't bother me enough to send you packing, and that in itself bothers me a bit."

Marin smiled.

"Do not gloat."

"I'm not."

"You are. You're quite proud of yourself, aren't you? You've played out perhaps every man's fantasy of taking a rambunctious woman in hand and walking away with your cockles intact."

Marin rested an elbow on the table. "It's not a game, Grace. You had it coming, and you didn't send me packing because you knew it. I didn't do it to score one for the blue team. I did it so you'd know that I won't let anything happen to you and tripping me up and making my job harder will have consequences."

"Back in the day, a man had the right to chastise a woman—rule of thumb, and all. We're in the twenty-first century now, John. You forget that."

"I haven't forgotten anything. You're a grown woman. At the end of the day, you're in charge. Say the word and we'll go back to the way we were before; you do whatever the hell you want, I get pissed, we argue, and you become less safe. I won't stick around long for that, though. I won't be your beta-male, no matter how much you pay me." Marin stared into her ice blue eyes. "Truth is, I think you feel better about things since our little talk. And before you throw that cup at me, that isn't hubris talking. I think you know that."

"Mmmm."

"Mmmm," he repeated.

"Oddly enough, all I can hear in my head is, 'This can't

happen again, Duchess'," she said, mocking his deep voice and inflections. "Yet forty-eight hours ago, both my lips and my breasts were trapped in your mouth, and..."

"And?"

"I never wanted it to end," she whispered, looking down into her coffee.

Heat suffused his gaze. "I didn't either."

"You're irritatingly arrogant, but I honestly feel you have my best interests at heart. And I also feel..."

"Yes?"

"Your interest goes beyond the paycheck you're receiving. Am I wrong?"

"You know you're not wrong."

Grace cleared her throat. "You..."

"What?"

"Oh, do shut up."

"Tell me," he said, chuckling.

"And stroke your ego to as yet untested heights? I think not."

"Tell me. Tell me what's on your mind, sweetheart. No judgment. It's just us here."

After a long, scrutinizing stare into a pair of earnest blue eyes, she dared the truth. "You tap into something deep in me that..." Grace stared at her hands, fingers fidgeting. "That no one else has, ever. You handle me with absolutely no thought to the law, or my feelings, or the bloody suffragettes, for fuck's sake! The smart, independent feminist in me is roaring like a damn tigress, and I find myself telling it to hush at every opportunity, because..."

"Because?"

"Wipe that damn smirk off your face!"

He laughed. "I'm not smirking. I'm fascinated." Marin lost the smile. "Go on, please. Because?"

"It turns me on. All of it. Every blasted thing about you. I feel..." Grace sighed. "I feel at my *most feminine* when you are taking charge of me, and when I'm sitting in that mountain of a lap of yours. What happened between us was incredibly intimate—all of it. And in an odd way it communicated to me that you cared, perhaps beyond that of protector and client." Grace held up her hand when he opened his mouth to speak. "And that is intensely erotic. And, as a woman grown, as you so kindly pointed out, I'm choosing *this*, for now."

Marin sat back in his chair, and in that moment he saw what a huge responsibility she was giving him, and he was taking on, as naturally as someone takes on air.

"You have me at a disadvantage, Mr. Marin. I hope you will take great care." Grace placed a hand over her heart, and Marin was certain she wasn't aware she did it.

"Grace."

"*Grace*, indeed." She fiddled with a lump of sugar resting in her saucer. "When are you going to acknowledge there's something between us?"

"Don't you have enough going on?"

"Yes, I have quite a bit going on, as a matter of fact, and perhaps a simple discussion of the matter will be a great relief to both of us."

"Or make things harder."

Grace had the audacity to scan down toward his lap, and Marin couldn't help but smirk just a little. "Eyes up here, Duchess," he said, barely above a whisper. Grace sat back, folded her arms, and stared at him.

"I...like you, obviously." Marin cleared his throat. "Very much."

Grace wanted to beam but forced it down. "See? That wasn't so hard, was it? I like you, too. Very much."

"Are we done?"

"Oh, I don't think we are."

Marin shook his head. "Nothing changes. I need to keep my head."

Grace looked into her coffee cup for guidance. "I ache for you, Johnny."

Marin's hand, flat on the table, curled. And then he stretched his fingers until they touched the tips of hers. "I ache for you, too, sweetheart," he whispered. He did not, could not, meet her eyes, for if he did, he'd have to strip her, here and now, and bury himself deep inside her until she screamed his name. And that would not be good for either of them.

Grace reached a slender finger over one of his—hers delicate porcelain, this thick and tan and rugged. Leather and lace, iron and velvet, magnet and steel. Tears pricked her eyes, and as she tried to blink them back, the stark contrast of their digits blended into one blurry amalgam, dark undulating against light, hard against soft.

"When do we land?" she asked.

Forty years or so, he wanted to say. Instead he sat back and let the steward clear their plates.

14

*T*he black Land Rover Sentinel sat on the tarmac next to the terminal at Teterboro Airport in New Jersey. The vehicle gleamed inside, the white leather fresh and pungent. The doors were heavy, the glass thick, and without explanation, Grace knew what the armored vehicle was capable of doing. Doc gave her the rundown anyway: it could handle off-road under the harshest conditions as well as it could on the smoothest highway; the interior was reinforced to withstand armor-piercing incendiary rounds, TNT explosions, and grenades going off both beneath the floor and on the roof. In addition, there was an anti-tamper exhaust, a self-sealing fuel tank, and an auxiliary back-up battery with a split charging system. Doc was particularly fond of explaining the fully stocked rear area for any medical emergencies that might arise. Given the man's medical background, Grace wasn't surprised in the least.

"Like an ambulance," he finished with a smile.

"You're like a boy in a candy store," Grace said.

"Yes, ma'am."

"How are you, Doc?" she asked after he turned in his

seat and put the vehicle in gear. Marin spent time at the rear of the vehicle, and she heard the familiar clang and snapping of guns being loaded. Soon, he took the passenger seat in front.

"I'm good. We're all set here." He turned to her. "I'm sorry about your troubles back home. You okay?"

"I'm getting there," she answered.

"And what the hell happened to you?" Doc asked his front seat passenger.

"My doing, I'm afraid," Grace said.

"It was an accident," Marin offered.

"I'm sure it was," Doc said. "I'll look at it when we get to the hotel."

Grace stared out the window as they crawled through rush hour traffic in New Jersey and would likely see worse once they got into Manhattan. Marin filled Doc in and they spent a good portion of the ride talking business in hushed tones. While they were stopped in traffic, Marin opened the passenger door, got out, and got into the back seat next to her. His black leather jacket was off and across the front seat he'd just vacated, and he wore a gun secured in a black holster around his shoulders; one side held the gun, the other held two clips within easy reach. Grace stared at the ensemble, and then caught his eye.

"The press will be at the hotel," Marin said after he settled in. "And you were right, Duchess. This is the right choice."

"Thank you."

"No need to thank me. When you're right, you're right."

"He's never said that to anyone in his life, Mrs. Coolidge," Doc offered. "He'll have to rinse his mouth out when he gets up to the room—twice, maybe."

"Shut up," Marin grumped good-naturedly. The men

had a bond, it was clear. Marin seemed more relaxed now that Doc was around—strength in numbers and all that, she figured.

Grace preferred Marin next to her, as opposed to up front. She'd never reacted to a man like this before, never craved the closeness, the protection, the safety net his simple presence, his masculinity, provided. She wanted nothing more than to put her head down on his shoulder. She was in trouble, and she knew it. Grace looked out the window. "Yes, I suppose the press will be there."

"We'll deal with it. We move through the crowd and through the lobby quickly as a unit," Marin said. "Stay on my hip."

"I know. I remember."

"You all right?"

"Yes, of course," she said, turning to face him. "Are you?"

Marin laughed, as did Doc. "Yeah."

"The press will wonder who you are," Grace said. "Those questions will be shouted, and all our non-answers will be reported on Page Six tomorrow morning as the God's truth, and you can expect that we'll be the topic of discussion until I leave the country again."

"It'll be okay."

"Mmmm." Grace looked at her phone. "Oh, I'd like to get my nails done before the party at the Levys tomorrow night."

"We'll arrange it when we get inside and we're in the room."

"Doc," she asked, leaning forward. "Do you need anything done at the salon?"

"Got it all taken care of yesterday, Mrs. Coolidge. But thanks."

"As you wish" she said. "But if you are shying away from

a pedicure because you believe it unmasculine, you're missing out."

"Oh, I've had pedis before, Mrs. Coolidge."

"You continue to surprise me, Doc."

"Yes, ma'am."

Marin grabbed his jacket and put it on as they pulled up to the entrance to the New York Palace Hotel. Doc shot out of the car before the valet and doormen could respond. Marin was out and pulling Grace out behind him as reporters crashed in on them and microphones were shoved in her face.

"How do you think President Bannish is doing?"

"How are you holding up, Mrs. Coolidge?"

"Who's the man with you?"

As they moved through the doors, held open by a doorman, and walked briskly through the lobby, they were met midway by the hotel manager and escorted to the Towers section of the hotel. As they passed through the lobby, other guests approached them, and Marin firmly kept them at arm's length as they made their way through a closed brass gate to a bank of elevators just for Towers guests.

"Mrs. Coolidge..."

"Grace..."

"Over here..."

People called to her and she didn't have time to look in anyone's direction, as she assumed was John Marin's intent. She would have to make time for the press sooner or later. She should have had Sterling handle that, and had he been with her as was the original plan, it would be one less thing she'd have to think about. She felt herself getting annoyed.

The manager got into the elevator with them and used a special key to get the elevator moving. Grace asked about getting a pedicure, and the manager reiterated the safety features the hotel put in place during her stay.

They exited the elevator and Marin held up his hand. "We'll take it from here."

"But, your bags...?"

"We'll manage them, thank you."

"Well, please, if we can do anything for you..."

"We're good," Marin said, scanning the area in front of the elevator doors and as far down the hall as he could see.

"Mrs. Coolidge, we are thrilled to have you here, and rest assured we will do everything in our power to make your stay a pleasant one. Unfortunately, the press cannot be barred from the sidewalk, but they will not be allowed in the hotel, and know that no calls will be sent up to your room."

"I appreciate that..." Grace squinted at his name tag. "... Darren. Thank you."

"Very well, then," he said, and left in the same elevator from which he came as Doc came out of a second one with Grace's two large bags. "I'll get the others and take care of the car," he said. "And get yourself ready for me to look at that eye." With a smile and a wink to Grace, Doc disappeared back into the elevator.

Marin looked down at her and raised his brows. "Let's move." He led her down the hall to the very end without another word. When he entered the suite, he pulled Grace inside behind him and set her in a small room next to the door, after scanning it. A desk, a couple of chairs and some end tables took up the space. It was a small office.

"Wait," he ordered, and then disappeared into a bedroom directly opposite. He came out a moment later and continued down a hallway into the rest of the suite. She heard the banging of doors and drawers, and then the growl of an indelicate swear word rattled the walls. Then she heard him on the phone. She sat in one of the chairs in the dimly lit room and waited for her orders. She was learning. Marin had moved through the suite like he knew it, and of course, he did. He'd studied the floor plans of every room in every hotel they considered.

Within moments, both Doc and the manager entered the room. Grace stood.

"Stay here," Doc ordered. What the hell was going on? When she heard Marin speak in *that* tone, she crept down the hall toward the main living area and listened.

"There wasn't supposed to be a terrace," Marin snapped at the hapless manager.

"Oh…"

"And I said no baskets. No deliveries, no nothing."

"I…you're right, I'm so sorry," the man sputtered. "I can… let me move you…"

"No, we're all set in here, but that terrace compromises my client."

"Yes."

"You'll tarp it. Now."

"Yes…yes, of course. Please, give me an hour and I'll have it done."

"Not good, Mr. Naser."

"No…"

"Get that basket out of here, now."

"Of course, right away." Grace looked after the delicacies with fondness as Mr. Naser passed her, clutching what appeared to be a goody basket filled with everything in the world she adored. Marin pressed a button that lowered a sheer shade over the bank of windows that looked out over a large terrace and the city below.

"What happened?" she asked from the arched entry into the living room of the suite.

"There's a hole in the boat, my friend," Doc smiled. Marin chuckled and swore.

"John?" Grace inquired.

"Come on," he said, gesturing her forward. "Look around."

Grace surveyed the suite. "Nice," she pronounced. And it was. Modern colorful furniture filled the living room, and a sliding wall separated the inside from a large terrace covered in furniture of all types. A glance into her master suite revealed a dark but glittery room. Tiny lights had been imbedded into the headboard of the bed to resemble stars. Whatever was black, silver thread seemed to run through it. She liked it. It was warm and comforting. Sexy.

Marin whipped through the room, looking under the covers of thermostats, under tables and beds, and inside closets and behind pictures.

"I want this swept for bugs. Now."

"I'll get on it," answered Doc.

Marin looked out at the terrace and sighed. "Why don't you go unpack and I'll fix you a drink. Then we'll talk."

Grace did as she was told and when she came out, there was a gin and tonic with a fresh lime sitting on the coffee table in front of an over-large chair.

"May I say something?"

"As long as it doesn't piss me off."

"I won't promise that. I have to meet with the press at some point, and had Sterling been here..."

"But he's not, and no you don't," Marin snapped. Procedure had not been followed. Of course he was upset. Nevertheless...

"But, I do."

"Why?"

"Because...because I'm here."

"And when the other living first ladies come into New York, do they meet with the press, too?"

"Well," Grace said thoughtfully, "I suppose it depends on why they're here."

"So, why are you here?"

Grace sighed. "You're being difficult again."

"No, I'm not. We're talking this out so we're on the same page."

"We're never on the same page," Grace pointed out.

"So, we're done, then, about the press?"

"We most certainly are not done about the press!" she snapped.

"Okay, then tell me why you are here, in New York."

"I'm attending a few parties, and an event at the Met..."

"And which of those requires a statement from you to the press?"

"None of them," Grace conceded, "But they'll expect access."

"This won't be the first time the press has been disappointed."

"John..." Grace thought for a moment. "The public appearances, like the event at the Met."

"Okay, and that's Sunday night?"

"Yes."

"It is an event where the press would normally be there?"

"Yes, I should think so. It's quite an event."

"Then I'll call Jarvis and he can arrange for some time for you with the press. Will that do?"

Grace sat back and smiled. Oh, it wasn't a happy smile, but rather an admiring one. He'd handled her brilliantly, and if she hadn't been so irked, she would have stood and applauded.

"It will do fine."

"Good. Drink."

"Bloody bumptious, bossy..." A chuckle from Doc ended her tirade.

"Grace."

This latest tiff happened in front of Doc, and she wasn't happy about that. Expecting a scowl to meet her gaze when she looked up, she was pleasantly surprised to see him relaxed yet full of concern, it seemed, for *her*.

"Everything's okay, and I don't want you to worry," Marin said, taking a seat on the couch next to her chair. "I want to explain what went on here."

"All right." For the first time Grace noticed a silver metal case in the middle of the table.

"We don't want a terrace because someone can see you from the air if you're outside. These shades are black from the outside, even though you can see through them from in here. The glass around the terrace outside is bulletproof, as is this wall of glass here—thanks to President Cornwell's visit during his last term. They never replaced it. That's why I wanted this suite—in fact, it sold me on this hotel, as you predicted. The tarp I asked for will give you privacy if you decide to go outside. I was angry because I expect that when I secure an agreement with the head of security in a prominent hotel, my orders will not only be met but exceeded. The basket put me over the edge."

"It looked good," Grace said.

"I'm sure it was, but it wasn't supposed to be here. No one was supposed to come in this room after Doc, Happy and Sneezy secured it, so now I'm concerned."

"Concerned enough to leave?" she asked.

"I'm having it checked out, and then we'll see."

"All right."

"Putting you in front of the press unless it's absolutely necessary doesn't sit well with me. I want to think about it further as regards to the Met event, okay?"

"Your Secret Service roots are showing." Grace took a sip of her drink and set it down. "What's this?" she asked, referring to the metal case before her. Marin opened the case to reveal several necklaces set in foam lined in dark blue velvet. "Oh, how lovely."

Grace lifted out a silver necklace in a teardrop shape, about as large as a half-dollar. Above the teardrop sat a smaller inverted teardrop with a one-carat diamond set in the center. The necklace was heavy, well-made. Grace turned it over. A faint cut-out the size of her fingertip lay flat against the metal.

"We turn it on like this—" Marin pressed something along the bottom edge. "And we know where you are at all times."

"A tracking device."

"Yes, and if something happens and you get into trouble, or you're scared, you press this flat button back here, and I'll be there."

"Whichever one of us is closest will be there," Doc amended.

"This is incredible, so beautiful. Which...? I mean...?"

"All of them, whatever goes with what you're wearing." There were gold square pendants with colorful jewels in the center; there were casual, fun pendants in hammered silver and brass; and there were classy diamond pendants. There were two cuff bracelets to choose from, and even a pair of gold teardrop earrings that were long enough to tap against the edge of her jaw.

"Take the case into your room and put it away." Grace nodded and took it to her room. When she glanced out, Doc was hovering over Marin cleaning the cut over his eye. Sometime later, Doc left, and Marin stood in the doorway of her room.

"I don't want to keep fighting with you."

"Were we fighting?" Grace said as she removed a pair of earrings and replaced them inside the metal case. "I thought it was a great discussion, a meeting of minds and mutual needs."

"Then why do I feel like I've gone ten rounds with you?" Grace looked up at the tone of his voice—tender, and dare she assume, hurt?

"You're not used to a woman asking questions or questioning you."

Marin chewed on that for a moment. "You challenge me."

"You challenge me, too, you know."

She met his eyes, and they appeared filled with a mix of confusion and capitulation. She liked it. "How's your room?" she asked over her shoulder as she dug into one of her bags.

"This is ridiculous."

"Would you like this one instead?" she asked with an arched brow.

"No. I mean this whole..." Marin waved his hand. "Look at this place."

"Yes." She looked around. "It's nice. I love this hotel. They also have a three-bedroom suite, which I expected Sterling to occupy along with us. Might have made things easier on you."

"Still not over that, huh?"

"No, but I believe Sterling is secretly thrilled, much as he loves to travel, especially with me. We have a grand time together. You, I'm sorry to say, make him nervous."

"His shadow makes him nervous."

"That isn't nice," she said with a smirk as she edged past him and crossed the living room. She turned down the hallway that led to the front door and Marin's bedroom.

"Oh, this is lovely," she said, poking her head in. Two queen beds and a large, masculine bathroom made up Marin's room, with floor to ceiling windows taking up an entire wall. "Are you sure you're okay here?" she asked. "I don't need to have that room. Either will do."

"I want to be near the front door."

"All right. Where's Doc?"

"In his room across the hall. I'm going to see him for a minute." Marin came up close to her and took her hand. "Are you okay?"

Grace looked up at him and nodded, offering him a ghost of a smile. "Mmmm hmmm," she murmured. She longed to have him bend slowly and take her mouth, the way he did at Shannonfield. A reassuring kiss, an *I'll never leave you* kiss. A *You're mine* kiss. Instead, he sighed, and resumed professional countenance.

"Okay. Stay put and make your appointment. I'll be right back."

"Drink when you return? I can order up some food."

"Sure. Whatever you want."

When Marin left, Grace arranged for a manicure and pedicure in the room in an hour, and then ordered a tea service for three, intending to have Doc join them. She went about her tasks without thinking, and then wandered the suite. The day was winding down and it was a dull gray outside, like her mood. Her thoughts turned to that morning and the carnage she'd seen in her precious stables. How would she ever go back? How would things ever be the same for her at Shannonfield?

GRACE WATCHED the New York skyline come alive as the sun set behind the buildings. Her feet were soaking and while one girl worked on her hands, another prepared to work on her toes. Doc sat in a chair reading; Marin had gone downstairs; why, Grace did not know.

"Doc, would you like to get your toes done?" Grace teased.

"Laugh all you want, but I just had one," the big man said. "I wasn't kidding. Taking care of your feet is very important."

All three women laughed at this rugged, burley bear, picturing him with his huge feet in a whirlpool bath.

"How do you and John know each other, Doc?"

"We were Rangers together."

"Ah, yes. And do you do anything else—besides his bidding?" she asked with a smile.

"A few things. I'm a medical training officer at Fort Benning, I do personal protection, like this, I'll go and spend months in some war-torn region as a doctor—I'm a lot of things."

Grace smiled and shook her head in wonder. "That's wonderful. Are you married?"

"Not anymore. This life has no room for a woman, I'm afraid." The woman doing Grace's nails was trying to convince him differently, shooting sideways glances at him he was finding hard to ignore. As the women worked, Grace and Doc chatted, but he never asked her anything or offered information on his own, only when asked. He was kind and funny, and Grace found herself telling him things about being in the White House and about her time spent as the wife and companion of a politician without prompting.

The manicurists were wrapping up when the door rattled, and she heard John come in. He entered the living room, and Grace gasped. He'd cut his hair; it was short and combed straight back off his face, one half falling to the side. And the beard was gone. If possible, John Marin was handsomer, sexier, than before.

"What prompted this?" Grace asked.

"You asked me to," he said.

"You look very nice."

"Thanks."

Doc stood. "You clean up good, ol' Hoss."

"Yeah."

As Doc passed Marin to leave, he asked, "What is the plan tonight?"

Marin looked at Grace.

"We can eat in the room if you like," she said. "I'm tired."

"Join us?" Marin asked Doc.

"Probably not, but thanks. Later, Mrs. Coolidge."

"Will you please call me Grace?"

"Unlikely. Night, you two." Grace stuck her tongue out at him in most unladylike fashion and settled up with the two girls before ushering them out. She stood in the doorway to Marin's room after he entered.

"You going to be all right for a bit? I have some calls to make," he said.

"Of course. I'll order up dinner when you're ready."

Marin nodded, and when she disappeared back down the hall, he went into the small office across from his room and sat down heavily in an upholstered chair. He could hoist his charge over his shoulder and carry her down twenty-five flights of stairs; he could rappel down the side of the building with her in his arms; he could administer CPR if she stopped breathing or apply a tourniquet if she was bleeding. But none of his training prepared him for resisting a client he was falling for. He wanted to feel her body against his. He wanted to taste her and then bury himself deep inside her. He wanted to set her in his lap and kiss her for hours. That mouth. Jesus Christ. He could literally kiss her for days; forget about all the rest. She tasted like air, like life. He thought he was done with the kissing, until she took off on her stallion. That mouth, those breasts; that was just the beginning; acknowledging his feelings for her was falling into dark territory. It wasn't good for her. None of this was good. *He* wasn't good.

It needed to stop.

Marin sat back and kicked a leg up over his knee. It was Friday night; the memorial was the following Friday. One week, and then technically he was done. But would he be done, really?

"John, excuse me."

He was so lost in thought that he jumped. "Yeah?"

"I'm going to a hot yoga class in the morning."

"Hot what?"

"Yoga."

"Where?"

"A few blocks away. I have the address."

"What time?"

"Five-thirty."

"Okay."

"There's no need to worry; I'm taking the class with a UN Diplomat's wife, a senator, the district attorney of New York, the mayor's wife and a famous author. It'll be like Fort Knox in there. And they don't open to the public until seven anyway."

"Okay."

"Will you tell Doc, or shall I?"

"I'll tell him. Five-thirty?"

"Yes." And then she came into the room and stood at his side. Before he could brace himself, she bent down and placed a tender kiss on his brow, where Doc had stitched him up. Marin closed his eyes as a warmth coursed through him and a snap of electricity shot south. She placed a delicate hand on his shoulder and squeezed. With no thought to consequences, he wrapped his arm around her waist and pulled her into his lap. Their eyes met, one seemingly more shocked than the other at the sudden turn of events.

"Well," Grace muttered, clearing a dry throat. "Look where I am."

"Clumsy, falling into my lap like this," he whispered.

"I should watch my step."

"Yeah. Damn right you should." Then he tipped her sideways, pulled her up so her head fell back, and he kissed her. Supporting her across her back with one arm, he roamed freely with his other hand, running it over her hip and across her bottom, encased in forest green denim. Her head unsupported, she wrapped her arms around his neck and pulled herself close. His hand stroked her bottom in sync with the slow sweep of his tongue along hers. He loved kissing her. Too much, he was learning. The hard way.

Marin ended the kiss, tenderly, with reverence, and he rested his forehead against hers.

"I'm going to have to stop doing that," he growled softly.

Grace ran her hand over his freshly shaven face. "Yes," she agreed. "Do you have a timetable on that, a goal of some kind?"

Marin shook his head lamely.

"We can work on it together, then."

He chuckled. "Okay." He lifted her off his lap and slid an arm over his bulging crotch.

"Mmmm," she muttered, staring at his attempt to hide. "I may find a bruise on my hip in the morning."

"Get out of here, Duchess," he ordered with a half-grin. "Now."

"Dinner's on the way up," she whispered.

"Fuck me," he hissed when she was out of earshot, adjusting himself.

15

*I*t was still dark when they pulled up in front of a
brownstone on E. 61st. Several black cars were
double-parked outside; dark, ominous, official, and all of
them had government plates. Marin got out first and opened
his arm to Grace while scanning up and down the small side
street off 2nd Ave. near the East River. Grace offered an
amused smirk, and he knew that he was probably being
overly fussy, but his Secret Service training was ingrained,
and she'd just have to deal with it.

Once inside, she was greeted with loud choruses of
"Grace!" "Gracie!" "Darling!" and one, "Oh, thank GOD!"

"I am here, at five-bloody thirty, and on time to boot!"
she shouted in greeting. Marin nodded to the other black-
suited men standing or sitting in the lobby. He was the only
one in jeans and leather jacket. He knew that between the
four men, they packed enough firepower to hold a good-
sized attack at bay. Nevertheless, Marin didn't know them,
so what they were holding and who they were protecting
mattered little.

A muscled guy in loose leggings and a sleeveless shirt

came out to greet the ladies and they all air-kissed, most behaving as if they knew the man intimately—including Grace. It took Marin all he possessed not to roll his eyes, but when the darkly handsome man placed his hand at the small of her back, leaned in and kissed her tenderly on the cheek and whispered something in her ear, he almost flew across the room at the guy, and had the guy not whisked her into the yoga room, Marin would have. The three agents introduced themselves, and one of them said, "You're private security?"

"I am now," he said, taking a seat on a molded plastic chair that was surprisingly comfortable.

"Interesting choice for the former first lady," he said.

"None of your concern, I'm guessing," countered Marin.

"Sorry," the agent said with raised hands.

Marin looked at the three men, standing or sitting in various degrees of alertness, and he knew immediately who was Secret Service and who was private. And he guessed the two who did not have protection were the author and the DA. He hadn't looked into the yoga room when they arrived. He'd been too preoccupied with the dude who put his hands on Grace. He mentally kicked himself for the mistake and strode to the door the women disappeared behind moments ago.

The six women were in various stages of setting up. Grace was standing next to a mat on the floor and laughing with two others. The room got quiet, and that prompted Grace to look over her shoulder. Marin had poked his head in and rendered everyone speechless. He ignored the silence as he looked around, noting if there were any closets he needed to look in, or rear doors he needed to open. When he saw nothing untoward, he stared down the yogi, who looked like a Dolce and Gabbana model, and then caught

Grace's eye. She gave him a smile and a confident nod, and Marin nodded back and closed the door.

"You think we missed that part, Chief?" the agent said, causing the others to chuckle.

"I'm sure you didn't."

"You're ex-Secret Service," he stated.

"Yeah." And then Marin placed himself between the other agents and the door to the room.

"OKAY...WOW," said Meg Arthur, U.N. diplomat Jake Arthur's wife. "Where did you find him?"

"It's a long story." Grace averted her eyes as a blush crept up her body. Her embarrassment was simply undeniable, especially in a room full of women.

"We have time," cooed Karen Perry. The best-selling author was the quintessential queen of romances, and she'd been at it for two decades, so she was particularly interested in Grace's potential love life, whether true or not. The woman was more than capable of filling in the blanks.

"No, we don't ladies," offered Axel, who was already sweating in the one-hundred-degree room. "I have another class at seven."

"Good God, Axel," sniffed Senator Gwendolyn Winkle-foos. "That's an hour and a half away. Just how flexible do you think we need to get?"

"Gwen, aren't we interested in the man squiring Grace all over New York?" mused Deanna Pierce, New York Mayor Jim Pierce's wife.

The senator tapped her index finger against her mouth. "This might not be the place, since Grace may not want to share her escapades with Axel in the room." The senator offered the patient man at the front of the room a sideways glance. "Perhaps a little breakfast after we're finished would be more appropriate."

"Since when do you have time for breakfast, Winnie?" said Grace, addressing her old college roommate by her nickname.

"Thank you, Senator," barked Axel. "Now, ladies, let's settle down and breathe. That means you, Mrs. Coolidge."

"You're all getting me into trouble," she hissed as she sat on her mat and waited for Axel's next instruction.

"Namaste, and welcome," he said in a low tone meant to relax his students. "On your backs, legs apart..." That elicited a giggle out of the author, which got the senator going.

"I can see I'm going to have to keep a few of you after class," said Axel with some humor. "Breathe..."

MARIN LOOKED toward the door when he heard Grace laugh. He could pick it out of a crowd of noise, and he leaned forward in his chair so he wouldn't miss it if it happened again.

Hot yoga. The smell of lemongrass and feminine mystique wafted through the studio on a humid cloud. She was in that room now, sweating and twisting in those tight black yoga pants that fit her ass just right, and a hot pink exercise bra with black trim that kept her together in one place. But she was safe. For the moment, here on a Saturday morning at 5:40 a.m., she was safe, and laughing. Given the day she had yesterday, he'd say that was good.

"Shit," he heard one of the agents hiss. "Fucking Constant Comment. What the hell is that?"

"Tea," another said, barely heard above the white noise of a fan and the underworld din of sitar music seeping from the ceiling speakers. Strategically placed Himalayan salt lamps cast a warm glow in a space where, for the time being, testosterone and skepticism ruled. The irony wasn't lost on Marin.

"Got that, Chief. Who drinks that shit?" This guy wasn't your regular, every day security detail. He was way too familiar. While the rest of the guys stood and paced, this one was bitching about tea and questioning the former first lady's choice of security. Marin smiled to himself. The agent was fucking his client. He spent the next hour wondering which one.

THE WOMEN FILED out of the room amid a cloud of steam. They turned down a hallway, none giving their detail so much as a glance—except Grace.

"We're going to shower and then go for something to eat," she said to him.

Marin nodded and brushed the back of his hand across the front of her shoulder, whisper light. "Wait here." He strode down the hall ahead of the group and entered the women's dressing room, the moisture from her hot body growing cold on his hand.

The women turned to Grace with raised eyes and devilish smirks, except for Meg Arthur, the diplomat's wife, who turned to her security man with a glare. Grace did not miss the exchange. Marin came out a moment later, set his hand on her shoulder, and mumbled, "All set."

"Thank you, John," she said, and the others echoed their praise, some in sing-song voices.

"Like junior high," Grace mused good-naturedly once they were behind closed doors.

"He had to know the detail out there already vetted the place," Senator Winklefoos said.

"None of that matters to him," Grace said as she stripped her wet clothes off.

"That is so hot," Karen Perry said. "One of my best sellers was about a bodyguard and an heiress. I wrote it back when you could get away with a good alpha-dog hero. They're all too sensitive and 'damaged' now, and it's the women who climb on top to make repairs. Phooey."

"Here here," Brooklyn District Attorney Ruth Wilson said. "I read the old bodice rippers all the time, longing for a return to knights in shining armor. And if he spanks her for being a shrew, all the better." Nude, with just a towel clutched in her hand, she scanned the faces of her friends. They all stared at the DA, wide-eyed. "That shit doesn't leave this room, bitches."

Grace entered the shower stall and thought about the man sitting outside, waiting for her, and the effect he had on these smart, successful women. She wondered what they'd say if she told them John Marin had already spanked her—and threatened to do it again. And she didn't say no. There was a reason women responded so viscerally to men like John Marin. It was ingrained, settled into a woman's DNA since prehistoric times, when the male protected the tribe while the females tended to their young. It was primitive.

She pictured Meg Arthur with the man in the suit, and the glare she gave him, and what made her turn to him and away from her husband. As Grace lathered her body and scrubbed away the sweat and toxins only a good hot yoga class could extract, she thought about Matt Coolidge, and about how easy it had been to turn away from him. It happened slowly; she hadn't even noticed, until the die had been cast. Now she regretted not having the time back to try again, to make amends, to see if perhaps their relationship could have gone back to the way it had been in the beginning. What had she done to make Matt Coolidge stop looking at her the way John Marin did—and Marin was nothing more than hired protection? What had Matt done, or perhaps *not* done, to make her stop caring? And why did every day feel like a new day since Marin came on the scene?

THEY HAD a quiet lunch in the hotel, and then Grace took a nap while Marin confirmed coverage and security for the party they would attend at the home of Sharron and Aaron Levy. Grace seemed nervous about the affair, mentioning more than once that people from the Coolidge's political life would be there. This was not a gathering of good friends. Grace hinted that it was a fundraiser of sorts for The Party, although no money would be collected this evening; it was more of a reminder of what the country had under Matt Coolidge, and what they lost when he was assassinated. Grace would be their touchstone, and she wasn't comfortable with it.

At six p.m. Marin heard her in the shower and started getting ready himself. An hour later Grace came out in a dress that made his mouth go dry. The black off-the-shoulder dress came to her knees in front, and the back fell in waves to the floor. The lining of the dress was pale pink, and the material looked smooth as butter, elegant. The gown hugged her body, accentuating her feminine curves. Pink painted toes peeked out of silver-pink strappy heels.

Her wildflower-honey hair was swept back off her face, the ends fanned out behind her ears, which were adorned with diamond drop earrings. She chose the pale pink rough-cut agate quartz geode necklace from the silver case, set in poured gold, the agate matching the inside lining of her dress. A sheer black ribbon held the pendant in the center of her chest. She'd applied a deep rose to her lips and little else to the rest of her face. A delicious floral scent, light and fresh, wafted off her whenever she moved. She was classy and elegant, and any man would be proud to have her on his arm. He felt overwhelmed.

He set a glass of chardonnay on the coffee table. "Come here. I want to show you something," he said. Grace, for the moment, could not move. Marin wore a charcoal gray snake-skin suit with a cerulean shirt, which he left open at the collar. A matching pocket square peeked out of the breast pocket of his jacket. His large body and handsome, ruddy features set him apart. At six-four and well over two-hundred pounds, John Marin was hard to miss, but the understated elegance of the suit would help him blend in. He took a small earpiece out of his ear.

"Feel behind the pendant for a rough spot and press it." Grace did as she was told. "Here," Marin said, setting the earpiece in her ear. His finger lingered on the delicate lobe of her ear, and the urge to bend her head and expose the tender area underneath—an erogenous zone for her—for his tender kisses was overwhelming. She quivered when his finger caressed the area before disappearing back in his lap.

"That's what I'll hear when you press the button, and I'll be there," he said, his voice soft and low. "Don't be afraid to press it. If you're uncomfortable and I'm not in your line of sight, you press it. No such thing as overreaction, no such thing as a stupid reason. Understand?"

Grace nodded.

"Promise me?" He caressed along her jaw with the back of his finger. Grace closed her eyes, wishing for that touch to never end. When it did, she removed the earpiece and handed it back.

"I promise."

"I can track you as long as you're wearing that, see?" Grace watched the black face of the expensive looking 'watch' he wore as a green dot flashed steadily to set, then shined a steady green. "I've found you."

Grace nodded and met his eyes. "You have, indeed."

"Sit and have your wine. We've got time."

Grace looked up at him, thought about how much had changed for her over the last year, and how she didn't have things like time to look forward to after the assassination. And now? Maybe she would finally find some closure. She wondered if this extraordinary man would play a role in that.

I hope so, Grace thought to herself. *I really hope so.*

16

*T*he apartment belonging to Sharron and Aaron Levy sat at the edge of Central Park, and had 360° views of the park, Manhattan, New Jersey, Queens and beyond. It was truly a 'Mansion in the Clouds'. The place was gorgeous, with high ceilings, entertainment rooms and a grand staircase of stained wood that climbed to the second floor in an undulating wave. A catwalk that looked down on the main living room led to five bedrooms and three bathrooms, and one more floor above that held more rooms for entertaining, and access to a terrace that wrapped around the entire apartment.

"What am I tonight, Duchess?" Marin asked in the car before they arrived.

"A friend. I don't want any of these people to know I'm..." She didn't know what she was, but she didn't want a room full of people, who were not necessarily her friends, to know either.

"Vulnerable?" Marin offered.

"Mmmm. Yes."

"I'll be the perfect 'friend', then. You know the drill, right?"

"I do."

Once at the party, and after the excitement of Grace's arrival died down, Marin stayed close, wandering away with the excuse of fetching her a drink or a hors d'oeuvre when a guest would beg for her attention. The crowd was tony, for sure; politicians, Hollywood people, Broadway people, old New York money. He'd seen several of these people before, during his time in the Secret Service and as the owner of a private security firm. Most weren't very nice; none could be trusted. His eyes were on all of them, he'd memorized almost every face, knew where everyone was situated, including Grace.

She stood off in a corner talking to a man she seemed to know, given her body language. Marin could not see the man's face. She was relaxed now that she was here at the party. He tried often to put himself in her place, think like she thought—but he couldn't. He chalked it up to him being a man and her being a woman. They thought differently, and they handled stress differently. Once he settled that, he was able to move past things and care for her without judgment.

Marin saw a roaming waiter take Grace's wineglass from her, and he turned to fetch her another one. He wanted to make his presence known, didn't want to leave her side for too long. Grace's tale of the asshole who whispered in her ear at the inaugural ball still irked him. He'd not let a thing like that happen to her again. An attractive socialite waylaid him as he took a glass of chardonnay off a tray, and he politely but firmly extricated himself and, turning to the room, scanned it for Grace. She was not in the spot she'd been before, and either was the man she'd been talking to.

A knot formed in his gut, but this was no time to overreact. She was inside a vast apartment among people who knew her and maybe even cared about her. She had tools with her she could use in case there was trouble. Still, they agreed she was to stay close by, where he could see her, and she was to let him know if she was leaving the area.

Marin moved through the room, looking between small gatherings of people in case she was sitting down. But as he passed by each group, he found Grace was not among them. He offloaded the wineglass and stopped the evening's hostess as she passed.

"Sharron, have you seen Grace?"

"Well, dear...I did a moment ago." The woman tapped a surgically altered cheek in thought. "You couldn't be more darling. She can't leave your sight, can she?"

"I'd prefer she didn't," Marin smiled. "I'll find her."

Sharron Levy nodded. "Oh, I know you will."

"I'VE WANTED to talk with you about this for a year, and then, well..." Evan Weld raked a hand through his chestnut hair. "Hell, Grace, what a thing. This country is still reeling, despite how hard Bannish tries to follow in Matt's huge, impactful footsteps. I wonder if we'll ever see recovery in our lifetime."

Grace stood on the expansive roof top terrace and watched the lights of the city twinkle while Senator Even Weld attempted to work his charm. The terrace was two levels separated by two steps and large Chinese urns filled with birds of paradise. Small tables and chairs were scattered on the upper portion, and the lower terrace, which extended the entire length and width of the Levy's vast apartment, was appointed with upholstered chairs, sofas, love seats, tables and even lamps. There was an entire other world out here, and Grace wondered why the party hadn't extended yet to the third floor. The fall chill might have had something to do with it.

Never mind. It was the perfect place to have a moment alone with Evan Weld. Weld had taken Matt's seat in the senate after Matt won the election, and he served his constituents in New York well. His agenda fully followed the Libertarian ideal of a free market economy and individual freedom. People were still getting used to the idea. Evan Weld was a good, credible man, but Grace could have written this particular speech herself.

"Oh, Evan, let's dream big." Grace pulled her silver-gray fur stole around her against the chill and secured the ends with a wide diamond broach. Weld moved to remove his jacket and Grace held up her hand.

"How are you holding up, kid?" he asked, his smile turning grim.

"I'm fine, just fine."

"Liar."

Grace arched a reproachful brow. "I beg your pardon. Do you know who I am?"

"If I have my way you'll be the new Chairwoman on Education Reform. Who knows? We sure could use you in the DOE. How does Education Secretary sound?"

"Something happen to Francine Gertz I am unaware of?"

"She's ineffective and you deserve a cabinet post, Grace. There'd be no one more qualified."

"Evan, you know damn well I'd push to get rid of that bureaucratic nightmare and hand it off to the states."

"Libertarian to the end." Evan Weld took her hand, and then let go, slipping his hand casually in his pocket. "I keep seeing you as ambassador to the U.K. You'd be great, and I can't stand Brandt Delacroix."

"Nor can I, I'm afraid. I don't trust him." Grace hesitated. "Someone killed my horse."

Evan Weld shook his head. "I heard. I'm so sorry."

"Word does get around," she muttered.

Weld took Grace's hand again in his. "Are you sure about this?"

Grace nodded. "The right people will know the truth, Evan, believe me."

"There's something else." Weld slipped his hand into his pocket and stared at her hard before he spoke again. "Howell's got something up his sleeve, and I don't like it. Be caref—"

"Grace?"

They both turned in the direction of the low but laced-in-steel voice coming from the open glass doors of the entertainment room. John Marin did not move. His face was set in granite, and the only movement was the slight twitch at the corner of his mouth. Separated by three steps and twenty feet, he kept his eyes on Grace, but spoke to Senator Weld.

"Excuse us, please." And in that moment, Grace realized the tremendous mistake she'd made.

"Of course," Weld nodded. "We'll talk later, Grace." She nodded in the senator's direction without taking her eyes off John Marin.

"I—"

"Get yourself together. We're leaving."

"What? Leaving? Why?"

"You know why."

A knot formed in the pit of Grace's stomach. "We can't leave. Sharron has yet to serve dinner."

"That's not my problem."

Grace stood in stunned silence as Marin pressed a finger to an almost invisible wire in his ear and spoke into the jewelry around his wrist. She saw his lips move, but outdoors, twenty-five stories above the city, it was hard to hear much of anything. When he turned back to her, she tried again.

"John—"

"This isn't up for discussion, Grace. Move."

"I am not leaving before the *dinner*, which is being given in my honor, is served. What is the matter with you?"

"There's not a thing the matter with me, Duchess. You, unfortunately, still don't understand the rules, so now we're going home. You've got three seconds to get inside so you can say your goodbyes, or this evening's guests will watch me carry the former first lady through the house and out the door over my shoulder, and then you can spend the day tomorrow on the phone explaining yourself."

"You can't mean this!"

"One."

"Seriously?" she scoffed. "You're counting?"

"Two."

"John!" She stomped her foot in frustration, and the clack from her expensive Jimmy Choos hitting the flagstone floor echoed in the semi-enclosed terrace. For the first time in weeks, Grace felt true panic. She stared at him open-mouthed, and it became obvious very quickly that John Marin was not giving in; she could see it in his eyes and in the way his jaw was set. She learned her first lesson when they left England a day behind schedule because of those damn letters and emails she kept from him, and no matter how much she argued and fussed, Marin had not given in. And going off with Shane without telling him set him off on another tirade and lecture, with more reminders of expectations and consequences. Now she was in trouble again, and she had no earthly idea how to get herself out of it. Her heart raced in her chest. What the hell was she going to do?

You will obey me.

"I can't do this! I can't just leave!" She brushed past him, unwilling to test him further. Marin followed her inside the large entertainment room off the terrace and closed the glass doors. Grace paced in a tight circle.

"I need a minute!" she hissed when she saw he was close to uttering that final number that would send her to her doom over his broad shoulder.

"Time's up," Marin said after a few seconds. "Get moving."

"You have no idea...!"

"Three."

"Wait! Stop! No!" An unladylike oomph whooshed out of her, followed by a decidedly more delicate screech, as Marin hoisted her over his shoulder and made for the door.

"John, no! Please!" She whacked him on his broad backside with her clutch. "Put me down! I'll walk. Please." He carried out of the room and down a long hallway toward the stairs to the second floor. If someone came upon them now, she'd positively die.

"John, please!" she whisper-screamed. He was steps away from the staircase when he stopped.

"Let me be clear; we are leaving." He hesitated, and Grace wondered—hoped—that he was entertaining second thoughts about humiliating her in front of two-hundred people.

"All right!"

He moved, Grace thought, to set her on her feet again. Instead, with his hand still attached to her derrière, Marin spun on his heel and returned to the room they'd just left. He set her down and as the blood rushed back into her head, she staggered. Tears sat unshed in her eyes.

"You're going to stop testing me." It was not a question.

"You need to give me a minute to compose myself," Grace said, raising a hand to ward off his looming form. Her mouth wobbled, and her hands shook as she scooted deep into the room and grabbed onto the back of a low suede sofa, taking several deep breaths.

"The hell I do."

She jumped as he closed in on her, the fabric of his jacket brushing her arm as he loomed over her again. My God, why wouldn't he give her a *minute*? What was he doing? What was *happening*? For every two steps Grace took, Marin took one big one, until she fell back into an oversized leather chair. He bent over her and placed both hands on the arms, trapping her in the seat. "Feeling vulnerable, Duchess?"

Grace's eyes went wide, and she nodded, unable to keep her lips from quivering.

"Having trouble thinking on your feet about what to do next?"

Again, she nodded. "What are you doing?"

"Trying to get through to you, lady. I'm the bad guy and your protection is two flights down surrounded by two-hundred people, and he has no goddamn idea where you are."

Grace stared at the thing around his wrist. The green light was steady; he'd found her. Marin looked at it, too, and then dispelled her of any doubts about how this worked.

"Fifteen seconds to scan the area for you from my position across the room, where I went to give you some privacy —a big mistake. Another full minute to walk the room to make sure you weren't sitting down, hidden by people standing around you. Another forty five seconds to wend my way through a room full of people to get to the kitchen, dining room, library, sitting room, office, den, and two bedrooms on the first floor without calling any attention to myself so I wouldn't create a panic, or get stopped and questioned, wasting more precious time; another minute-twenty to alert my men that you were missing and make my way through two additional floors, playing the 'you're getting warmer...no colder' game, because the fucking tracker wasn't working. You curious how long three-and-a-half minutes is when someone's hurting you?"

Grace stared at her lap and fingered the quartz geode around her neck, feeling the rough spot in back that she was to press in an emergency.

"And I'll bet you never gave a thought to pressing that button, did you?" he asked, taking the exact thought from her head.

"I wasn't in danger," she whispered, realizing as soon as the words were out of mouth that it mattered no one iota.

"Still feeling that way?" he growled.

Her heart slammed into her ribs and heaviness befell her. She brought her hand up and placed it over his, still gripping the arm of the chair. "I...I wasn't thinking, John. I'm...I'm sorry."

Marin pulled his hand out from under hers and backed away. "Get up." When she did, he jerked his head toward the door. "Say your goodbyes. We're leaving."

"But..." Grace was stunned. He'd scared the hell out of her, taught her a lesson; she got it. And she believed, for some reason, that he'd let this go. Exercise in diligent thinking reemphasized, she would walk out of here duly chastened and free to enjoy the rest of her evening.

"For the last time, Grace," he said through clenched teeth, hand raised, finger jabbing the air for emphasis. "We are leaving. You will pull yourself together and start walking out that door. You can do it with dignity, under your own stream, or you will take a ride through this house, kicking and screaming, over my shoulder. If that's the option you choose, I promise you that before I throw you over my shoulder, I will throw you over my knee—"

"John!"

"—I will pull up your dress—"

"How dare you!" He was speaking so loudly that someone—anyone—on the other side of that door would hear him clearly.

"—And I will spank your shapely ass until you are speaking in tongues. It shouldn't take me more than three-and-a-half minutes." He arched one determined brow, and Grace got his message, loud and clear. What others heard at this juncture was of little concern to her now. "Considering that this is about the hundredth time we've been over this, you're lucky I'm not doing it now."

"Hundredth—how charmingly hyperbolic—I'm going, you bully," Grace snapped when she saw him stiffen as if to make good on his threat. She scooted around him and walked, albeit slowly, down a long hallway to the first set of stairs, then down to a second set. And as she made her way to the first floor and the main part of the house, where the guests congregated, she realized just how big the house was, and she understood better what Marin must have gone through to find her. The place was a veritable maze. Head down, the fist of her free hand against her mouth, she struggled for what possible excuse she could make to her hosts at this late moment. Sharron and Aaron Levy were good friends, and very influential in politics. Their social status was top-tiered. Most of all, Grace adored them and would die before upsetting or embarrassing them. Grace turned around to plead her case one more time.

"Isn't there...?"

Without a second's hesitation, he moved into position to hoist her up when Sharron Levy entered the hallway. Grace spun around and leveled a pleading glare at her friend. The woman's very presence felt like a stay of execution, however brief. By the look on Sharron's face, however, she knew something was amiss. Grace had to act fast. Her hands found the woman's shoulders and she steadied herself as if she were about to swoon.

"Grace, there you are." She looked over Grace's shoulder. "You've found her," she said to Marin. "What's wrong, darling? You look pale."

Grace certainly felt sick; it appeared as if she looked it, too, and for that small favor, she was grateful. "Oh, Sharron, I'm so sorry. I...I don't..."

"What? Please, tell me." She looked over Grace's head. "John?"

"I'm afraid I'm not well," Grace snapped before the beast behind her could offer a word. "I've been battling a bitch of a headache all day, and now it's turned sour on me."

"Darling, I'm sorry. Would it help if I moved dinner back half an hour, maybe you can...?" She stared over Grace's head at Marin.

"Oh, Sharron, I don't think so. I..." She felt Marin's hand on her shoulder.

"Sweetheart." His voice was barely a whisper. *Oh, please, oh, please...* "Let's take ten minutes someplace quiet, huh? You have some water, and maybe Sharron can push dinner back, like she offered." Sharron's eyes meet Marin's, and the woman almost fainted from relief.

"Oh...oh, yes. Yes, Grace, dear, do you think that would work?" Sharron said. "I so want you to be well. This is your party, after all."

That amused Grace, for it wasn't *her* party at all. It was the Party's party. "Well," Grace muttered, not wanting to appear too excited. "Maybe ten minutes, and then we'll see."

"Yes. You come right down this hall to Aaron's office. Not a soul will bother you here, and John, there's a fridge right under that cabinet with water, flat and sparkling. Oh, Grace, I hope you perk up. Aspirin? A little bicarbonate?"

"No, I think dim lighting and some sparkling water will do it. Thank you so much, Sharron. I'm so sorry to be a bother."

"Not at all. I'll close the hall door and have an imposing hors d'oeuvres passer block the entrance, so no one comes in to bother you. Take as long as you need. I'll tell whomever needs you immediately that you're on an important call with POTUS and cannot be disturbed. That usually impresses people enough to forget about why they wanted you in the first place."

Her friend and hostess behaved now as if her mouth had taken a tumble down the stairs, so scattered was she. Grace knew that a change of plans this serious—the guest of honor having to leave before dinner was served—would throw Sharron Levy back into therapy, or into rehab, by tomorrow.

"I'd move dinner to midnight if that would help," Sharron finished with relief. She placed a tender kiss on Graces cheek, and Marin watched her disappear down the hall, closing another door behind her.

Grace walked to the large wooden desk and gripped the

edge. Through an unshaded window lights from another high-rise across the way bled into the large room, which smelled of old books and woodsmoke from the fireplace. She slammed her eyes shut to stem the flow of frustrated and embarrassed tears.

"Thank you," she whispered.

Marin closed the office door and locked it. "I'm not a monster, Grace. But this is far from over."

Grace nodded without turning around. "I'll agree to anything you say." She wondered if she would come to regret those words, but at the moment, she was desperate. And she was sorry, truly. How it must have felt to him to have her in his sights one minute, and then gone the next—given what they'd agreed on, and given the challenges she was facing with whomever was sending those missives.

She heard him move and then she felt his heat at her back. Barely touching her from behind, she nevertheless pressed her pelvis into the edge of the desk. Now that the fear of being dragged from the party had passed, Grace was inexplicably turned on. As if sensing this, Marin pressed against her. He laced his fingers between hers and pressed them into the desk, pinning her down. She shuddered, and Marin felt it because he sucked in a breath and spread her arms wider.

"Yes, Duchess," he whispered in her ear. "You will." She dampened her panties at such an authoritative statement. After what he'd done for her, it would be her pleasure. "You find obeying me difficult?" he asked.

"I seem to," she whispered. She sighed with relief. They would play a little game, enjoy a little flirting, some sexy banter to ease the tension while she settled down. She must remember, she said to herself, to find a mirror and check herself before rejoining the party. All this stress made her look a fright.

"Sweetheart," he said, his voice suddenly menacing. "You're about to learn the true meaning of difficult." And then she felt his hot breath in her ear. "Take off your dress."

17

*G*race gripped the edge of the desk until her knuckles were white. She didn't see this coming, and she'd have to sit with the whys of that later. For now, she had some negotiating to do. His close proximity pressed Grace against the desk, her hips against the edge, his erection hard against her ass, his spread legs forcing hers closed between his knees. Whatever did he mean, *Take off your dress*?

"Why?" she whispered.

"Because I'm going to spank your ass red, and then you're going to return to the party. And I will watch you squirm every time you sit on one of Sharron Levy's hard chairs." He pressed her into the desk. "I told you, this was not over."

So this was how he'd make her pay for not being dragged home like a naughty child who'd misbehaved in a restaurant. "Surely, there's another way," she whispered. Not able to look into his eyes, it was hard to gauge the seriousness of the situation.

"I can tear it off you, and once I'm finished you can

return to the party with that dead animal around your shoulders. No one'll notice, I'm sure." They both glanced at her gray stole, tossed on the desk next to her bejeweled clutch.

"You're determined, then," she muttered

"I'm determined to prove to you that my warning about consequences, and your agreement to that, wasn't just talk."

"I didn't think it was."

"Good. We're on the same page." Marin grew quiet, his big body still pressed against her back. "I don't ask twice, Duchess," he finally said. "Do you need me to count?"

Grace was getting nowhere. "I'm sure we can discuss this," she said.

"One."

"This is insane," she whispered. "I'm not going to...going to..." When no response was forthcoming, she finished with, "I never agreed to *this*."

"Two."

Her stomach fell. He was actually counting. There was no getting out of this. He'd let her off the hook once; he would not let her off the hook again.

"Wait."

"Three." He grabbed the top of her dress and tugged.

"All right. Please." She reached up and snatched him by the wrists. His hands on her shoulders, the dress was low enough to expose the top of her bra.

"What did you expect?" he asked. "Did you think I wouldn't keep my word? That I'm like you?"

Her eyes flashed, the cut hitting its intended mark. Grace placed a hand over her heart where it appeared to hurt the worst. "I'm known as someone who keeps her word," she protested.

"Then show me. Show me you're a woman who can be

counted on. Show me now, like you couldn't seem to show me earlier, that when you agree to certain rules, I don't have to worry that you'll break them. Show me that I can trust you. You can certainly trust me. I think you know that."

She was out of time, and she knew it. "Someone will hear us. I...please, John. I c-can't."

"I know that. You've proven yourself tonight over and over again."

Grace's heart sank, and a pain sat low in her belly. He was right, of course.

"You've lived through the assassination of the president, and an attempt on your own life. You've kept secrets of threats against you for months, and you've navigated public life with class and dignity through it all. And you're telling me that you can't take your dress off and hand it to me?" Marin shook his head and narrowed his eyes. "Obey me, Grace."

She blinked in surprise, allowing a tear to escape. Her breathing quickened, and she set her mouth in a thin line. She gripped the desk again for balance, if nothing else. How could she do this? She'd be giving up everything, all of her power, and certainly every ounce of her dignity. But how much power and dignity could one truly have if one couldn't keep her word? Grace had assured him before they walked into the party that she understood the rules, and she agreed to obey them—assured him, actually, more than once. What would the harm have been to simply ask him to join her and Weld, but stand inside the entertainment room, while they talked? She would have maintained their privacy, and Marin would have been satisfied, and proud of her for doing as he'd asked: follow the rules and keep herself safe.

Grace had not handled this properly. As Marin stood behind her, stoic and determined, she realized there was no escaping what she had coming. He was right; she'd survived two assassination attempts, along with other crises Marin knew nothing about. She would survive this, too.

Her hands gripped the fabric around her thighs, and she lifted the dress up her legs. Still behind her, still pressed against her, Marin didn't move as she worked the clingy garment up and over her bottom. He backed away, mere inches, as the dress ascended her body, brushing against his erection and resting around her waist until, with a resigned sigh, Grace took it the rest of the way and pulled it over her head. Marin took the dress from her. It felt soft, smooth and heavy in his hands. It held her essence in every fiber, and he wanted to bury his face in it. Instead, he laid it over the back of one of the two armless chairs in front of the desk. Then he stood back and squinted into the dim light. He set his hands on his hips and stared. And in those moments that felt like forever, his silence told her everything.

Grace turned around, leaned back against the edge of the desk, crossed her legs and folded her arms. One professionally shaped brow shot up, and she smirked at him. She actually smirked.

"What the fuck?" Marin muttered, raking his eyes up and down her body.

"Mmmm. Indeed," she countered.

"What exactly am I looking at here, Duchess?" What he saw was a black lace over cream strapless cat suit type garment that began at the tops of her breast, pushing them high and together, then contouring down her body to midthigh. Upon closer inspection, the contraption didn't close around her hips like a slip, but rather split between her legs like long underwear. His cock jerked. He'd never seen anything sexier. But he had no idea what to do with it.

Grace raised her chin in haughty hubris. "It holds me in."

The controlled dominance Marin held from the moment he saw her outside with Senator Weld completely disappeared. He was at a loss.

Hold it together, man. You had it once. Find it. FIND IT.

"Take it off," he barked. "Now." That was it. He had nothing else.

Grace's arched brow flew higher. "I will not. I've had to pee for two hours. If I can't get it off, you certainly won't be able to." And then she smirked again.

"Wanna bet?" he challenged.

"I do, yes."

He stalked to her and spun her to face the desk. He raised his hands in confusion as he inspected the garment for straps or eyehooks—any hint as to how to get it off her. And he vowed that when he found a way, she'd not sit comfortably for a week.

Her ass looked different; it was raised, pressed into a rounded shape that wasn't her own. He ran his hand over her, from front to back. He felt no buttons, no ribbons, no locks or keys. Frustrated, he gave her encased bottom a sharp slap. His hand bounced off like he'd jumped on a trampoline.

She giggled.

He swatted her again.

Grace snorted. And then she guffawed.

"Get this off, young lady, right now."

"I can't," she said. "I'll never get it back on again."

"That is bullshit. You're lying to me." He swatted her again, hard, and spun her back around, grabbed her upper arms, and gave her a good shake. His hand stung.

"I *am* sorry," she blurted, and then covered her mouth to

prevent another indelicate snort. One squeaked through anyway. He stepped back and slammed his hands on his hips again.

"Who invents this shit for you people?" he snapped.

"An intractable, and figure-conscious, woman, no doubt," she answered.

"It's like a fucking suit of armor." His eyes roamed over every inch.

"Mmmm."

"Should be illegal."

"Yes," she said, hiding another smirk.

"Be quiet," he snapped.

"All right."

"I've completely lost the upper hand here."

"Oh, dear. Well..." Grace stepped forward and slung her arms around his neck.

"Don't butter me up," he growled.

"No."

"This shit's got to come off sometime."

"I don't know about that."

"And when it does, you won't sit for a week."

"Oh, well..."

"You think this is funny, woman?"

"It is, a bit. You have to admit..."

"It's not." His changed countenance sobered her. "We could have had a real problem tonight."

"Whatever do you mean?"

"Happy and Sneezy had just gotten off the elevator when I called them off. We were seconds away from a three-hundred-pound Samoan and an over pumped Irishman with anger issues crashing through the front door of this fine apartment to find you."

Grace slammed her eyes shut. "Muffy and Randolph would not have taken kindly to that."

"No," Marin agreed. "Look at me." When she did, he continued. "These men have lives, Grace. They work hard, and they're damn good at what they do; they're the best, or they wouldn't work for me. And because they work for me, and because I've asked them to, they will throw themselves in front of a bullet for you. I take that very seriously."

"I know. I—I do, too. I just stepped outside for a moment; we couldn't hear each other speak. I wasn't thinking."

"That excuse stopped working for me about a week ago." He ran his hands down her body, the tight suit smooth under his hands. "It's getting too hard for me to protect you."

"What do you mean?" Grace's heart pounded in her chest, fear shrouded her. Had she finally gone too far?

"My words and logical reasoning aren't penetrating with you."

"I know. I've a good hiding coming, as you've said. Indeed, you're right to be cross with me in every respect. I suppose I've pushed you—"

"We're past that now, much as I agree that's exactly what you need, delivered long and hard, by a man who knows how." His brows crashed together. She didn't believe she'd seen him this serious. She was, indeed, in trouble. Her core ached.

"You think I do this all the time, with all my clients?" he said. "You bring something out in me, lady, that has been sitting dormant a hell of a long time. I'm wondering why now, and why you." He sighed. "We've crossed a bridge, turned a corner." He backed away from her and paced in a tight circle.

"Why? Because you can't admit I mean something to

you, that there is something between us?" Grace threw her hands in the air. "Look at me! Who does this kind of thing to a woman he cares nothing for?"

"No one said anything about not caring, sweetheart."

"Perhaps if you took me to bed, you'd feel differently."

Marin chuckled. "You ever wonder why a doctor doesn't treat his own family, why a lawyer doesn't defend a spouse or a parent? Because they're too close; they can't think objectively. We've been pretty intimate, and I haven't officially made love to you yet. You think I'm in the same place mentally that I was the day we arrived in London? I'm fucking worlds away from that now! I can't protect you this way!" For the second time since Grace set eyes on him at his sailboat, he shouted at her. She worried about who could hear them. Their ten minutes were about up, and she expected Sharron Levy, or the imposing tray passer, to bust through the door any minute, she still in her undergarments.

"Are you saying you can't handle this, handle me?" she snapped. "You're a goddamn liar. And a coward."

"This isn't about wanting to take you to bed anymore—you know damn well I do. I don't work this way!" Marin sighed. He had to gain the upper hand again, do what was right for her. "There's no future for us, Grace, and you know it." He waved his hand in her direction, took in her attire. How the fuck did they get here, to this moment? "This is insane."

"I know nothing of the kind. How dare you presume to know what's in my mind and in my heart? Despite your callous, Neanderthal ways, I've never wanted a man more, and I've never met a man who has made me beg for it so wantonly as you. I'm in my bloody knickers, begging you to fuck me. Jesus, what a fool!" Grace snatched her dress off the chair and pulled it over her head.

"Taking this job was the last thing I wanted," he whispered.

"Yet, take it you did." She ran her fingers through her hair and pulled a compact mirror out of her clutch. "Why?" She checked her lipstick, closed the compact with a snap, and threw it back into her bag.

"There were a number of reasons, not the least of which was my fucking attraction to you!" He snatched her at the elbows and pulled her close. Her clutch fell to the floor. "A man fails at his job, he gets out. He sells everything, buys a boat and a pair of flip-flops and disappears. Then a very stubborn lady comes along and all he can think about is how he'd give it all up to stand in front of a bullet for her."

"Matt was not your failure."

"You have no idea."

"Oh, but I do, John. I've watched you; I've seen your face, haunted over something that was out of your control."

"You are within my control, lady, and now you haunt me."

"Good. I'm glad." She grasped his strong shoulders and squeezed. "Do it, John. Stand in front of a bullet for me. I'd do it for you; in a heartbeat, I'd do it for you."

John Marin loved her. He knew that now. All he had to do was get her out of this hell-hole of a party, get her back to the hotel, and take her to bed. He'd paddle into next week, exact a promise never to cross him up again, and she'd be his. She'd be safe. That simple. He'd make it happen, he'd break the mold; he'd prove it could be done. And then he looked deep into her eyes and realized what he'd lose if he lost her to his own stupidity, selfishness and lack of self-control. Never before had he been this outside of himself. Time he reined himself back in.

"Time for a new face, some new personalities. Let's stop this right now, before we hurt each other."

"I made a mistake."

"As I said, we're past that."

"So, you've taken the least chivalrous approach, allowing me to remain the rejected." She paused in an attempt to control her anger. "You're taking revenge."

"That's a hell of a lot *I'm* doing, Duchess." He'd take it; he'd take that burden on. It was him, all on him. That was fine.

"Very well, then." Grace stepped back and squared her bare shoulders, the gown accentuating their beauty.

"Grace…"

"Deny it! Go on, deny that you don't care for me!"

"I can't."

"Then stop this!"

Marin shook his head. "Sweetheart."

"I hate you for making me feel this way!" Emotion shrouded his face, moisture form in his eyes, and for a moment she thought she stood a chance.

"My life is on a boat with a bottle of rum and women whose names I can't remember the next morning. I can't do this with you."

"You *won't* do this with me."

"No. Better you get someone else. I'll make arrangements tomorrow. You'll be able to return the clothes I haven't worn, and I'll refund…"

Grace reared back, closed her eyes, and swung. Her hand cracked hard against his face, and Marin took it; he never moved. She took one full step back and raked her eyes over him from head to toe. A sneer found its way to her mouth before she could stop it.

Marin locked his eyes on hers for several seconds before he spoke. "Grace."

She closed her eyes, tears slipping through despite her determination not to shed one more tear over this man.

"I guess that's it, then," he whispered.

"Yes, I guess so."

Marin sighed, and in that moment, he was back in protection mode. A shroud of gray descended, and when the fog cleared, a woman stood before him. It was no longer Grace Coolidge; it was a client. Only a client. Just that quick; just that easy.

Because it was better that way.

"You'll stay on my hip for the rest of the evening. Trip me up, and I'll take you home, and I'll do it in front of the whole room. Do you understand?"

Grace opened her eyes and stared at him. His left cheek glowed where she'd slapped him. His eyes were clear and dark, and she knew in that moment it was over; she'd lost him.

"Perfectly," she said. And then Grace bent down, picked her clutch up off the floor, grabbed her stole, and walked out.

18

_G_race managed to walk with dignity through the hotel lobby and into the elevators, never giving a hint to the folk milling about that she'd just slapped a man and had her heart broken. The ride back to the hotel had been deathly quiet, the tension coming off Marin like a fog. She missed him already. Once in the elevator alone with him, she felt awkward, embarrassed, vulnerable. She no longer had people fawning over her and begging for her attention; she no longer had the luxury of forgetting he existed, even though he kept her glued to his hip the rest of the evening. She had no more distractions, only him, here. Alone. She wanted to lash out, hit him, kick him. She wanted to fall against him, bury her face in his shoulder and cry.

As Marin ushered her in and closed the door, Grace dropped her clutch and her stole on the floor and stalked into the living room. She was behaving horribly and she knew it. She wanted to go back to the moment she suggested to Evan Weld that they take their discussion outside. She wanted that moment back more than anything. She removed her shoes as Marin came down the hall holding his jacket, her clutch and mink stole, his rig, and what appeared to be a hotel envelope. He set it all on the dining table. Everything she wanted to say to him flew out the window. Fresh rage got the better of her. She threw her Jimmy Choos at him with all her might. He batted away the first, and caught the second. Taking the flat of the expensive shoe to the tight seat of her gown wouldn't be out of line. He glared at her, believing he needed to say something, or better yet, *do* something. And then the gray shroud descended once again, and she ceased being Grace. He tossed the shoe aside and turned away from her. And Grace's heart split again. With her head high, she spun on her heel and closed the door to her room behind her.

MARIN WATCHED her disappear into her room. The evening started on such a high note; procedures in place, he'd felt confident that things would go boringly smooth, but the lady had other plans. Once procedures went askew, he acted with speed and efficiency to see his charge safe. Ah, those best laid plans...He managed a chuckle. He didn't know how.

Marin rubbed the ache that had formed in his chest in the Levy's library, and hadn't let up. The sting of her slap had faded hours ago, yet he still felt her slender hand on his face, felt her deep inside him. What was done was done. It was for the best, what was best for her—and for him. He was sure of it. Quite sure.

He'd done the very thing he swore he wouldn't do: get close to a client. How could he protect her now? What set a protector apart from a lover was the detachment, the lack of emotion the protector felt. The protectee was a job, nothing more. When the protectee became more than a job was when shit went down and went down bad. He'd seen it before. It never worked well. He had no idea how he'd break away from her now, but he knew he needed to. It ended, in that office, the way it needed to. It didn't matter that he wanted to put a fucking baby in her belly, for Christ's sake. Jesus! Where did that come from? But it's what he thought of now, like it was a given, like it was etched in stone and it was only a matter of time. His little girl would be blond and headstrong and sassy and intelligent, like her mother, in need of a spanking at least once a day, like her mother— although he'd cut off his own arm before he ever laid a hand on his child. The boy would be honest and strong and bold and brave, and he'd love his mother something fierce.

Fuck, stop it! He screamed at himself until his head ached. He was lost, and he needed to end it before he started naming the children.

Bryce and Angela.

Sonofabitch!

The right thing to do would be to assign someone else to her case and get the fuck out of her life. Yeah. That's what he needed to do. The thought made him sick to his stomach.

As he headed toward the hallway and his room, he noticed her fur wrap on the table next to his rig. Soft, feminine, she looked so damn elegant with that thing wrapped around her shoulders with that fucking diamond-crusted broach she wore in front to keep it closed. It sat unassuming next to his holstered gun, a weapon designed to kill. The pistol was not soft, or feminine or elegant. It was hard and cruel and deadly—like him. Like he should be.

He reached for the rig and his jacket, and spotted the

envelope he'd picked up when they came in. Another procedure askew, he thought, as he turned the plain white legal sized envelope over; nothing written on the front and it wasn't sealed, but it definitely wasn't empty. He didn't like this. Nothing should have been shoved under their door for any reason.

"You up here yet?" he said into the watch on his wrist.

"I'm parking. Be up in a minute," Doc replied. "How's our lady?"

"Down for the night. Come in when you get up here. We've got a problem." Marin disconnected and went to the bar, where he and Grace had sat over a glass of wine earlier. He grabbed the corkscrew and a pen and returned to the envelope, where he used the two implements to open the envelope and extract what was inside without touching anything. Bad enough he'd touched the outside of the envelope. When he opened the single folded paper, he tossed the pen and the corkscrew down and gripped the side of the heavy wood dining table until it threatened to crack in his hands.

"Sonofabitch!"

GRACE PACED HER ROOM. Whatever hope there had been for anything more than the most superficial relationship with John Marin died with that horrid disagreement and a single slap to his face. God, he was infuriating! She'd never done anything like that before. He'd been so final in his pronouncements, and honestly that had not been expected. To see things end so disgracefully stabbed her like the dullest knife.

She had to admit she'd been nothing but trouble to him

since London. What was it about him that was different
than the Secret Service protection she'd had to endure
while in the White House? Grace had not yet known the fate
of her husband, sitting on that deserted road outside New
Orleans a year ago, but she had a good idea. John Marin, a
$160,000 a year Secret Service agent, had saved her life, and
had been relentless in his efforts to protect her. She recalled
that night, sitting with him on that dusty back-road that
used to be lined with homes, and where residents had
floated down on doors and chairs, waiting to be rescued,
after Katrina hit in 2005. Grace had not thought about those
moments in the limo for some time. She'd forgotten about
John Marin until Brandt Delacroix insisted she take on a
detail. He came to her mind like a breath of fresh air. She
knew in that moment she'd have no one else. She still felt
that way.

Grace shook her head free of the memory and removed
her jewelry, and then her gown and the suit of armor, as
Marin called it. She hung the gown in the closet, smiling at
the folly of it all. The look on his face when confronted with
something as simple as a body shaper. And she wasn't about
to help him. Her smile faded. They'd never have a moment
like that again. She'd never have the pleasure of his good
humor, his utter maleness, his goodness, again. They'd
never laugh together, he'd never hold her in his lap, he'd
certainly never scold her again. Not ever. Her duties in
Washington would not happen for another week, and for
the first time since leaving London, she considered going
home, and flying in next Friday for her appearance. How
would she go another week without him by her side?

Nude, she stood in front of the mirror in the bathroom
and washed her face of the little bit of makeup she wore, the
cold cream and water mixing with tears she'd not allowed

herself to shed until now. Grace sighed and slipped on a silk violet floor length kimono robe with hand painted cherry blossoms down the front and walked into the bedroom. She stared at the closed doors to the suite and wondered what Marin was doing now. Was he packing, getting Doc set to watch her until someone else came along? She wouldn't have it. She'd not have anyone, and Bannish and Delacroix could pound sand. Suddenly she was sick of doing what others wanted her to do. Blessed freedom. She'd survive it. She had no choice. She dabbed at her eyes, feeling the really, profoundly good cry was still buried deep and not about to show up for a while, and set about pulling her clothes out for the next day. Perhaps a morning swim in the pool, or a workout in the gym, or another yoga class was what she needed. She was free to do that now without a word to anyone.

Grace pulled her bedding back and grabbed up her book and her reading glasses. She heard his voice outside her doors and imagined hearing someone else's for the remainder of the trip. It made her want to go home. This wasn't what she wanted. Guilt overwhelmed her. She could not let this lie. She'd not allow things to end this way. If he was leaving, he was leaving, but not like this.

Grace opened the door and stepped into the living room. Marin stood at the large oak table between the living room and the hall to his room and the front door, his back to her. A lamp on one of the side tables spread dim light around the area, and a modern chandelier was lit over the table casting his big body in shadow. His gun and her stole sat side by side on the table, like an old couple; the lady and the alpha, steel and mink, hard and so vulnerably soft. Grace stepped fully into the room.

"Do you have any idea how insulting it was that you

reduced the end of our agreement to the returning of clothes and monetary refunds?" Grace saw his shoulders rise and then fall. "Those things are the very least of my concerns." When he didn't respond she took a few cautionary steps toward him. "I'm speaking to you, Marin. Don't ignore me."

Marin straightened and, without turning around, placed his hands on his hips. "Grace." He sounded defeated. Grace supposed being slapped would do that to a man.

"I've never slapped anyone in my life," she said, her voice barely a whisper. "John, I'm so very sor..." The suite door flew open, and Grace took several steps back in shock as three large men entered the suite with purpose, their ever-present guns attached to their hips. Their demeanor matched Marin's—dark and on alert. The large Samoan, Happy, entered first, and his normally congenial countenance was anything but. Sneezy followed, and Doc came in last.

"What is it?" Grace asked. "What's happened?" She approached the table and the first thing she saw was a single sheet of paper. *Oh, no,* she thought. *Another email.*

Three colored photographs covered most of the single page. The first was of a woman in front of what looked to be the Levy's building, and this woman appeared to be wearing the same gown Grace wore tonight. A man's hand was barely visible at the small of her back, where it always was. The second was taken of this same woman, from the side, as she spoke to a man—Evan Weld. Her hand was sitting in his and she was looking up at him with a smile on her face—almost intimate.

In the third picture, this woman looked stricken, her face turned toward a shadow in the background. And then Grace realized the woman in the pictures was she. Someone had photographed her on the Levy's terrace, and as they entered the building upon arrival. Grace looked over Marin's shoulder. Above the three pictures, the two sentences made her blood run cold:

You looked beautiful tonight. A beautiful corpse.

19

"*H*ow the fuck did they get up here?"

Grace stared out the windows at nothing. Marin's words startled her. Someone was watching her. Was he watching her now? Could he see her through the windows of her suite, situated at the top of the world? Where, if not right here, right now, was she safe? She backed into the shadows as the murmurs of hyper-focused men continued behind her. Something about not involving local police, something else about summoning Grumpy and Bashful from Shannonfield, their words were running together into an amalgam of curses, warnings and dire outcomes. Marin raised his voice, his tone angry. Grace jumped, as if his ire were directed at her. She should tell him; she should tell him right now.

She did not know how long she stood there, and she did not hear the three men leave. She did not feel the tears wet on her face, and she did not hear her own sniffles as she tried to keep her emotions at bay. She felt nothing, until his fingers caressed the back of her neck, feather-light.

"Baby." He said it on a whisper, reverent, like a prayer.

She closed her eyes. Her left arm, protectively wrapped around her middle, propped up her right as she gnawed on a manicured nail. She was a strong woman, but she knew she wouldn't survive it if John Marin left her now. She could smell him behind her, feel the heat of his large body through the thin fabric of her robe. He grabbed her shoulders and turned her to face him.

He'd rolled the sleeves of his dress shirt up in the time she was in her room feeling sorry for herself. His dusty blond hair had lost some semblance of control, and bits threatened to flop over his forehead—from raking his large hand through it in frustration, no doubt. His gray suit pants rested conservatively at his waist, a black leather belt keeping them up and his shirt, for the moment, tucked into the waistband. They fit every inch of his wide hips and long legs, and despite all that happened, he still looked put together in a way she didn't come close to feeling. His over-large hands flexed on her shoulders, and he stood, feet apart, ready to pounce. Grace was stunned into paralyzed silence by the figure standing close enough to kiss. He smelled of vetiver and lime, and something underneath it all advertised he was not a man of this world. She'd known it all along.

"I won't have anyone else," she whispered. "I simply won't."

Marin shook his head. "No. No, you won't."

He fixed her with a hooded glare; she'd seen the look before, but now the intensity had her knees going weak. He was going to fuck her; she saw it in his eyes, in the set of his jaw, in the temporal vein that pounded at the side of his head. She felt his heat through her thin robe. His shoulders rose and fell on audible breaths, and if he were bare from the waist up, she was sure she would be able to see the pounding of his heart through his chest.

Grace's choices in men had been safe and free of excess emotion and drama; even Matt Coolidge was as safe as any man she'd ever been with, despite his political ambitions—in short, he was as regular as a man could be. But from the moment she set eyes on John Marin almost two weeks ago, after a year spent forgetting, she felt all of that reserve, all of those comfortable rules she'd set up for herself as first lady, all of the self-preservation she'd built around her heart and her soul come tumbling down, piece by carefully cultivated piece. In this moment, standing in a robe and bare feet in an expensive New York City suite, she felt neither safe, nor sorry. She wanted this man like she'd never wanted another, with a fierceness that would tear her soul to shreds if she allowed it. She'd seen the worst he had to offer; now she wanted the best.

Without taking his eyes off her, Marin tugged at the sash of her robe, and as it fell open, he separated the lapels and brought them to rest on the outside of both breasts, exposing her fully to him. They contracted and pebbled, tingling in anticipation of his touch. His hands, his mouth— she could feel it all before he touched her, as if her breasts had a mind of their own. A meaty hand cupped her jaw and lifted her face to meet his. His eyes, previously focused and locked on hers, roamed freely now over her face, as if seeing her for the first time. A pair of full lips parted, and his head moved almost imperceptibly from side to side, as if he were trying to talk himself out of something.

At last he snatched her up by her arms and pressed his mouth to hers. Her legs went weak and his hands tightened. His tongue swarmed through her mouth mimicking the fucking she knew he would give her before the night was through. He tasted masculine, dominant. She would do anything for him now. Anything.

Marin separated from her mouth by yanking her head back, and his hand drifted from around her jaw to her shoulder. With an imperceptible sweep of his hand, he sent the robe cascading down her body like a waterfall to pool on the floor at her feet. His mouth covered hers again as he dragged his right thumb across the bead at the center of her exposed breast. Both grew hard and her nipples pebbled. Grace cried out into his mouth when he took her breast in his hand and massaged, the glide of his palm over her aching globe determined yet gentle. She missed that hand, had felt it across her breasts for days, like a missing limb— there but not really. He paid equal attention to its twin as he swept his tongue through her mouth. Then a hand dropped down and down and down until his fingers reached the close-cropped and professionally shaped triangle above her pubic bone.

Marin pushed her back until she was up against the glass the door to the terrace. Grace cried out as first her bottom, then her back, came in contact with the ice-cold glass. With his free hand around her throat, he braced his fingers against the glass behind her. His eyes screamed, *Say no. Say it now.*

I'll do nothing of the kind, her eyes answered, and with that, Marin slid a thick digit between her folds and caressed her slick and semi rigid bundle of nerves. Back and forth, back and forth his finger drifted. Grace closed her eyes, bracing her upper back against the cold windows as her hips jutted forward into his hand. A high-pitched gasp escaped. She was dewy, slick with want, and his finger traveled effortlessly over her clit and down each side between the creases, then over the entrance to her core. He watched her, his hand around her neck holding her against the glass, not so tightly that she was unable to swallow, but attempting an escape at this moment would prove uncomfortable, in more ways than one. Her head wanted to thrash from side to side as pressure between her legs built, but Marin held her still, watching.

"You'll come," he whispered. Never one to obey an order without considered thought, Grace did just that. She held onto his broad shoulders as her entire body quaked, and her hips bucked against his hand and her ass bounced against the glass door. Just like that. It took seconds, and already she was doing his bidding.

"Open your eyes," he ordered, his voice hoarse, his hand working slowly and efficiently between her legs, drawing out the torturous orgasm on his terms, not hers. Grace cried out, tears blurring her vision of him as she rode the climax Marin drew from her simply by stroking between her legs.

As her descent began, Grace unbuckled Marin's belt and unfastened his slacks, the outline of his cock visible as he pressed his hips into her hand. He managed the rest, and with his cock jutting straight and heavy, he pinned Grace against the door, lifted one leg in the air, and set the pulsing head against her slick core. His eyes begged her to fight, to say no, to resist. *Last chance*, they said. *It's now or never*, they warned. When all she gave him was a slight tick at the corner of her mouth, Marin lifted her and pulled her legs around his hips. With gentle determination, he positioned his cock at her center. His hands gripping where her thighs and bottom met, he spread her wide, his finger stroking her entrance, vying for space with his cockhead. Without taking his eyes off hers, he entered her.

"God," he whisper-growled. "Oh, God, Grace." Grace's eyes flew open, her head jerked back, hitting hard against the glass as she let out a high-pitched yowl. Marin entered her to the hilt, then pulled halfway out, and impaled her. Her ass slammed against the bulletproof glass door as he retreated only far enough so he could thrust into her again. Marin fucked her with precision, and determination, every thrust ending with a twist of his hips to burrow in deeper before retreating and doing it all over again. With every thrust her back flattened into the glass door, and with every retreat he held her still so he could pound into her again. Grunts, mewls and muted expletives were the only sounds coming from them. Marin buried his face in Grace's neck and slowed down, moving himself in and out of her with touching tenderness, only to straighten again, pierce her with lustful eyes, and pound into her again.

Grace smiled, relaxed, and Marin widened her eyes with one particularly impressive thrust that had her riding on a second orgasm that began deep within her and caused her to scream his name. She wanted to feel him banging against her clit; she wanted to feel him ramming her cervix. She wanted him all the way in.

Marin covered her mouth with his and continued to pound relentlessly into her. As her climax squeezed his cock, he slowed. An arm still supporting her, he cupped her jaw with a free hand and held her eyes as he glided in and out of her. John Marin was making her come again and he was watching her do it. She nude, he still dressed, Grace Ashton Coolidge was fucked to a second explosive orgasm by a man she never thought she'd have. She snatched up handfuls of his shirt and pulled, sending buttons flying in every direction as she screamed his name into his mouth. Tears glistening in her eyes, Marin drew the deep orgasm out of her with hard thrusts followed by gentle strokes. And as she rolled down from the explosion, he closed his eyes, pulled out of her and settled his cock between her labia. In one, two, three strokes, he roared his release between her legs.

Still holding Grace aloft, Marin remained attached to her, her heat almost too much for him. She smelled like rain, newly mown grass, the beach. She was soft and slippery, and her skin was hot and velvety soft. Now was the time; now he needed to reiterate his plan to place her in the hands of someone who didn't *care* the way he did. If he stopped now, if he let go of her now, he could quite easily help her make sense of it all because, dammit, it made sense! He was no good for her. He couldn't protect her from beneath her sheets, from between her silky legs. Instead, he took one look into her ice blue eyes, fear, hurt and confusion resting easy in them—too easy—and all thought flew out the window. He'd never been with a woman sexier than Grace Coolidge. Her eyes spoke volumes.

What now?

Will you still leave?

Love me one more time.

Marin eased her down until her feet found purchase, and he wondered what to do next. He never wondered what to do next, he just knew—as if the very idea of what to do next at any given time had been solely invented by him. The woman in his arms wobbled as she found her footing, and he pulled her to his chest, one hand pressed into the middle of her back as the other eased her head into his chest. The top of her head came to just under his chin, and he kissed her there, her hair smelling like a tropical spring. Her small hands gripped his ruined shirt and she shivered in his arms. Marin swallowed hard and tipped her chin, scrutinizing her countenance to determine exactly how much trouble he was in. One look at those barely pinked lips and those eyes, and he knew he was in serious trouble. No woman, ever, had made him feel so unhinged.

Stop this now! screamed in his head. He couldn't; not yet.

Marin kicked his pants away, swept Grace up in his arms, carried her to her room and laid her down on bed linen that smelled divinely of her. Pride settled in his chest at the idea that she wore him on her body, his seed slickening her inner thighs. Her own moisture was copious, and her musky scent drifted up and filled his head again. His cock danced and lengthened, impeded by the length of his dress shirt. Grace shivered, and her delicious woman smell caressed his senses. He pulled his shirt off and used it to wipe between her legs, removing their mingled lust. He needed to taste her, so after tossing the shirt aside, he bent his head and did just that.

Her hands dug into the sheets as Marin took her swollen and still pulsing bud between his lips. He licked up her slit and toured through her folds and around her wonderfully scented clitoris with his tongue. Grace spread wide and weaved her hands into his hair as Marin took the flat of his tongue to her core, and entered her. He fucked with his tongue like he fucked with his cock: sure, hard and dominant. Her honey slid over his tongue like the rarest treat, and he spread it around her lips and her clit simply so he could take it up again, enjoying her a second and third time. Their comingled tastes lingered on her and it drove him crazy. He felt Grace go rigid and he knew she would come again. Setting her ass at the edge of the bed and holding her legs around his waist, he slid himself deep inside her, and this time he fucked slow. He took her to the edge, backed off, and then brought her to the brink again. Curses sat behind her eyes as he teased another climax out of her, riding her hard as she pulsed around his cock, until he, too, roared his own release again into the quiet of the dimly lit room.

GRACE WOKE GENTLY, in Child's Pose, her hips raised. She was filled completely, covered from behind in the soft-hard warmth of Marin's body. His arms were over hers, his hands laced on top of hers, as he moved slowly, gently, in and out of her. With every easy thrust, he went deeper. She felt possessed, owned, wanted. He tortured her with deep penetration followed by slow withdrawal, until only the wide tip of his cock breached the tight ring of her vagina. He kissed her shoulder, nipped at her neck, licked behind her ear. And Grace bowed her back, spread her legs, and felt his labored breath in her ear.

"You. Are. Magnificent."

His fingers caressed the edges of her lips with the barest touch, teasing her, coaxing her to beg him for more. His cock irritated something deep inside her, something between an itch and an ache. She needed it relieved; have it seen to. But he had other ideas. On her back, his mouth between her legs, he took her to the top of the hill, and threw her back down again. With every touch, her climax built, only to be denied. Over his knee she went, her clit aching, her core pulsing, her body aching for release as he spanked her, hard, his hand clapping off her bare bottom, exacting promises that she would obey him, or there would be more of the same. Then he spread her legs and spanked her core, his ridged fingers slapping relentlessly. She screamed out as he lectured, reminding her who was in charge. Still he would not let her come. He put her on her knees, told her he was going to fuck her throat, then he held her head back by her hair and did just that. She allowed her hand to drift between her legs, and he threatented to take his belt to her if she came.

Finally, after taking her greedily, he set her at the edge of the bed and fell to his knees. His mouth hovered over her spread legs and he took her, slowly, gently, teasingly, until she cried tears of frustration, called him Daddy and begged to come. As it built, from deep inside her, Marin moved over her and slid inside her.

"Deeper, darling, deeper," she begged, and he filled her, until his balls slapped against her ass with every thrust. And when she let go, he held her steady, taking control, removing it from her, making her come with such force that she believed she would die, right here in a fancy New York hotel room. And as Grace Ashton Coolidge fell back to earth, the warmth of his breath in her ear settled her, the words melting her like butter.

I love you, baby. I love you.

GRACE DRIFTED up slowly from the depths of sleep, from a place she hadn't been in a very long time. She let her leg drift behind her, hoping to feel a hard shin or a long, bony foot. When she felt only the cold sheet she turned over and stared at the empty space next to her. Light peeked through a gap in the curtains and underneath the closed double doors of her bedroom. The clock read nine a.m. Normally a six-a.m. girl, she felt guilty and lazy and indulged. She wanted Marin back in her bed. She imagined him, dressed in black or faded jeans, the forest green or the maroon Henley, and his go-to boots, sitting on one of the overstuffed chairs in the suite's living room reading the paper. Bent at the waist, ever on alert, never sitting back in relaxed repose; John Marin was always ready to pounce, to act, to protect.

Perhaps he was in the office opposite his bedroom, at the desk, coffee cup and newspaper covering the glass top. Grace smiled and pushed the covers halfway down her body and slid a hand behind her head. In that room, the office, he would be dressed in suit pants and a dress shirt. She wasn't sure why he was dressed differently in that room, but he was. He will have had breakfast by now. She imagined appearing in the doorway and being raked over by his potent brand of scrutiny.

"You overslept, Duchess," he would say. He'd sit back in the ergonomically correct desk chair and fold his large arms over an even larger chest. *"You know how I feel about laziness. Now Daddy's going to have to spank you."* Grace's clit pounced at the fantasy. *"Now, drop that robe and come here. This one's going to sting."*

Daddy. Oh, lord.

Perhaps he was across the hall with Doc, both doors propped open, Marin situated in a spot where he could see into their suite while he chatted with Doc, maybe sharing a meal while allowing her to laze the day away.

God, how she wanted him again.

"Johnny?" She wanted him to come to her; she wanted him to *want her*.

He'd made love to her last night, more than once. Grace chuckled out loud. No, John Marin *fucked* her. A tingle raced through her body at the memory. Every place he touched awakened from a dormancy she didn't realize was there, a complacency that sat deep and content, until he came along. She retraced with her fingers every inch of herself that he caressed hours ago. His fingerprints and her body oils and perspiration would be evident on the glass door to the terrace in the new light of day. She would attempt to clean the glass so the maids wouldn't gossip after they checked out of the hotel on Thursday. Grace smiled, remembering his big body on top of her, the helpless way she felt as he held her hands over her head and fucked her without taking his eyes off her; how her hands felt grasping the feather pillows as she lay still, as ordered, while he took her from behind. The way she felt so exposed as she stood, nude, in front of him, while he looked at her, admired her. Smiled when she fidgeted. The man was wicked.

Grace smiled at the memories he'd left her with, and willed him to open those double doors now, grin indulgently at her and then tell her to get her ass out of bed. She would shove the covers off her and coax him to join her with a sassy grin and a few choice words. He would not indulge her, but rather scold her on her laziness. That idea turned her on more than him returning to the bed on her whim. Why? She hated to be bossed around, told what to do, made to adhere to rules. But with this man, she seemed to fall right into line—eventually.

"Johnny?" Grace called again. She sat up and drew her sheet-covered knees to her chest. She stared at the double doors and wondered if she'd dreamed John Marin standing there in the middle of the night, the light from the city coming in through the windows, casting him in a dark shadow and just the silhouette of his large body taking up most of the doorway. He'd been dressed, and he stood there staring at her. In her dream she thought she called out to him, but he stood there, silent, unmoving. Then she felt him move farther away, until he was just...gone.

"Oh, God, no!" Grace jumped out of bed and grabbed for her robe. Evidence of their coupling still lingered in the creases and folds between her legs, then gravity took hold and she felt the telltale trickle leak down her inner thighs. Not caring a wit, she stood before the double doors and slammed her eyes shut before opening them.

Doc sat where she imagined John Marin sitting, except instead of the newspaper spread out on the coffee table, there was a map, and a sheaf of papers, and a large bottle of water. He looked up when she stepped into the living room, the wide grin that would have normally greeted her nowhere in sight.

"Good morning," he said.

"Good morning. Where is he?" But of course, Grace required no answer, for she knew by the silence in the suite and the look of—was it pity? —on Doc's face, that John Marin was gone. She raced through the living room and down the hall and stood in the doorway to Marin's room. The bed was made with military perfection, and had she been in the mood, she would have actually attempted to bounce a coin off the bedcover. His toiletries weren't sitting in a neat and orderly fashion on the bathroom counter, his go-bag was not sitting on the spare chair in the corner, nor was the tuxedo he was to wear for the event at the Met laying out on the second queen bed. The room still smelled of his soap—cedarwood and lime—and moisture still hovered from a shower taken probably hours ago.

Grace braced herself in the doorway as she fought back tears and willed the deep, pounding ache in her chest to disappear. John Marin said they weren't to be. He said there was no room in his life for her, for this. He said he could not —would not—protect her *like this*.

She moved with purpose into the room, opened the closet, and what she saw didn't surprise her in the least, but had no bearing on the pain she felt: the large suitcase stood closed in a corner, as did the duffle she'd purchased in

London for him. The clothes she bought him—the suits, the
tux, the shoes, the pants and shirts, were hung like little
soldiers in the closet. She checked the drawers, and only his
underwear, socks and a few t-shirts were gone. The silk tees
he liked so much, the Henleys, the half-dozen cotton tees in
assorted colors she'd bought him sat folded neatly in the
drawer. And she knew that if she checked her bank account
now, she'd discover that the $160,000 check she'd written
him at the start of their arrangement, had not been cashed.

In a fit of temper, she pulled everything out of the
drawers and threw them about the room, her screams of
rage bringing nothing more than echoes in the quiet room.
Not even Doc bothered to come to her aid. When her anger
had been spent, Grace sat heavily on the bed and pressed a
hand to her chest, so her heart would not come flying out
and run away. She'd never felt such pain. Humiliation had
not found its way in yet, and she doubted it would, for she
wanted last night as much as he did. Every minute of it was
sincere, of that she was certain. No, her pain came from
believing that because of how wonderful things were last
night, that he'd seen his way clear to being with her, found a
way to love her and protect her at the same time. She
believed he'd changed his mind. What almost killed her
now was the realization that love had nothing to do with it.

"Fool. Damn, damn fool!" she chided herself. A deep
moan came from someplace, and she realized it was coming
from her. The pain was unbelievable.

"Pull it together, damn you!" she scolded aloud. She did
not know how long she sat there, and she blessed Doc for
giving her space. She came to, laying on her side on the
same bed he slept in when the front door rattled. Her heart
soared when he walked in. He stood in the doorway to the
bedroom, and Grace's insides melted. He had the same hair

—albeit a bit more reddish—and the same blue eyes—albeit a bit lighter—and she realized why she took to the man the way she had, from the very beginning. He looked a lot like John Marin.

"Mrs. Coolidge," he said. And then Grumpy walked into the room and set down his bag.

20

*G*race stood in the middle of the suite, having showered and changed her clothes, and then cleaned up the mess she'd made in Marin's, now Grumpy's, room. Saying her piece to two formidable men with John Marin's love juices running down her leg donning nothing more than a silk robe wasn't going to cut it. Her black sleeveless cashmere sweater and tan boyfriend-cut khakis felt casual yet serious enough for the five minutes it would take to kick the two men out of her suite. Then she planned to sit in the restaurant bar for the rest of the day.

"I am under no obligation to have protection until the memorial on

Friday. I will see you both at the plane on Thursday for the flight to D.C." With a single nod punctuating her statement, she headed toward the door to lead them out.

"You have your scheduled appearance at the Met tonight, and other plans throughout the week, Mrs. Coolidge," Grumpy reminded. "Our orders are to remain with you until further notice."

"Further notice—ha!" Grace blasted out, a sneer

forming where an amused and patronizing smile belonged. She was losing herself. She knew better. "You're not understanding me," she tried again, remaining ever-so polite, as was her breeding. "I am a free woman, and I choose to remain—how to put this? —alone and unattached to protection until I am forced to by...law, or whatever Charles Bannish has put to this silly mess. Do you understand?" She punctuated the sentence with the most endearing smile and batting of eyes, while the stabbing pain of John Marin's departure dug deeper and deeper into her very soul.

Grumpy and Doc exchanged looks, and then Doc gave it a try. "Grace, we hear you, really we do. But John left us strict orders..."

"Since *John* is no longer under my employ, he has no jurisdiction over me. If he has some over the two of you, then that is your problem and certainly none of my concern. Stay out of my way and we may be able to remain friends once this nightmare is over." And with that, Grace snatched up her purse, slipped her feet into a pair of open-toed black suede slides, and headed for the door, not caring any longer to see them out.

"Christ," exclaimed one.

"Fuck," said the other. And by the time she'd flounced down the hall and reached the elevator she was flanked by them both.

"Ma'am..." Grumpy attempted.

"No," Grace snapped. "No 'ma'am' or 'Missus Coolidge' or anything else. I want you both to leave me alone." And much to their credit, the men said not another word to her for the rest of the day but remained within fifty feet of her at all times, their eyes not leaving her once.

AFTER BEING INFORMED that he would not be sharing her suite, and then being threatened with incarceration if he did not leave immediately, Grumpy gathered his things and trudged across the hall to bunk with Doc. He spent the needed seconds to drop off his bags, then plunked himself in a chair outside her door and wore an open scowl that made her teeth ache.

Grace stood at the long dresser in her bedroom, fresh from a shower and wearing only her robe. The dress she would wear to the Met this evening—a floor length velvet dress with a deep V neckline, fitted waist, and elegant wide cap sleeves in a deep, rich red—hung over a hook outside the closet. The Harry Winston-designed diamond and ruby cluster necklace sat on the dresser next to the silver metal case Marin and Doc had presented to her on their first night in New York. It sat open on the long dresser, the intricate pieces of jewelry made to keep track of her every move and gave her a way to call for one of them were she to get into trouble, rested gleaming against the blue velvet lining. She picked up the silver teardrop necklace with the diamond and turned it over in her hand. Then she picked up a gold square pendant with a cut amethyst in the center, then the hammered silver, and the funky brass one. Then she lifted the rough-cut pale pink agate geode necklace she wore last night, a lifetime ago, when John Marin told her he was leaving, and she slapped him. And then he made love to her. And then he left her.

Grace held the necklace aloft by the black satin ribbon. It was a beautiful piece, like the others in the case. When this was over she would ask for this one, buy it if she had to. As pieces of jewelry went, it was probably one of the less expensive in the case, but she loved it. It was rugged and beautiful—like him.

She could not decide whether she was most angry, or hurt, or sad: perhaps all three equally. She hated John Marin, yet she wanted no other man. Only about a hundred times that day did she will him to appear, while she was at the bar, or on her way out of Bloomingdales, with some outrageous explanation about where he'd been, apologize for the confusion and for scaring her. She wrote elaborate, scathing rebukes in her mind, but all she could settle on as a reaction was to throw her arms around him and cry.

She pressed the button on the back of the agate geode.

Did John Marin really think she'd allow Grumpy and Doc to just take over, that somehow their mere charm and presence would make up for him leaving her, that somehow she'd believe she still needed protection after him? That somehow this was about anything and everything except him?

She pressed the button behind the silver teardrop pendant.

What made him think that she'd just toss this off as some amazing one-night stand and forget about him? How could he go back to his life before, after her?

Grace found the rough spot at the wrist of a wide brass cuff. She pressed the button.

She pressed all of them, every button she could find, on every single piece of jewelry in the case. Petulant? Yes. And when she heard the thump and clomping, like a herd of buffalo, crossing Doc's suite and then the hallway to her door, followed by the keycard in the door, and the bang and rattle as the door met with a deadbolt and the metal security barrier, she came out into the living room and stood. She heard curses and shouts, her name being called, followed by fierce kicks to the door. Her cell phone rang, as did the suite phones.

Silence filled the suite before new shouting and banging resumed. She could see the terrace through her open bedroom doors. Suddenly Grumpy appeared like some cartoon Spiderman from she didn't know where. He stumbled over the terrace furniture and grabbed on to the French doors into the suite—the very one John Marin fucked her against the night before. The imprint of her bottom and her shoulders, so clear and so obvious, sat dull on the otherwise clean glass. Grumpy rattled the door and shouted at her as she walked into the living room and stared at him. He glared at her, his light blue eyes on fire, his mouth set in a thin line that came close to the one Marin affected when she got like this. Grumpy was a formidable man, and he was livid. He pinned her with a heart-stopping glare and without taking his eyes off her he spoke into his wrist, like Marin had done the night before while she stood on another terrace across town, wondering what she'd done wrong. The noise at the front door ceased. While she was sure the man outside wanted to pick up the nearest chair and throw it through the window like a scene from *Body Heat*, instead he sat in one of those chairs. Grumpy was as angry as Grace had ever seen a man, and she cared not one damn. She raised her middle finger and kept it there a full ten seconds before retreating to her room to dress, and the formidable strawberry blond did not move until it was time for him to dress and attempt to escort her to her scheduled appearance at the Met.

21

"*W*hat the hell happened?"

"You mean at the fucking event, or the bullshit before," Grumpy snapped.

"All of it," Marin snapped back.

"She took a goddamn cab to the Met..."

"So, hang on. You couldn't get a hundred-twenty-pound woman into an SUV for a ride to the Met? Do I have that right?"

"Yeah, asshole, you have that right. You want me to physically move her from one place to another?"

John Marin squeezed the phone so tightly he broke the case. As much as Grace Elizabeth Ashton needed a firm and unyielding hand, the idea of another man touching her—even if the man was his best friend—made him insane with rage.

"Not that she fuckin' doesn't deserve it," Grumpy went on. "You know what she did this afternoon?" Grumpy gave an accounting of Grace's actions throughout the day, which included setting off all the tracking alarms and then locking him and Doc out of her suite, and ended the report with, "A full ten seconds she flipped me the digit. She's a handful, man. If she were mine…"

"She's not." Marin's mouth twitched at the imagined indignant glare in her eyes and the defiant gesture.

Had he not left, they'd have probably spent most of the day in bed, because goddammit, the woman smelled and tasted too delicious for her own damn good. He'd delight in taking her into the shower, cleaning him off her, only to take her back to bed and dirty her up again. He'd have stayed and watched her dress for the event, dressed already himself. He wanted to know how she dressed, in what order she put on her clothes. He wanted to watch her put on her panties, and her bra if she were to wear one. And then he wanted to watch her slip on the gown she'd chosen, and had shown him, for the Met event. Her shoes would come next. Then, maybe, he'd intervene and choose one of the tracking necklaces for her, taking away one small choice from her, just because he could. And she'd let him. Because she was his now, dammit!

No. She was as far from his as a woman ever was.

"Was she wearing any security items at the event?" Marin asked.

"She refused."

"What happened at the event?"

"She's fine, John."

"What happened?"

Grumpy sighed. "She was in front of the press, taking a few questions, and the guy pushed forward and yelled something. He knocked her down, I knocked him down, he's talking to the NYPD and someone from Homeland Security, and I'm wondering why the fuck she was allowed to attend this event in the first place."

"It's been part of the itinerary since the beginning," Marin answered. What his friend wanted to say, and didn't, was, *Why weren't you here?* And he wasn't wrong.

"She's fine," Grumpy repeated. "We've got her."

"Okay." Marin signaled the bartender, pointed to his glass, and the man dutifully hit him with another shot of Ol' Number 7. "Is she in, now, for the night?"

"She damn well better be."

Marin sighed. "Put her on."

"Yeah. Okay. This should be fun."

Marin sipped whiskey as Grumpy attempted to get Grace to come to the door of her suite. That Grumpy wasn't in the suite with her infuriated Marin.

"It's John," Marin heard Grumpy say. Silence for what seemed like an hour was followed by a terse, "Yes?" and the slam of a door.

"What the hell are you doing?" he snapped.

"It doesn't appear to be your concern any longer."

"Let's be clear: no matter what happens between us from this moment forward, what you are doing—hell, what you're fucking *thinking*—will be among my biggest concerns."

"Words, John. Pretty words coming from a liar!"

He was silent for a long time. "I deserved that, I guess."

"Are we through here?" The dual meaning cut Marin to the quick. He knew what he had to do. Still, it hurt.

"I handled this wrong, Duchess. I'm sorry."

"Why?"

"Why did I handle it wrong?"

"I know why you handled it wrong. You're a coward."

"Yeah," he capitulated. "I deserved that, too."

"I have to go," she said, *before I start crying and never stop*.

"Before you do, I want to say I'm sorry I hurt you. I still

believe you're better off without me. But, fuck if I can shake free of you."

"More words."

"You're going to make me pay for this, aren't you, Duchess?"

"You just...left.

"I did. I was wrong." *I'll do it again soon, I'm afraid*, he thought to himself. It was for the best. He'd keep that mantra up until it stuck. For now, he wanted nothing more than to hold her in his arms and bury himself so deep inside her that he'd lose himself forever, taking choice out of the picture entirely. That's what he wanted, to rid himself of the have-tos. He was fucking tired of the have-tos.

"Forgive me," he whispered. "A man worth anything makes himself clear to a woman he cares about."

"You don't give a bloody damn."

"Stop being petulant." His voice was soft, low, intimate. "I have something I need to take care of. In the meantime, I want you to stay off the phone, off any social media, off email. Just stay quiet today. Can you do that?"

"Why?"

"I can't say now. Can you do as I ask?"

Grace hesitated a long time before offering a terse agreement. She wasn't giving him an inch, not that he deserved it. "Good. Thank you," he said. "We're changing venues for your dinner with your lady friends tomorrow night."

"Why?"

Marin chuckled to himself. "I'll explain later. I need you to follow Doc and Grumpy—"

"Oh, for heaven's sake," she snapped, "what is the man's name? I'd like to leave the Happiest Place on Earth out of this, if you don't mind."

Marin smiled and took a sip of his drink. "Brian. Brian Dean."

"Brian. I can see that."

"Cooperate, please." When she didn't answer, his voice got low. "Grace."

"I'll do my best."

"Thank you. Now," he said, his tone lowering an octave. "You took a taxi to The Met?"

Grace's stomach plummeted to her feet. "I was upset—not that I answer to you any longer."

"Stop being a brat," he ordered. "And Saturday night you 'weren't thinking'. I told you I was done with those kinds of excuses."

"This is different."

"How?"

"You left me."

Marin was quiet for a moment. "Still."

"Still, indeed."

"I'm not arguing the whys of it with you, Grace. Anything could have happened to you tonight. You had a tantrum to get back at me, get my attention. Well, now you've got it, lady."

Grace's stomach rolled. "I'm fine."

"Yeah." Marin paused, his voice low. "You haven't dealt with me on this yet."

"Meaning?" Grace thought they'd gotten disconnected, he was quiet so long.

"You'll come to me and ask to be punished."

"Ha!" she scoffed, right before she soaked her panties.

"Naked."

She snorted. "You are—"

"While holding my belt." That last part he whispered.

She heard him loud and clear. "The rules elude you, for some reason. We'll work on that. Together."

"You're high," she sassed.

"Not yet, babe, but I'm working on it."

"So, I will see you again," she noted, tears welling in her eyes. Embarrassment shrouded her, even as she heard the clinking of glass and the murmur of voices, telling her he'd said all this while in public.

"Yes, eventually." He paused. "Nothing's changed, Grace. I can't be what you want."

"Yet I'm expected to...oh, dear, this is rich...to come to you and ask..." Grace laughed. "You've lost your mind."

Marin chuckled. "We'll see. I'll make it worth your effort."

"We'll see, indeed."

"Behave like a reasonable adult, please," he implored.

Grace chuckled. "Of course. It's what I do best."

"Let Grumpy back into the suite where he belongs, and put him back on. And I'll see you soon."

"Maybe I no longer what that," she snapped.

"Put him on, babe." There was humor in his voice, and Grace could see the corners of his eyes crinkle in amusement. She saw it rarely, but she could see it clear as day now.

"Goodbye, darling," she whispered, instantly feeling foolish.

"Bye, baby."

In a moment, Grumpy came back on the line. "Yeah."

"I think everything will be all right now."

"Uh...huh. She's crying," Grumpy noted with a sigh.

"Yeah. My fault."

"I'm back in the suite, so there's that"

"That was the goal. Stay put. Call me if she isn't cooperating. No calls, no communication with anyone except me. Not until I'm through here."

"Roger that," Grumpy said.

"I'm sorry, man."

"Yeah."

"She's got a lot going on." Marin finished his whiskey.

"Yeah."

"And I'm part of that."

"Yeah. How are things there?" Grumpy asked.

John Marin sat in a dark corner of a Brooklyn hotel bar. It, like the hotel, was clean, modern and off the beaten path, which, to him, meant private. It was also where Sterling Jarvis was staying. Grumpy's call about Grace was the first opportunity Marin had to move Jarvis to the back burner. Marin knew the lady wouldn't take this lying down. But it was his way of staying close, doing something to solve this issue, without sharing a room, and a bed, with her. He could act, with his head firmly intact and focused. Her life, her safety, was his priority now. He'd handled it wrong; he'd hurt her. For now, it was best this way.

"Fine," Marin answered. "He's here; I'm on him. I told her we've changed venues for her dinner tomorrow night with her girlfriends, and nothing more. The less she knows now, right?"

"Yeah.

"We're changing her itinerary until D.C, and I should have enough on Jarvis before then to get him out of the picture."

"Right."

"She'll want to shop tomorrow, or something else. Let her go but stay on her. If she gives you trouble, I want to know about it. I don't think she will."

"Roger that. I wish I had better news for you."

"Yeah. She's a handful. But this is on me. Give her a break, huh? This isn't about you guys."

"I know." There was a long pause before Grumpy spoke again. "I won't be too sad when this gig is up. The sexual tension between you two is killing me."

"Shut up."

Grumpy chuckled. "Okay, then."

"Later."

"Later, asshole."

22

*T*he uninhibited laughter of eight women filled the cozy room upstairs. The owners of the tiny Hoboken restaurant closed their doors at eight p.m. on a Tuesday for the former first lady and her guests. While Doc remained with the car, as he always did, Grumpy sat at the bar with Meg Arthur's man and Senator Winklefoos's detail.

Upstairs, the laughter turned raucous; the more the women drank, the more they shared. Grace reminisced with Winnie Winklefoos and Eleanor Cabbish about their college years at Middlebury, and she talked politics and men and sex with Meg Arthur, her author pal Karen Perry, and Sharron Levy. DA Ruth Wilson announced her run for mayor in two years. "That's why Deanna isn't here," she said. "I'll be running against her husband."

"Why take it out on me?" Grace said petulantly. "I love Deanna."

"And she loves you, dear. It's me she ain't too fond of."

"I am sorry, Ruth—about Deanna, I mean, not about your run," Grace returned.

"I know. Me, too. When she sees I'll make a better mayor

than Jim, she'll come back to me, and I'll welcome her with open arms."

"Put her on the city council, Ruth," Winnie suggested. "She can be a real bulldog for you."

"Good point, Gwen. I'll think about it."

And as the women talked, Grace's mind wandered.

John.

Such a common name, for such a common man. *Ha*, she laughed to herself. There was nothing common about John Marin. She missed him. He should be here, downstairs at the bar while she gossiped a flight of stairs away. She'd have made sure she laughed a little too loudly on occasion to remind him she was up here. Instead, he was off doing God knew what. And without benefit of the truth from her.

"Where you going, Lou?" Winnie said, slurring her words a bit. Grace smiled at the college nickname she'd been given since the first day of orientation at Middlebury.

"The loo." The women fell about, laughing.

"Careful, those stairs are steep, honey," called Karen Perry as Grace slipped on the edge of one and stumbled down two more. Grumpy was on his feet in a second, waiting for her at the bottom of the stairs.

As he raked his eyes over her in concern, Grace wished with all her heart it was John standing there. And then she remembered his tone, and his warning of what was in store for her, and she amended that wish, ever-so-slightly.

MARIN SAT in a white Jeep across from Le Bernadeaux on the Upper East Side, where Grace and her friends were supposed to go. Their reservation had been for eight p.m., and he'd been sitting here since six, waiting for Sterling Jarvis to show up.

The photos of Grace, standing on the terrace at the Levy's, had been taken from the building next door—both post-war towers with easy access to the roofs. How did the photographer know she'd be there? Grace's parents and the Whipples were the only people who knew Grace's general itinerary. Jarvis, Marin, and the 'dwarves' knew every detail. Happy, in his imposing Samoan way, showed a picture of Jarvis to the doormen of both buildings, and all reported seeing Jarvis lurking around on Saturday.

But why? Why would he stalk Grace? She said Jarvis had been loyal to the family for a decade, and he seemed fond and very loyal to Grace in particular. Why would he hurt her? Why would he threaten her? He, Marin, was good at spotting crazy, and he saw none of it in Sterling Jarvis.

At ten minutes to eight, a car passed him. Jarvis was bent over the steering wheel looking for parking. Finding none, Marin watched the nondescript compact car go down the next block. It was dark, and Marin lost sight of the car in traffic. He got out and jogged down E. 71st, past York, and ducked into a doorway as Jarvis, hunkered down in a jacket and wool stocking cap, trotted past him. Marin let him get fifty feet away before he stepped out of the doorway and followed him. Jarvis was heading to the restaurant, and the streets were just crowded enough that Marin could not take his eyes off the man without losing sight of him.

Jarvis waited at the light at the corner of 71st and York, and then crossed against the red once it was clear. Marin did the same, and almost got clocked by a speeding taxi trying to make the light. The cabbie honked at Marin and screamed accented obscenities at him while he ducked behind pedestrians, hoping Jarvis's focus was on Grace and that restaurant, and not the typical noises of New York City. Jarvis glanced over his shoulder and sped up. Marin was surprised that Jarvis wasn't in place sooner, and then he remembered that the man knew Grace intimately, knew she'd be ten minutes late, or more. What was his plan? Sit in the restaurant in plain sight and wait? And what did he expect Grace would do if she saw him? Nothing Marin was seeing now made sense.

A green awning over the entrance to the restaurant was Marin's point of focus, so when Jarvis disappeared through a door two addresses from that entrance, Marin turned around and went down York to a narrow alley behind the shops and restaurants on the 300 block of 71st. He saw Jarvis standing outside what Marin assumed was the back of Le Bernadeaux; he, Marin, had not vetted the place; his men had. He wished now that he had been the one to scope the place out, so he'd know what he was looking for.

Jarvis looked around, as if waiting for someone. Marin had enough. The man hadn't done anything yet, but he'd sure as shit get out of him what the fuck he was doing there.

Marin crept down the alley, hugging the side of the brick building, while Jarvis squinted into the dark, and then squatted down on his haunches. He was looking straight ahead, to the flat brick wall of another building. What the fuck was going on? Jarvis was so focused on whatever it was he was looking at, or waiting for, that Marin simply grabbed him by the jacket and pulled him to his feet. He shook the diminutive man like a rag doll, and Sterling Jarvis looked up into the angry eyes of Grace's protector.

"Mister Marin," the man Friday said. "I was wondering when you'd show up."

"WHAT'S THE MATTER, darling? You're not yourself." Sharron Levy turned to the remaining women. "Gracie wasn't well Saturday night." Sharron took Grace's hand and patted it firmly. "But she perked up and was the life of the party." Karen Perry, Jane Harrison, and Ruth Wilson looked at their friend with concern. Karen leaned in conspiratorially.

"There's something else going on," she said. "That hunk of meat we all saw at yoga isn't downstairs. What's going on, Grace? Spill, honey bun. Immediately."

"There's nothing to spill." Grace fiddled with her demi-tasse spoon.

"Horseshit, babe. Talk."

Grace shot a glance at Karen and sighed. "I must swear you all to secrecy." She eyed each woman in turn, knowing she had their loyalty without having to say the words; yet say them she did.

"Of course," Ruth said. "You know that."

Grace put her hand over Sharron's. "Sharron, I am sorry about Saturday. John Marin was not my 'date'; he was my protection. Bannish would not allow me to come to the states without it, and I wasn't about to trust Secret Service, for reasons I'm sure you all understand." Grace closed her eyes and then speared each women with moist eyes. "John was Matt's agent. He got me out of the convention center the night of the assassination."

"Oh, my God, Grace," Ruth exclaimed.

"No wonder you trust him," Jane said.

Grace had to acknowledge how much her close circle of friends did not know about her, especially over the last year or so.

"Marin is...very particular about how I handle myself," Grace continued, "and, well...I broke one of his rules at your party, love, and we had a terrible row. He was going to take me home, immediately. Like a naughty bloody child. And then, by the grace of God, he managed a change of heart. I wasn't ill, darling. I was...in trouble. We ended up having a terrible fight in Aaron's office, and I barely got through the party." She felt miserable. She must have looked it, too, for all three women fell into peals of laughter.

"What is so damn funny? It was awful."

"I bet it was," Karen said, her eyes wide and a very knowing smile on her face.

"He was very upset with me," Grace reiterated.

"Uh huh," offered Ruth.

"Oh, never mind!" Grace snipped.

Ruth glanced at Karen and gasped. "He spanked her ass, I'll bet my next orgasm on it!"

"Ruth!" Grace hissed.

"Oh, lord," gushed Sharron.

"You're damn right he did, babe!" exclaimed Karen with a smile.

"Well, if this isn't beyond the beyonds," sniffed Jane Harrison, "I don't know what is."

"And you fired him," Karen finished, wide-eyed.

"Oh, God, why, Grace?" Ruth gushed. "You clearly deserved it."

"I *what*?" Grace bellowed. And with that, the normally quiet Sharron Levy guffawed. And then she snorted.

"The English love a good spanking," Jane announced proudly, "And not from some mousey man, either. You may wish to start at the beginning, love," she soothed, patting Grace's hand. "And don't leave a thing out."

"I certainly will not," Grace huffed. "And *he* certainly did not!"

"Grace, come on," Karen countered, rubbing Sharron's back to calm her while the rest supported the request for details with nods and vocal affirmations that left Grace little choice. And for some reason she wanted to talk about it. "Nothing wrong with it," Karen continued. "In fact, it can be very cathartic. I know."

"Good God!" Grace bellowed, and then she laughed. She couldn't help it. It was all so ridiculous, and sad, and hot. She had to tell someone. Who better than these bitches. Grace sighed. "Fine. I was chatting with Weld out on the terrace..." And as her friends leaned in close to listen, Grace went into detail about that fateful Saturday night, including Marin's intentions in Aaron's office, and his confusion over her body shaper from Spanx. She wrapped up her story with, "...and when we got back to the suite, I was so furious —at him and at myself, of course..."

"Of course," echoed Karen, patting Grace's hand.

"Oh, if this goes in one of your books, Karen Louise Perry, I'll..." Grace threatened.

"Read it," Ruth Wilson interrupted. "We all will."

Grace sighed. "Then, with all the talk of leaving, and we were both so upset, and I was so upset that I'd struck the man—"

"I cannot believe you did that, Grace. My God. So unlike you," Jane offered.

"Indeed," Grace capitulated. "And, so, one thing led to another, and..."

"And?" Sharron Levy nudged. Her mouth hadn't closed since Grace began the sordid story.

"We made love." Grace eyed each of the women. "And the next morning he was gone."

"Oh, Gracie," Ruth said. "Was it good?"

"You're in love with him, aren't you?" Jane asked.

"So, he didn't spank you?" Karen asked, somewhat disappointed. "You slapped him, for God's sake. No heroine of mine would get by with such a thing." With that, Sharron put her head down on the linen covered table and laughed and snorted so hard she cried. Grace drained the wine glass in front of her and gestured for Karen to pour another. Sighing, she took a large swallow, and looked at Ruth.

"Yes, it was everything I dreamed of, and more."

Then she looked at Jane. "I'm quite sure I am, yes."

Then Grace looked at Karen and raised her chin proudly. "He did, during..." Grace swallowed hard and demurred. "You know."

"Sex?"

"Mmmm," Grace affirmed with a nod.

"So, he let you come," Karen said, her mouth set in an uncharitable moue

Grace's brows shot up. "Karen, for heaven's sake!" Grace rasied her chin proudly and speared her friend with an awful look. "I'll not be inspiration for one of your sordid heroines."

"Oh!" Sharron gasped when she looked up from the table. "Please stop a minute. I'm going to pee!"

Grace slapped Sharron's thigh with the back of her hand. "Oh, do get hold of yourself, Sharron, please."

"Honey, why did he leave?" Ruth asked.

"Well," Grace sniffed, "It's possible," she continued, looking down at her hands, "that a part of him is wary of something more—" She looked at her friends. "—with me."

"Oh darling," Ruth whispered, holding Grace's hand. "Why, I never saw you this overwrought, even when you were first dating Matt."

"I never, at any point, felt this way about Matt."

Ruth took a tentative swipe at her eyes, as did Jane. Sharron snapped her head up and her smile waned. "Oh, shit." Karen, hyperfocused as ever, had other things on her mind.

"The one downstairs at the bar looks just like him," the romance author noted. "Was that deliberate?"

"Oh, don't let's start with that one," Grace countered.

"Is he single?" Karen asked. "His hands are big."

"I'd hardly know about either of those things," Grace sniffed.. "Go down and ask him, and you can distract him while I slip away." And that was all she wanted; to slip away for a few days alone, until she caught her plane to Washington.

"I think I just might do that," Karen said, setting Sharron off all over again.

"I DIDN'T like what I was seeing, and hearing—and this was long before you became involved, John." They sat in the white Jeep in a vacant lot overlooking the Hudson. "Ever since the shooting at the library in May."

"What didn't you like?"

"Lady Grace was surreptitious," Sterling Jarvis said. "She'd go into the library at Shannonfield and lock the doors, and I would hear her talking quietly on the phone— and not the house phone, either. It was out of character. And those missives you found in her desk—I knew about those." Jarvis hung his head. "Then the accident happened, and she was dealing with Scotland Yard. Sometimes she would speak of the accident—mind you I only heard her side of it, I never eavesdropped on the phone...I'd never do that..."

Marin held up a hand. "Tell me more."

"Well, as I was saying, she would speak of the accident

over the phone, but I knew she wasn't talking to Scotland Yard."

"How do you know?"

"You know how a woman speaks differently—her tone, mind you—when she's speaking to the waiter at Crumbs rather than, say, a lover?"

"I suppose, yeah."

"Not that she was necessarily speaking to a lover...what I mean is, sometimes her conversations on the phone, about the accident, were more...intimate, familiar. I knew at those times she was not on with one of the inspectors."

"During these calls, did you ever hear the name Evan Weld mentioned?"

"I don't recall, although I know who he is. Grace seems fond of him. I believe they're friends."

"How about David Howell—Senator David Howell?"

Jarvis thought for a moment. "The name Howell sounds familiar. Just Howell."

"And was she mentioning him in a positive or negative light, given your penchant for tones?"

"Hard to say. I'm sorry."

"Why didn't you say anything to me about this, especially as I was throwing you out?"

"I wasn't sure of myself, and, forgive me, John, but you can be a bit intimidating. I did, however, contact Ambassador Delacroix."

"You did?"

"Yes, and as far as I know, Lady Grace knows nothing about that. I was afraid for her, and I knew that if she went to the states without protection, well, I didn't know what else to do. I thought the ambassador would put a stop to it all, and in fact he assured me he would, and get someone on investigating those threats. I believed once he did that, Lady

Grace would show me the door. But I didn't care. The ambassador told me he'd get her off the agenda for the embassy dedication, and the U.S. trip, which I knew would disappoint her greatly. Then suddenly she's having me call you. When I asked what happened, she said the president was insisting she accept Secret Service protection in order to go to the states. It was then I knew Delacroix had no intention of helping, or if his intentions were good, they were for naught. I did her bidding and called you, of course—and happy to do it."

"I see."

"Is the ambassador in on something nefarious regarding Grace?"

"I don't know."

"Hmmm. And I wonder, did you happen to ask Lady Grace why those threatening letters, et cetera, weren't with Scotland Yard to begin with?"

"I didn't have to. She was hiding them, for some reason."

"There's more to it, I'm certain."

Marin sighed, certain of it as well. "Yeah. They weren't tough to find."

"Did Delacroix lie, then, about getting her out of the two events? He certainly did nothing with regard to those threatening missives, surely," Jarvis sniffed.

"I don't know."

"I see."

Marin laid out the pictures from the Levy's, as well as some from the emails Grace had received. "So, you didn't take these pictures?"

"No," he said. "But I found one you might be interested in." It was a picture of Grace in the back of a car, a limo, it appeared. A man was driving. Marin stared at the picture in horror.

"This was taken after President Coolidge's funeral. Grace was on her way back to the White House to...to pack."

"Jesus."

"This picture is significant for two reasons: it appeared in all the papers to play on emotions—as you can see, the lady is, well, heartbroken." Marin saw that clearly enough. He'd seen the look, sitting in the back of a similar car on some New Orleans back road, while she lost her mind.

"The other reason?"

"The other reason is the picture that appeared in all the papers shows a different man behind the wheel. The man shown behind the wheel was African American. This one, the original, I found as I was sorting through pictures and archives for the library. Why? Why show a different man behind the wheel when, with some digging, the original, true picture can be found?"

Marin shook his head. "I don't know." But, of course, he did.

"The frightening part is I have seen this man lately."

"Lately?"

"Lady Grace was sitting at an outdoor café last month. This was after the accident in Piccadilly, so I had the car— the Jag. I'd done some grocery shopping and I was arriving to pick her up, and this man was sitting at a table next to her." Jarvis tapped the picture. Marin did a quick calculation and surmised that could have been about the time that the threatening note was placed in her purse. Pure speculation, of course.

"I've also seen him in town, in Plaistow. He looked so familiar to me, and I about died when I saw this picture again. He's following her."

"I'd say he is."

"Is he the one sending the threats?"

"I don't know."

"How did you know I'd be here?" Jarvis asked.

"I called London to discuss how to handle the press for Grace's appearance at the Met Sunday night, at her urging. You weren't in London."

"And you traced me here."

"Yes. It wasn't hard."

"And I wasn't trying to hide. I meant no harm."

"I know that." Marin stared at the pictures.

"You know this man." Jarvis stated. Marin knew him and had known him for years. And he knew how good he was, and how, if whoever hired him wanted Grace dead, she'd be dead already.

"I do," Marin said. "His name is Jason Weber," Marin whispered. "We call him Dopey."

23

"*A*ll well there?" Marin called Grumpy as soon as he saw Jarvis off with orders to lay low until further notice.

"Yup. The stragglers, led by the former first lady, are getting moving. One or two, oddly enough, have joined me at the bar."

"Watch for distractions," Marin warned.

"What have you got?" Grumpy asked.

"Interesting shit. Goes with what you found with the threatening letters and emails."

"I'm all ears."

And Marin told his partner all he knew. He finished with, "So, plan A."

"Yeah. Plan A. You ready?"

He wasn't. Not even close. It was the part he'd been dreading. He had no idea he'd fall so hard for the lady, so dread hadn't been a factor—until Saturday night. In light of this new information, he wasn't leaving her side—until the very last second.

"Of course," Marin said. "No problem."

GOD, she was good. Karen Perry was a beautiful woman, but more than that, she had a sex appeal Grace would have paid top dollar to be able to emulate. Karen stood next to Grumpy now, and the man, despite his attempts to thwart her, was not, at this moment, having a lot of success—or so Grace thought. The newly appointed protector was the only one left at the bar, and he'd been on his phone when the ladies came downstairs. Grace's three comrades all stood around Grumpy now, and Grace saw her moment.

"I'll just run to the ladies, and then…"

"Don't you move," he growled. Then he looked at Karen Perry, who managed to distract the handsome man from the moment he disconnected from his call. "You stay put, too. I'm nowhere near finished with you." And while Karen patted her heart and batted her eyes, Grumpy brushed past Grace, opened the unisex bathroom door, pronounced it safe, and gave her a curt nod.

Damn that man. He was worse than Marin, she groused as she dabbed around her eyes and contemplated a pee she did not have the strength or notion to attempt. But attempt she did, and as she washed up and exited the bathroom, she found her substitute hired gun surrounded by her beautiful friends. Of particular note was Karen Perry, who did not understand the word no, or the meaning behind such phrases as, *I'm nowhere near finished with you*. She sat on a barstool next her target with her hand on his knee and her cleavage in his face. Grace eyed the kitchen and an exit route through the round portal in the swinging door. It was time. She'd had enough. She simply could not function in captivity.

She trotted through the kitchen, navigating around a

man who was mopping the floor, and another who was scrubbing the steel counters, and exited out the back of the restaurant. She ducked between the buildings to the street. Traffic was quiet at the late hour, and Grace searched for an available taxi.

Hoboken on a Tuesday night seemed closed up tight. It certainly wasn't Manhattan, but Grace found it homey and sweet nevertheless. Despite her promises to Marin, she was in no mood for bossy tonight. She'd had a bit too much to drink, and she was feeling feisty. She wanted to be alone, and a few moments of just that in the back of a taxi to the hotel across the river was all she was thinking of. She'd be fine.

She stepped off the curb and into the street. A pair of taxis whizzed down a side street, and one turned onto hers. It pulled over to let a passenger out and Grace trotted forward, wondering if Grumpy had yet figured out she was gone. Her friend Karen was indeed that good. Grace might even like to see them together. They'd make an amusing match: she was a harbinger of fun; he was the annoying black cloud that signaled fun's demise.

"Not one more step, Duchess."

Grace's hand froze in mid-reach of the cab's door handle, and her heart stopped cold. She did not need to see him; she could feel his heat, his dominance, his body on hers as if he were pressed up behind her, his voice touching her, stinging and caressing in unison, like nothing she experienced before. Grace turned her head and saw him standing in the shadows a few feet from her.

"Come here."

Oh, dear God.

"Hey, lady! You gettin' in, a'what?"

"Grace?" His voice was laced with warning. She hesitated only a moment. Deal with the man standing behind her or run for the hills.

"Yes, I..."

"I don't think so, babe," he growled in her ear. Just that quickly he was behind her, his hand on her arm while the other banged the top of the cab. "Get out of here," he barked as his grip tightened, and Grace watched her escape disappear into the night.

Grace turned slowly and looked up at him. "Hello," she said.

"Hi," Marin smirked. He admired her spunk, that was for sure. Then his brows crashed together. "Move." He pushed her ahead of him, his hand still around her upper arm.

"Back to normal, I see," she sassed, her boots tip-tapping on the sidewalk as she attempted to halt her forward momentum.

"Like you never dreamed," he said, ushering her along like an errant child.

"May I walk on my own?" Grace inquired.

"Nope. And you keep fighting me, I'll spank your ass on the street." As he said this, Doc appeared out of the shadows. Marin threw him a set of keys. "White Jeep at the corner." Grumpy came up behind Doc and seared Grace with a glare. Grace gave him a sly smile. When they moved on, Grace speared him with a glare.

"Is there no end to the humiliation you enjoy heaping upon me?"

"No end in sight, Duchess."

"How lovely."

They came alongside the familiar SUV, door locks snapped open, and Marin shoved her into the seat. With no Doc to protect her, she felt even more vulnerable to this man's knuckle-dragging ways, as evidenced by his uncouth treatment of her on the street, in front of God and man. Dragging her about, indeed, she groused to herself as she reached for the door handle.

Marin slid his big body behind the wheel of the SUV and started the engine. He smelled like crisp fall air and cedarwood. He shot a sideways glare at her and held it.

"I wouldn't. And put your seatbelt on," An ache formed between Grace's legs as she snatched her hand off the door handle as if it were red hot.

Marin pulled into traffic, and they were silent for a full minute, which felt like an hour. "Are you drunk?" he asked, breaking that interminable silence.

"A bit." She hiccupped and stared out the window.

Marin bit back a smile. "What happened?"

Grace snapped her head around and pierced him with an angry sneer. "You! You happened, you...you!"

"Watch it, Duchess."

"Oh, do shut up," she said, turning away from him to look out the window.

"You ditched your detail."

"Don't be ridiculous. My *detail* had his eyes glued to my girlfriend's tits instead of me, and I had no idea where Doc was. You really should have a word with them. So clumsy."

Marin speared her with a dark look. "Grumpy can multi-task. Your tag-team efforts could use some fine tuning."

"Hmmm." Grace tried not to smirk as she looked out the window. "I do believe I've been set up."

"You are predictable. Add a little alcohol, and you get downright dangerous."

Grace turned to him. "Where have you been?"

"We'll talk about it later, believe me."

"Is that some sort of threat?"

"When have I ever done *some sort of* anything?"

"You do tend to be an all-or-nothing type of fellow."

"There you go, then."

"There I go, then," she mumbled.

His wrist rested over the gear shift and his overlarge hand dangled casually over the center console.

"Why are you here? Didn't I fire you? Or did you quit? I can't recall."

"It's the gin."

"It was three vodka martinis and four bottles of wine," she offered, staring out the window. "Amongst eight women," she said, noting his frown of disapproval, "So get back in your cage, tiger."

"Keep smarting off, lady, and I'll pull this car over."

Grace raised her chin and folded her arms. Marin took her hand and she thawed immediately. Damn fool! As if such a simple gesture could undo the hurt... she was a dimwit, it was that simple.

"I'm wondering..." she reflected.

"About?"

No longer wishing for an answer she wasn't prepared for, she stared out the window.

"What were you wondering?" Marin prodded.

"If you missed me at all."

He shrugged and stared straight ahead. "I don't know. Maybe. A little."

"Bastard." Grace threw his hand aside. "I don't like you."

"Yes, you do. Hey, come on, Duchess," he said, taking her hand. "I'm kidding." He squeezed. "I missed you, more than you'll ever know."

"If you tell me, then I will know," she reasoned helpfully. "Not that I should believe you," she snapped, pulling her hand away again.

He held it out to her again and snapped his fingers once. She placed her hand in his, like Pavlov's goddamned dog. Silence filled the vehicle. "I've had this pain—" he finally said, gesturing toward the left side of his chest with the hand that held the steering wheel. "Thought maybe heart attack—"

"John..."

"—angina, maybe something I ate. Since Sunday." He gave her a look.

"You're scaring me."

"Funny thing, it went away a few minutes ago." He laced his fingers with hers. "That's how much I missed you." Marin sighed. "You drive me insane, Duchess, but you've wedged yourself under my skin like a little bug." He turned to her. "I can't seem to burn you off."

"Isn't that lovely?" Grace mused. "I'm a bug." She stared out the window while her nose stung and her eyes watered, just a bit. Truth be told, he'd wedged himself as well, right in the bloody middle of her believed-to-be-frozen heart. She looked down at their hands, intertwined. "Your hands are very big. I feel swallowed by them sometimes." She turned his hand over and glided her fingers across the palm. "They've held me down when all I've wanted to do is run— like New Orleans; like tonight. I like these hands."

Marin nodded. "We'll see how you feel in about fifteen minutes." He entered the Lincoln Tunnel into Manhattan without another word.

---

24

*T*he clink of ice hitting crystal echoed in the suite as Marin tossed in one more cube and filled the old-fashioned glass to half with scotch. He took a sip and ran his right hand down the leg of his jeans. The sting lingered like an amputated limb ached when it rained; the feel of her ass, soft and firm, sat imbedded in his palm like a second skin. Against his better judgement, he took her as soon as they entered the suite, not waiting to see if she'd obey him.

He rolled the chilled glass over his hand and rested his foot on the brass rail behind the very efficient granite bar, which, to him, was one of the highlights of the suite he'd fought so hard against. Because Grace was the guest, the bar had been stocked with a few bottles of top shelf hooch, and he was imbibing now. God knows he needed it. He stared into his drink and gave the glass a shake. He loved the sound of clinking ice in a well-made glass; it made him feel right with the world.

Something flashed in his peripherals and he looked up to see Grace leaning against the doorjamb of her bedroom.

Her silk robe hugged her body, the hem skimming the floor, the deep violet color bringing out her eyes. His belt dangled off a delicate finger. She swung it back and forth, a sassy smirk pasted across her mouth.

"Hello" he said.

Grace studied him as he stood behind the bar; confident, sexy, dominant. His jeans were slung low on his hips and his black tee was untucked in front and on one side, making him look devil-may-care; like he'd just rolled out of bed; like he'd just fucked someone; like he'd just won a war. He was indeed Satan, for what he had done to her was surely a sin.

"Hi," she answered.

Marin came out from behind the bar, barefooted, his hair tousled, his cock still a visible outline at the front of his jeans. Grace came into the room and met him half way.

"You left this behind," she stated.

Marin's cock stirred. He took the belt from her and wrapped it around her waist. Resisting him was futile. He held both ends and pulled her to him. "How about I have it framed?" he suggested.

"You think you're quite funny, don't you?"

Marin nodded. "Are you okay?"

"Why do I war constantly between wanting to kill you and wanting to fuck you?"

"I'm no good to you dead, love."

"No, unless necrophilia is another *bête noire* you'd like to introduce me to."

Marin brushed his nose over hers. It was a tender gesture from a man who had been anything but for the last hour.

"I take it you weren't fond of the strap."

"Not at first, no."

"Tell me," he said in her ear, "where you were the least fond—across your thighs or against your cunt."

He'd spanked her. He seemed to enjoy it; seemed to think she needed it. First, his hard hand, and then his belt. And yes, he'd strapped her cunt, light taps that sent bolts of electricity through her body. She came as the barrage became overwhelming, right before she entered subspace.

"I hate you," she whispered, head back, her eyes closed, neck raised in offering. He ran his tongue along that soft spot behind her ear.

"Don't lie to Daddy, baby," he whispered in her ear.

"God help me," she managed.

"You were screaming that earlier, if I recall." He breathed her in. "You showered."

"You said we'd be having a serious discussion, and feeling you trickling down my leg would prove distracting."

"Christ." Marin lowered his head and took her mouth, possessive, filled with want; apologetic. He drifted away from her lips and wandered, leaving lingering kisses to her cheeks, her brows, her forehead. He was hard again. He moved his hand over her silk covered backside.

"Sore?"

"No. I prefer you playful, given the choice."

Marin smiled. "You'll always have a choice, Duchess." She gave him everything, and more. Denying him wasn't in her DNA. He liked that. She took his hand like a woman, and his belt like a fucking warrior. She'd wear his mark for days. He liked that, too.

"May I have a drink?" she asked.

"You mean water?"

"No, I mean gin."

"I think you've earned it."

"Oh, I think I have, too."

"Sit," he ordered.

"I'd rather not."

"I guess you'd rather have water, too, then."

"Sadist," she muttered, lowering herself onto the wooden barstool with a wince.

He leaned in. "You lied to me," he whispered, noting the grimace.

"Only if one views 'sore' as a negative."

"Touché." Marin smiled in admiration as he grabbed a glass from behind the bar. He filled it with ice and poured two fingers of Bombay Sapphire. He speared a few olives and set her drink down in front of her. "You need to learn to follow the rules," he noted.

"Now, what fun would that be?"

"Keep it up, sweetheart, and we'll go opposite of fun."

"And you say you want to leave me," she sassed with a smirk. He didn't want to, not at all. But that wasn't important. Not anymore.

Grace took a sip of her drink and ran a finger around the rim of her glass. "You didn't show up at the restaurant because I ditched my detail, John. The fellas and I had found our way—begrudgingly. I wasn't going anywhere in that taxi, except here."

"I know. Still."

"Indeed." She took another sip. "Something's happened, then. Where have you been?"

Marin leaned on the bar. "The only people who knew our full itinerary, from the moment we left Shannonfield, were my men and Sterling Jarvis, correct?"

"Yes, as far as I know."

"So, when I called Jarvis about the press situation at the Met, like I said I would, he wasn't in London where he was supposed to be."

"He and the Whipples returned to Shannonfield the day we left," she said. "You know that."

"Jarvis didn't. Turns out he came here. He was seen in the vicinity of the Levy's Saturday night." He let that sink in.

"And you suspect him of something?"

"I didn't know, so I found out where he was staying." When Grace arched a brow, he amended, "In a hotel in Brooklyn."

"How?"

"It wasn't hard, mostly because he wasn't trying to hide, it turns out. We changed the venue for your dinner tonight, arranged to pick up your friends, and the only people who knew the details of that were Grumpy, Doc, and I."

"I know."

"I waited for Jarvis at the original restaurant, and of course he showed up."

"For what purpose?"

"Turns out he was worried about you, and for good reason." Marin opened the envelope and spread the pictures out. Grace's heart dropped into her stomach.

"I've seen this man," she said, tapping a manicured nail on Weber.

"I'm sure you have."

"He's one of yours," she said.

"Yes. The one we call Dopey. His name is Jason Weber."

Grace studied the photos thoroughly. "He was at Winfield House when I arrived for my chat with Delacroix; I know that now. When he came to the house with your men I knew I'd seen him before."

"Explain."

"Which part?"

"All parts."

"He was sitting with another man when I arrived for my

meeting with Delacroix, before I came looking for you. I thought they were there for me. I was fairly certain that my meeting was not about the embassy dedication. I thought Delacroix found out about the threats I'd received, and about the accident."

"He had; Jarvis told him."

"Well," Grace sniffed. "That is a surprise." She would take time to process Sterling Jarvis's thinking later. "When I saw these men, I figured Delacroix had taken it upon himself to secure a detail for me—or they were from Homeland Security and they would be accompanying me home." Grace tapped the photo. "This one sent a chill up my back, as he did when I first met your men at Shannonfield. I didn't put them together until just now."

"And, of course, you said nothing."

"I felt silly. After all, he was yours."

"Yeah."

"I should have said something," she conceded. "This one here—what's this?" Grace tapped the picture of Weber driving a car, with Grace in the backseat.

"Jarvis came up with this, when he was going through stuff for your husband's presidential library. Do you remember this?"

Grace studied the photo again. "The way I'm dressed, and the driver is on the left, see? We're not in the U.K., we're in the United States." Grace looked up at Marin. "This was taken days after Matt's funeral. I was going to the White House. I had to make way for Bannish and his wife."

"Yeah. Weber's been on you a while. Odd thing is, this is the picture that ended up in the papers." Marin showed Grace the photo with a different man in the driver's seat.

"Why?"

"Someone doesn't want Weber seen. Good news is, if he

meant you harm, he'd have done it already. What I think, Grace, is that Weber has been on you since your husband's assassination to protect you; that's why he was at Winfield House and why he was driving you in this picture." Marin tapped the photo again.

"If that's true, then where was he the day of the shooting at the library in May?"

Marin shrugged. "If I were to take a guess—and honey that's all I can do now, until you tell me what's going on—I'd say he was there. And he shot and killed the right person."

"The agent? Adelson?"

"Yes—if I were to guess."

"Why?"

"Why did two agents assassinate the president at the convention?"

"My God."

"I don't know who hired Weber, but whoever it is, they're good; he got past me. Why he's on you and who hired him is our next discussion." When Grace grew quiet, he said, "Duchess, you came to me for protection, and for whatever reason the people in charge allowed it. You have any thoughts on that?"

"No. I don't, actually."

"I'd like to know what you're involved in. We're not just going to Washington for a memorial. There's more going on here. Grace?"

"I'd say you're safer not knowing, but I don't think that's something you'll accept."

"No. And believe me, you're safer with me knowing —everything."

Grace smirked and drank the entire glass of gin down.

"Impressive," he said, taking the glass out of her hand and setting it down. "Puke, and you'll be sitting on pillows 'til we land in Washington, and that's a promise." Grace gave a delicate hiccup and nodded for him to continue.

"Let's start small." Marin filled the now empty glass with water and pushed it toward her. "The pictures of you at the Levy's—entering and exiting the building, and you with the senator—weren't taken by Jarvis. I think they were taken by the same person who's been inundating your email and sending you threatening notes. I think that the reason you never told anyone, be it Homeland Security or Scotland Yard, or me, about those threats is because they aren't threats at all. Are they, Grace?"

"What...whatever do you mean? You saw them."

"I did." Marin looked down at his hands, steepled in front of him as he rested forearms on the bar. Eye-level, gaze serious. "Remember, I said I'll have the truth. I won't tolerate obfuscation, or distraction, or half-truths or untruths any longer."

Grace nodded. Her head started swimming, the gin having an effect, but she wasn't so sure it was the desired one.

"Okay, so as I was saying, I don't think they are threats at all, so I asked Grumpy—"

"You mean Brian? I think we're past this now."

"I asked *Brian* to look into it. He's a forensics expert, after all. It didn't take him long—minutes actually—to see a pattern, a code of some kind. He hasn't gotten back to me on any more than that, but he will. Someone else was supposed to see those—unless you know how to read code."

"I don't."

"Okay. And you're telling me the truth that you believed these were legitimate threats."

"Yes."

"And you hid them because...?"

"I wanted no distractions from the...trip."

"From the trip. Which there is more to than just a memorial for your late husband."

Grace nodded.

"Tell me about that."

"I can't." Tears welled in her eyes.

"Yes, you can. You have to now. I have to know what's going on. It isn't fair to keep me in the dark any longer."

"I know. You're right."

"You're safe. I give you my word."

"I know that, John."

"Then talk to me. It's time."

Grace took her water to the sofa and sat down. Marin came over and joined her. "The truth is, I've wanted to tell you since the day we got to Shannonfield. However, it should come as no surprise to you that, at the time, I trusted no one—not even you, fully."

"Okay."

"Do you remember me blurting out, in a moment of weakness, that Matt had a mistress?"

"Yes."

"Yes. Well, that *person* was Catrina Cornwell."

"President Cornwell's—"

"Daughter, yes. She was also Senator David Howell's wife." Grace sat back in the sofa. "Get comfortable. This is a long story."

25

"Sweetheart, I haven't been comfortable in over a year," Marin confessed.

It was hard to miss the pain on his face, and it was a pain that never seemed to go away, to Grace's mind. She wondered how he endured this latest operation, where he had to care for her under less than honest circumstances, all the while trying to redeem himself from a past he'd never get away from. She was, indeed, being most unfair; however, these were trying circumstances not of her doing. How much could she—*should* she—say? One wrong move, to the wrong person...

And as much as she adored him, she had no idea who he was, really.

"Well, then at least unfurl your brow," Grace muttered. When he remained stone still, she sighed. "You may recall that during our first campaign for the White House, there was some speculation that the Libertarian Party, the LNC, Matt, and me personally, were being spied upon, through moles who were planted in strategic campaign offices, through computer hacking, and through video surveillance."

"Of course."

"It was laughed off as the ramblings of an inexperienced politician, but the truth of the matter was that during our first run for office, information was gathered and fed not only to the media, but it was used to garner a warrant to spy on us, the campaign and our campaign staff. When they found nothing, they accused Matt of collusion with foreign entities for the purpose of nefariously winning the election. When they couldn't prove that, the other side began a campaign of their own. None of this should be news to you; you practically lived it with us."

"Right."

"The other side refused to work with Matt on anything; they spread rumors about him to the press, including him with other women. The trouble he had reaching across the aisles wasn't because of me, or because of him. The wrong man won. The truth was, however, that their distress had less to do with Matt winning than it had to do with Jeff Scott losing."

"Jeff Scott—the Democrat candidate."

"Yes.

"How so?"

"Scott made promises to the deep state, and to certain foreign entities."

"What kinds of promises?"

"The usual kind that weakens the citizenry and strengthens the government."

"Such as?"

"High positions for people who could change the course of our history and our very laws; perhaps a nice new war for the military oligarchs. After all, war is money. I don't know the details, of course, but the vitriol was so staggering that one has to conclude people were promised the world had Jeffrey Scott won."

"That's a little far-fetched."

"You've been away; you know nothing." When she caught the look on his face, she demurred. "I apologize. I could have been gentler," she sniffed. "But the rum-induced coma you've been in shows. A lot has changed. In short, the rights of Americans are being taken away in slow, calculated ways that, unless you are really paying attention, you won't notice until they are gone. You are being distracted by a lot of noise on the streets while your rights are being destroyed behind the scenes. And the organizations that used to serve and protect us are being weaponized. But you already know that, don't you?" When Marin didn't answer, she went on.

"A Republican sitting president, James Cornwell, and the then Democrat Speaker of the House Jeff Scott lost the White House to a third-party first-term senator from New York. Who'd ever heard of such a thing? This was not only a stinging blow to the whole two-party system, but to a very dangerous, imbedded group of people who are still reeling because the wrong man won. And that wrong man was set to win again, after four years of solid winning, for everyone. So many in the Deep State lost with Matt's win that the Department of Justice and the FBI got involved. The plan was to get enough on Matt to impeach him at the very least, and to de-legitimize his presidency and have him removed at worse.

"There was no doubt in anyone's mind, except the egomaniacs behind all this, that Matt Coolidge would defeat David Howell in November, and become the first third-party two-term president in history. So, get rid of the sitting president, Bannish takes over as president until the election in

November, and Howell beats him then. Turns out, as you know, that Bannish beat Howell in a landslide in November for the same reason Matt beat Jeff Scott four years ago: both were horrendous choices."

"And how does all that lead us here?"

"Two things happened in those four years Matt was president: Senator Evan Weld didn't like what was doing on. He was not a huge fan of Matt's, but he respected the office of the presidency and didn't think trying to oust a president just because you didn't like him was good for the nation. He wanted the truth to get out, but he needed to head or at least be on a committee to investigate the allegations against Matt and put a stop to it. This, of course, was on the news every night; it was no secret."

Marin shrugged. "Okay. And the second thing?"

"Catrina Howell fell in love with my husband." Grace sighed. "Matt certainly wasn't the first president to carry on an affair in the White House, but I am quite certain he was the first to continue the affair in order to expose a conspiracy. Shagging the opposition's old lady was a nice way to imbed the knife deeper, to Matt's view. But Mrs. Howell didn't care for her husband or his antics, either, and as she was about to bare all to the investigative committee, she died."

"You're kidding."

"No. A very rare brain cancer." Grace smirked, her voice dripping with sarcasm. "She died days after discovery. There was no autopsy, and she was cremated."

"Wow. I have been away."

"It gets better. Prior to going on record with the committee, she went on record with me."

"With you." Marin sat back.

"Yes."

"Why?"

"She was dying. And she knew, I think, how dangerous her husband was," Grace finished.

"Was the cancer legit?"

"Cancer is usually man-made—weaponized, in this case. But David Howell's chicanery was becoming transparent."

"How so?"

"James Cornwell was a one-term president, and one of the many things he will be remembered for in his four years is his relationship with Said El Farad of Bahldar. It's a small, insignificant country. The deal happened quickly. El Farad was installed as a U.S. government puppet when it was discovered that the tiny province was oil-rich. It was cheap oil, as well, coming at great expense to a people rich in culture and religion, and not the kind we go to war over. As soon as Matt took office, he put a stop to it all. He pulled the U.S. out of the deal and sent troops in to restore the country. A major investor in that endeavor, among many other endeavors that only served him, was Senator David Howell. You can see now why he hated Matt, and by extension, me."

Marin nodded.

"Matt knew what he was up to, and was quick to put a stop to it all. Weld headed a committee to investigate not only Cornwell and the oil deal, but other senators and a few high ranking military officials who were involved as well, including Howell. The company that was hired to go into Bahldar and do the drilling was Shaefer-Kaye, who, as you may recall, was responsible for that major oil spill in the Gulf of Mexico a decade ago."

"Right."

"The company's chief lobbyist at the time was Catrina Howell."

"No shit."

"Yes. She seduced a sitting president—and apparently Matt needed little coaxing—in an attempt to influence his decision not to pull out of the Bahldar deal. When her efforts failed, Matt was assassinated. It was the final straw."

"With members of the Secret Service being in on it."

"It was the FBI. But again, you already know that—if we're being honest." Grace stared down her nose at him. "You know more than you're saying, as well, Judson. May I call you Judson?"

"Not unless you'd like to feel my belt again."

"Tell me what you know about the Secret Service agents who killed my husband. John," she said in a scolding tone when he didn't answer. "Or perhaps you'd like to feel *my* belt." Grace had never seen Marin turn red before. His mouth turned up and his eyes danced. Then he got serious.

"They were recruited like any CIA operative is who hasn't gone to school for it first: they'd gotten themselves into compromising positions, were in debt for a lot of money and their lives and the lives of their families were being threatened."

"And I am assuming their troubles were set-ups."

"To some extent. They'd gotten stupid, but not to the extent that they'd have to resort to murdering a sitting president to get out of it."

"They knew they'd die, then."

"I don't know if they're dead. Do you?"

"Sadly, no. Regardless, I'm assuming they'll never be heard from again."

"But at least their families are taken care of."

"That is disgusting."

"Yeah. Welcome to politics. So, what are you giving Weld, or what is he giving you in the picture here?"

"My testimony in case I'm killed."

"So, now we know what the threats are about. Except, why go that route? It's amateur hour. Why not just kill you outright? You're careless enough about your safety that a ten-year-old could do it."

"How kind," Grace simpered.

"Who are you protecting, while I protect you?"

"I don't know what you're talking about."

"Catrina Howell didn't unload on you. She was sleeping with your husband; you'd be the last person she'd talk to. So, either the president told you everything, and you're on your way to Washington to sit with a special prosecutor to discuss pillow talk, or she confided in Weld, and you're playing decoy until he's called before a special prosecutor. Which is it? Because I don't like being used."

"You're not being used. You're being paid to protect me. Does it matter why?"

Marin thought about that. "No."

Grace nodded. "Go, John. Go back to St. John, or back to Cody. Get out of this. You've taken me this far. It's enough."

Marin laughed. It was throaty and mocking. "Now? After Saturday night, and your screaming that I'm being unreasonable about us being together, you want me to go, just like that?"

"God." Grace sat forward with her face in her hands. "I am so tired. So bloody tired."

Marin stood. "I know. We're almost done. It's almost over." He pulled her to her feet and swept her up into his arms.

"I'm sorry I ever met you," she whispered in his ear.

"We'll see about that." He stalked with a purpose to her room.

GRACE WAS ENAMORED with the sight of him. He stood, nude, at the foot of her bed, cock heavy and half-hard, his wide hips, broad chest and flat stomach on display to her. She was in love with the way the golden hair on his body glowed against his tan skin. He'd spent time on that boat of his naked, for the tan lines above his knees were there, but faint. There was no spot on him that was stark white.

She was in awe of the confidence he displayed as he stood in front of her, one side of his mouth ticked up in that knowing way of his. There was nothing sexier than a confident man, and a kind, heroic confident man was sexiest of all.

She was aroused at his control, within himself and of her. His moral compass would not be altered for anyone, and he expected of her only what he expected of himself. She wanted to please him, make him proud of her, secure his admiration. She craved the solid wall he made around her and especially in front of her when she wanted to test limits, when she wanted to go too far.

He was the head and the hand; she was the heart— something she'd always wanted.

How much time did they have? Plans had changed—she saw it immediately on the threat that had been slipped under their door Saturday night. Weld was nervous; Howell was up to no good. Of course, she should have known; Grumpy, the foremost forensic expert in the world. He'd seen the patterns in the missives right away. Simple enough for her to pick up at a glance, unremarkable to anyone else. Marin and his men had to know what was going on, at least partially. How long did she have with this wonderful man? What strings could she pull to feel this way every day? He was an addiction she could not kick. Sudden emotion overwhelmed her, and she blinked back a flood of unexpected tears.

"I'm thinking about how I can please you further, but I find I'm not that inventive," she stated.

"You please me fine, sweetheart. Pull the sheet down. I want to look at what's mine."

"I can't," she whispered.

"None of that. Lose the sheet, darling."

"I fear my imperfections are glowing," she said as she eased the sheet down her belly, then down her legs, and let it rest across her feet. Marin reached down and pulled the linen completely off the bed.

"You," he said, with unveiled admiration, "are beautiful. Anything contrary to that from you will get you into trouble."

Grace felt her body jerk at the threat.

"I love that your lips can't quite contain all of your clit; I love that I can coax it out with my mouth while your legs are closed, get you to come like that."

"I like it, too."

"Turn over. Please."

Grace did as he asked, turning over onto her belly. She felt his weight behind her as he crawled onto the bed. She felt his fingers brush across the sensitive area between thigh and bottom. She was still tender. His hand slid over the crest, his palm cupping and kneading still hot skin; she felt sunburned.

Marin's cock lengthened as he brushed his fingers across the small of her back, and she arched against his hand, pushing her bottom high. Her beautiful ass was red, all over.

"Daddy spanked his baby hard," he whispered, raking his nails over the wide red lines that striped the lower half of her bottom and upper thighs, the edges welted where the thick leather bit her flesh. Grace jumped at his touch, and then settled as he planted tender kisses across her lower back, an erogenous zone of hers, he learned. He moved down and kissed every inch of red his hand painted on her formerly alabaster bottom, twirled his finger in circles at the crest, where his hand spent most of the time in an agonizingly slow, methodical rhythm. Sometimes the hardest lessons took the longest.

Marin raised her hips and pulled her back against him. Fully erect, he set his cock at her core and, as she sat in his lap, he entered her slowly, with reverence, and made love to his woman. He'd do whatever it took to keep her safe.

His woman.

"I'M GOING to miss New York. I've always loved it." A gentle snow fell Thursday morning as they drove through the city on their way to Teterboro. Unexpected, and it would not stick long, but it was beautiful coming down. A first snowfall cleaned the city before it turned brown and dull, like the island's very worst self. Marin slipped an arm around her in the backseat. He didn't seem to care that Doc and Grumpy sat in front, oblivious—or not.

"What happens...?" she said softly and nodded in the men's direction.

"They're flying with us," he said in her ear.

"That doesn't give us a lot of privacy," he muttered.

"You mean, on a private plane with two pilots who can hear everything with one flip of a switch?"

"Oh, live a little, Marin." Grumpy chuckled, and Grace reddened. Not as quiet as she thought she was.

"How's my friend Karen?" Grace asked.

"I don't know," Grumpy answered.

"I don't believe that."

The man turned around. "She was more trouble than she was worth."

"Those are the very best types of women, Mr. Dean."

"You playing matchmaker, Mrs. Coolidge?"

"It's not too terribly difficult, two attractive, headstrong people like you and Karen. You'll find your way without my help. Don't mind me." Grace waved her hand dismissively. "You do you, Brian."

"Thank you, ma'am."

"Just don't dismiss her out of hand."

"No worries there." He paused. "How long have you known her?"

Grace smiled. "We went to high school together. She was a year ahead of me. She sold her first romance while I was still searching for a major my sophomore year at Middlebury. She's quite talented."

"Yeah. She told me. Meanwhile, you became first lady. Got a few things going for you yourself, ma'am."

Grace laughed. "You're very kind."

When they pulled up to the small terminal at Teterboro, Grace checked herself in the mirror and applied some lipstick as the men got the bags. Grumpy and Doc moved through the terminal and out an opposite door to the plane. No one was around to greet them; no porter, no agents. Not even a mechanic. Grace thought that was odd.

Marin stopped her inside the terminal and turned her to face him. He brushed his fingers down her cheek.

"I've been wanting to say something to you, Duchess."

"Yes? What is it?" Grace looked up into his earnest eyes. She'd say it back; she was ready. She loved him; there was no doubt in her mind. She'd see this through in Washington and then they'd be together. She'd take time off; they could return to London, or stay in D.C. Or they could go to Cody. Whatever he wanted. She would defer to him. John Marin was all she wanted. Yes, it had been just a couple of weeks together, but people fell in love in mere hours, and that was not some fact taken from one of Karen Perry's novels. She'd seen it. And they'd been through so much. Their intimate encounters were unlike anything she'd experienced with another man. That had to account for something. They could, and would, endure anything together. That aside, John Marin had indeed ruined her for all other men.

Marin looked over her shoulder and then at her. "We end here, Duchess."

She felt her body weave. A hot flush moved through her, as if she'd just been notified of a death. "I—I don't understand. We're not flying together?"

"No. We end here," he repeated.

"I—I'm sorry." She tsked and shook her head. "I'm not following you." She blinked rapidly and gave a small chuckle. So silly. *Concentrate, Grace*, she chided herself. He didn't really say... And then Grace saw them; three men, dressed in black cargo pants and tight-fitting shirts, weapons at their hips. One was Jason Weber. They blocked out the sun that shone through the opposite terminal door.

"I've taken you as far as I can," he said, and she missed the pain in his eyes because hers was so overwhelming it superseded all else.

"I still don't—" Her eyes filled.

How?

"I know."

"John?"

"Go, now. These men will take care of you now."

"No!" A pain—and lord, was it sharp—stabbed into her side, and she felt her legs go.

"They'll explain everything on the plane." Marin nodded to the men, and they came forward.

"No!" Her legs wouldn't move. She looked around her for help. Doc, Grumpy, a lone airline porter who never came along to grab her bags. Anyone. What was happening? What was *happening*?

"Mrs. Coolidge, my name is Agent Jason Weber, and on behalf of the President of the United States I am here to take you into protective custody until your scheduled meeting with the special prosecutor. Please come with me now."

Grace turned to Marin. She saw it then, the stoic expression, the dead-in-the-eyes look he got when he was determined to see things go his way; that countenance that told her he hadn't been fooled for a second. "You knew. You've known all along."

Marin cupped Grace's cheek. "Everything will be all right now, Grace." No *love*, no *Duchess*, no *darling*, no *babe*. Just...Grace. So final. "Go."

The rumble of the jet engines grew loud in Grace's ears as Agent Weber took her arm and led her to the door. And as Grumpy and Doc reentered the terminal, Agent Weber swept the former first lady in his arms and sprinted for the plane; Weber had heard it before Marin, the roar of the black Hummer as it careened across the tarmac and screeched to a stop behind the idling plane.

"Grace!" Marin shouted, and pulled a Browning Hi-Power from his hip. Grumpy and Doc drew weapons and ran onto the tarmac as the plane started to move, a steward still trying to get the door latched. Marin could see Grace's face in the small window; she was crying.

The roar of the jet engine was deafening. What was she

seeing? A black vehicle that looked like it belonged in some war zone was chasing the plane—her plane. And then Marin and his men drew their weapons as cars with lights and sirens converged on the group. Who was who? She did not know. Confusion overwhelmed her; she wondered if the men holding the guns felt the same.

As her plane turned into the entrance to the runway, weapons jerked in determined hands and men started to scatter and fall to the tarmac. Inside the plane, her protectors surrounded her, war weapons raised, testosterone and intent wafting off them. Jason Weber was closest; he was almost sitting on top of her. Grace tried to push him away, as if that small act would stop it all from crashing down around her. She knew what this was, and in fact, was stunned it hadn't happened back in London, or at Shannonfield, or on the streets of Hoboken. She'd become complacent in John Marin's arms and under his protection. Most of the time, she forgot about the tasks that lay ahead, so comfortable was she in her surroundings. And Grace understood in that split second why Marin had been so hard on her. He'd known her story all along.

The G-force sent her back in her seat as the plane started its taxi down the runway. And as it arched toward the bright blue sky, yellow-orange cartoon sparks spewed from the gun muzzles on the tarmac. John Marin danced and jerked like a marionette, as her husband had done on that stage over a year ago. In slow motion, he fell to the ground and ceased to move.

Her screams drown out the roar of the jet as it climbed into the bright blue sky.

26

Four Months Later

"Sorry, Grace. I'll just be a minute."

Grace Ashton Coolidge paced back and forth across the Presidential Seal in the Oval Office while Charles Bannish signed some documents his secretary passed to him, one after the other. She should be sitting respectfully while the president worked instead of behaving like a nervous rabbit. She'd known Charles for too long to play games. And she was here because he wanted her, not the other way around.

A snow storm had blown through Washington D.C. for days, typical of weather in February. Snow blanketed the grounds of the White House, which Grace could see clearly through the open drapes. The sun was attempting a show, but Grace didn't hold much hope; she knew D.C. too well.

"Sorry about that. Sit, please," said the president, indicating a spot on the sage sofa. "I think you know why I called you in."

"I think I do."

"Are you interested? Our needs aren't being served right now. Delacroix seems to irritate people. Not sure why." He gave Grace a wry smile and she returned it. Both knew exactly why. "You actually have a personal relationship with the queen, and Prime Minister Flannigan practically begged me to give you the ambassadorship when I saw her in December."

"I've known Maeve Flannigan for years. I like her very much."

"So, you see? It's like a perfect storm right now, Grace. Things are moving in the right direction. Please take this job so the U.K is not someplace else I have to worry about."

"I have to be confirmed, Charles, and you know how the senate feels about the part I played in David Howell's downfall, and President Cornwell's censure, for lack of a better word."

"You're wrong. The democrats are embarrassed over Howell, and James can take care of himself. His role, while fool-hardy, was minor compared to Howell. Imagine if that sonofabitch was sitting here now?"

"I can't. Please don't make me." Grace sighed. "This is a diplomatic post, not an appointment to the Supreme Court. Forgive me, but I will not sit in front of a room of overaged lawmakers and be skewered just for this. I have opportunities elsewhere." Grace realized she sounded petulant and ungrateful. "I'm sorry, Mister President. It's been a trying few months. My tank is full."

"I get it." The president smiled warmly. "Don't apologize. Say yes. Deidre says she'll come in here and help me tag team you if I sense any hesitation." That made Grace smile. Charles and Deidre Bannish had been wonderful, and she felt strongly that if it couldn't be Matt sitting here now, Bannish was the best choice, for now. Oh, how she loved coming in here, sitting on the comfortable burnt umber sofa (Matt liked those fall colors), and waiting for him to sign papers, as Bannish had, before coming to her and joining her for a drink before they retired to the residence. When did that end? When had Matt stopped allowing her to come in at the end of the day, using late calls overseas, and last minute meeting as excuses? When did she stop missing it? Stop caring? Grace shook herself free of the memory.

"How is Dee Dee?" she asked.

"Dying to have lunch with you. What do you say, kid?"

"May I have a few days to think about it?"

"Take a week. I'm leaving for Prague tomorrow, and then I've got the State of the Union when I get back. I'd love it if you'd attend." Bannish stood. Their meeting was over.

"Thank you. I'd like that."

"We'll talk in a week, and I'll look forward to making the announcement."

"Thank you for asking, Charles, really. I am honored."

"You're perfect for the job, Grace. You must know that."

"Thank you."

"One more thing." Bannish pulled a single piece of paper out of a folder in his hand. "You've been asking about John Marin."

Grace's heart skipped a beat and her stomach fell. She swallowed past a lump. "Yes?"

"He was badly hurt in the shooting on the tarmac. His recovery was rough—a few surgeries for infection and the like. He spent weeks at New York Pres then went home—"

"To Cody?"

"Yes. As of December he was pushing to get back to work, and the CIA was courting him."

"The CIA."

Bannish arched his brow. "From what I know of John Marin, that acceptance wasn't likely."

"I'll say."

"He's back to running Marin and Associates. Did you know about that prior to his run in the Secret Service?"

"I did."

"According to my sniffers—and rest assured I have sniffers—"

"Good to know. I have one, too. His name is Sterling Jarvis."

"Invaluable. Anyway, my sniffers tell me he's not running around protecting diplomats just yet, but he's running the company from behind a desk—very efficiently, I might add."

"Less than four months seems an awfully fast recovery."

"Some people heal fast; other think they do." Bannish handed Grace the piece of paper he was reading off. "He's based in London. Wonder if that will seal the deal on my offer."

Grace wanted to weep. "It certainly helps." Her lip wobbled, something she did not want the president to see.

"At the risk of sounding like a Dutch uncle, honey, do you have feelings for this man?"

"I have tremendous feelings for this man, Charles." Grace brushed away a tear. "Thank you for this."

"You're welcome. I don't want you to think nagging pays off, but in this case I had a method to my madness." The president opened his arms for a hug. "See you at the State of the Union. I'll put you next to Dee Dee."

"We'll only giggle."

"I'd expect nothing else. Goodbye, dear."

"Have a safe trip, Mister President."

MARIN AND ASSOCIATES was located in an old Georgian home on a quiet residential street in London Fields. Wrought iron fencing surrounded the home, located on a corner and well back of the road. An armed guard sat in a small shack at the entrance.

"Is Mister Marin expecting you?" he asked.

"Well, no, he isn't."

"One moment." The man closed himself inside his shack and picked up the phone. He spoke little, nodded once, and replaced the receiver. Then he slid open the door and said, "One moment, please," and closed the door again. It was chilly, but the sun was out. The warmth from the shack drifted out with each opening and disappeared upon closing. Grace wanted to step inside with him, but his grand size took up all the space. In less than a minute, a man Grace had come to know fairly well jogged down the walkway from the entrance.

"Grace."

"Brian." Grumpy hadn't changed. That he was in London didn't bode well for her friend Karen Perry, as she was a New Yorker through and through. Sadly, Grace hadn't spoken to Karen since October.

"I've got this, Tom," he said to the guard, who gladly returned to warmth and a hunting magazine. Grumpy stared at Grace and smiled, but it was not genuine. "This isn't a good time," he finally said.

"I imagine not. Please take me to him."

Brian Dean stared at something over her head. "He, uh..."

"Doesn't want to see me," she finished.

"It's not what you think."

"No?"

He opened his mouth to explain and closed it immediately. Like John Marin, Brian Dean did not like to explain himself, she imagined—or ask twice.

"Grace, I'm sorry—" Grumpy looked down at his phone, then chuckled and turned it toward Grace.

Get her ass in here before she catches her fuckin death read the text.

"See there? He does care." She offered a smirk, which Grumpy didn't appear to appreciate.

"That wasn't the issue," he said. "I hope you know that."

"I do now. Lead the way, if you don't mind."

No matter how John Marin looked, Grace would not react. She knew him; he was proud, and he was anything but weak. But gunshot wounds could lay the strongest men low; Grace knew this first hand.

The front door was a good one hundred feet from the street. John Marin was taking no chances; the armed guards, the long distance to the entrance, it was all for enhanced security. She wondered if he, himself, was in any danger. The walkway that bisected the garden was made of flagstone, and the plants and flowers that had not yet bloomed, but would soon, covered the nicely landscaped front. Tall copper beech trees served as above-the-fence hedging along the wrought iron that spanned the width of the property and down both sides, their wine-rust leaves complementing the brick façade of the house. But there were no tall hedges in the garden or close to the house. Again, security was tantamount to John Marin. The symmetrical five sash windows above and below, as well as the gabled roof, the half-fan window over the doors, and the chimneys at each end were pure Georgian.

Grumpy led her through the double forest green doors

and into a black and white tiled foyer with a curved stair-case leading up to the second story. A crystal chandelier hung over the entrance from the ceiling. Chrysanthemums of the purest white sat high and full in a large black lacquered vase atop an antique table against a facing wall. Not John Marin's doing; he was too practical. Grumpy looked to the left as a blip in Grace's peripheral moved.

He was dressed in gold chinos and an ink black sweater and leaned on a hazel wood walking stick. Grace thought she'd prepared herself, tried to envision what months of recovery after being shot would look like. Nothing prepared her for this. He was half the man she remem-bered in New York. His clothes hung on a thin frame. His cheeks were hollow, made more so by the clean-shaven face and the military short haircut. Four months ago, John Marin was a strong, robust, solid man who weighed north of two hundred pounds and carried it well on his six-foot-four frame. Grace estimated he'd lost a quarter of that. His blue eyes were sunken in his head. They held pain, and lots of it.

One side of Marin's mouth hooked up; at least that was the same. He looked over her head at Grumpy. "He tried to tell you." His normally strong, confident voice was gravelly and weak.

"But I wouldn't hear it, would I?" she said, her eyes fill-ing. "Typical of me."

"I'll be right outside," Grumpy said.

"You shouldn't have come," Marin said in time with Grumpy's exit and the snick of the door closing.

"Why?" Grace whispered. "Why would you say such a thing?"

"I should have stopped this while you were still in Wash-ington," he said.

"You couldn't have." Grace took two steps forward. "I'd have come anyway."

"Still petulant. Still dis—" Marin closed his eyes and winced. "Disobedient."

Grace moved closer. "You're in pain."

"I'm fine."

"I'm here."

"Bad time."

"Best time." Grace reached him just as his legs gave out, and the only two things keeping him standing were the walking stick, and Grace's body, wedged between him and the floor.

"Help! Somebody help me!" she screamed.

"HE JUMPED BACK in too soon. If I didn't sit on him, he'd be in the field escorting come A-lister to the Oscars." Doc stood in the large room off the foyer that should have been the living room, but instead was a warm and very efficient office for John Marin. One side of the room housed a desk, chairs, and a round meeting table off in a corner near a bank of windows. A pair of comfortable sofas and matching chairs were situated in the middle before a blazing fireplace, and on the opposite side of the room were two cozy spots for more intimate meetings, with comfortable club chairs and small tables between. A full bar stretched for six feet along the side wall, and books and *objets d'art* filled a floor to ceiling library style bookcase from the corner to the heavy doors to the room. Grace easily pictured herself curled up in one of the chairs, reading while John worked. The room was stylish and comfortable. Despite time and distance, the room held his familiar scent.

"What happened that day at Teterboro?" Grace asked. "The FBI wouldn't tell me. Even the president is pretending he doesn't know."

"They were trying to stop you, obviously."

"Who's 'they'?"

"The same 'they', broadly speaking, that you spoke to the special whatevers about in Washington."

"I figured."

"The original plan was to fly out much later in the day, and out of JFK, but we intercepted some communications that led us to believe that wasn't safe. We dodged that bullet by seconds."

"But John didn't." Grace paced the room.

"No. John didn't."

"This is my fault."

"No, Grace, it isn't. Don't go there, please." Doc sat on the arm of a sturdy club chair. "We all go into these things knowing that we might not make it. It's not like going to war, because most of what we come up against is pretty predictable, but still things can happen. John knew exactly what he was getting into when he agreed to this."

"No, he didn't. I never told him about the threats—that weren't really threats. I couldn't be honest with him, for obvious reasons, about what was really going on. He thought he was coming in to fill a role so I could do the embassy dedication and the memorial, and satisfy Charles Bannish. I never meant to mislead him or involve him in all this." Grace sighed. "That's not true," she amended. "I believed I could keep the two separate, that John would take care of me while I took care of this other...shit."

"Grace, there's something you need to know."

"What is it?"

"After the president was assassinated, they approached

Marin about killing you."

Grace staggered and grabbed on to the back of a chair. The room seemed to undulate, and she thought she was going to go down, much like Marin had not thirty minutes ago. "I beg your pardon?"

"His father was in some IRS trouble and they promised to make it all go away if he went along. Stupid."

"What happened?"

"John paid the IRS bill, removing their leverage. They figured, he got close to you for that short time when he got you out of the convention center and out of town, and you'd easily trust him again. He never said a word about it. Instead, he disappeared to St. John."

"Is that why Brandt Delacroix seemed stumped when I asked to find my own security rather than use Secret Service?"

"I can't say for sure, but I wouldn't rule it out," Doc said. "If he was privy to any of this, you'd just done half his job for him."

"John said once that he was with me because 'they' allowed it. He was right, of course. So, had John stuck by his original *no* to me in St. John...?"

"They already had someone else on you. He took the job because he wasn't going to watch what happened to the president happen to you, too. When he asked us to get involved, he told us everything, including what he suspected you might be involved in, which was more than an embassy dedication and a memorial. He didn't know what, exactly. That the threats were so easy to find spoke volumes. If you'd really intended to hide those away, you'd have done it."

"But I did. They were hidden away in my flat in London."

"Who else knew?"

Grace shook her head. "Sterling Jarvis. He put them in the desk for John to find."

"You're one of the lucky ones, Grace. You're surrounded by people who care about you, and that's why you're standing here now."

"Tell me the truth: how's he doing?"

"Not well. He's in pain and he won't take anything for it —shows weakness, he thinks. But I can't get him up and moving without some pain management. And he's got to move. He's getting weaker every day, as you just saw."

"His injuries?"

"He was damn lucky. Both bullets penetrated on rico-chet, one hit him in the torso and the other hit him in the groin. Where they hit, at full speed and he wouldn't be here now."

"Oh, my God."

"The groin injury is what's giving him the most trouble."

Grace swallowed past an uprising of emotion that threatened to shake the walls. "Is he...is his...?"

"He's intact, Grace. The bullet hit him where the thigh meets the pelvis. It was bad because it nicked an artery. He lost a lot of blood and then an infection set in." Doc sighed. "I think, too, that he misses you. He was fine until you started asking about him. I think he'd pretty much settled on moving on, hard as that would have been. But when you started inquiring, and of course it got back to us, he sort of took a few steps back. You cared, and he didn't want you to see him like this. Now, the war between wanting to see you and not burdening you takes over. It affected his recovery."

Grace blinked rapidly as tears fell. "Be that as it may, Doc, I am not leaving him."

Doc grimaced. "You may have to, Grace. John was very clear: he wants you to go."

27

April

The dapple mare was gorgeous; a heavy horse, her poise was striking, and her sweetness was unmatched.

"Hello, darling," Grace cooed, rubbing the animal's nose. "You are a beauty, then, aren't you? There's a girl."

"Oh, I right like her," Jasper Whipple said.

"How are the legs? She's not delicate," Grace noted.

"She's good, heavy stock, my lady," Jasper said, feeling up and down the animal's sturdy legs. "The sire must have been a beast."

"Indeed. Her lineage is impeccable." Grace knew as soon as she looked into this animal's eyes that she was ready to try again. She hadn't been on a horse since the day she lost Shane. Dreadful. She'd been taught from the crib to get back up on the horse, metaphorically speaking. This behavior was unlike her in every way. Grace chalked it up to not finding the right one. She hadn't been out with a man, either, for the same reason.

"Let's have her fully looked over, then."

"Very good. I think you'll be very pleased with her. She'll fit right in." Jasper Whipple knew horses, and he'd gushed about Annabelle Lily of the Valley from the moment he saw her a day ago, and then talked Grace in to attending the auction.

Spring had come early to Vermont, and the day was bright. A mild sixty-nine degrees at mid-day promised that flowers would bloom three weeks earlier than normal, as there was no rain, and certainly no further snow, in the forecast. In gray leggings, riding boots and a plum sweater, Grace had no need for a jacket. She turned her face up to the sun and closed her eyes.

"That's the one then, darling?" Grace opened her eyes at her father's voice. He rested his hand on her shoulder. "Does this mean you're staying in the states for a while, granting your papa his wish?"

Grace smiled and rested her head on his shoulder. "Yes, I think so, if you and mummy are sure you don't mind."

"Darling, come now. You know better. I wish you'd move into the main house, but I know you want your privacy. The guest house is too far away."

"It's a thousand-bloody-feet from your front door," Grace scoffed.

"That's almost two-tenths of a mile, love, and at that distance I may not see you for an entire day."

Grace turned to her father. "I may take the ambassadorship. Bannish isn't pleased with Delacroix."

"I know. But we still have time." The Duke patted his daughter's hand. "Once you accept, then there's the confirmation, and then a transition." Bill Ashton looked at the dapple gray his daughter had her eye on. "And what of this one?"

Grace looked at her new charge fondly. "She'll go where I go."

The man sighed. "I'm off in search of your mother, before I find another addition we don't need to my own stables."

"As if you'd deny her," Grace smiled.

"Indeed." He kissed his daughter's cheek and walked away with a spring in his step, no doubt anticipating a good-natured argument about why Delilah Prentiss Ashton needed a new horse when she already had four. Jasper Whipple approached.

"If you've decided, I'll secure the sale and we can take her tomorrow," he told her.

"That will be fine, thank you. I'm going to look in on the stallion auction."

"Very good. Shall I join you?"

"No. I'm not buying."

"Meet you at the truck, then?"

"Yes. See you in a bit."

Grace strolled between two corrals where horseflesh was paraded out and auctioned off, one by one. People stood around with numbered paddles in their hands as the rapid-fire speech of auctioneers battled to be heard over each other, the whinnying of horses and the general whoops, hollers and conversation of the crowd.

Grace entered the closed arena, which was the size of an airplane hangar. The stallions were being led around the ring by their handlers so the crowd of oglers lined up along the fence could get a look.

"In the market for a stallion, Mrs. Coolidge?"

"Not today, Don." Grace smiled up at the pot-bellied president of the Horse and Hounds Foundation, the sponsors of the auction. "I'm just looking."

He smiled. "Well, stay 'til the end. You won't be sorry."

"Why?" Grace found herself getting excited. "What have you got?"

"Galileo is being auctioned to stud."

"No!"

"After winning the Kentucky Derby his owner acquired another horse sired from Mortal Thunder. He's sticking with the lineage, proven winners."

"Oh, now I am intrigued."

"We have an internet billionaire in the crowd, and the Sultan of Brunei's niece, Princess Alyra. I expect them to go head to head."

"How exciting."

"Come with me; I'll get you a seat in the front row. I'm auctioneer for this one."

"Oh, good show! Back to your roots."

"A nice end to the week. Here we go." Grace took a seat at the end of the front row, and Don gestured with a nod toward a young man who stood at the fence as the horses were led out of the arena and into a waiting area. He wore a hoody and sported a mop of messy hair. The internet billionaire, no doubt.

"End of the row, the woman in blue," he pointed out. The woman was dark and exotic, beautiful and young. She sat forward, anxious. Grace understood the feeling; the virility and strength of these animals alone would put anyone in a state. But the reason why this woman was here, for an animal like Galileo, was stunning. All the way from Brunei to little ol' Vermont.

The first five stallions were auctioned off, and then, for added drama, there was a full fifteen-minute lull before Galileo was escorted out to gasps from the crowd. He was a stunning animal, and Grace felt honored to bear witness to the first-time sale of this animal for stud. The bidding started at $50,000, and it didn't take long before the billionaire and the princess got into a bidding war. Grace was pulling for the princess; she didn't care for the hoody. He was young, and it didn't take him long to give up. He didn't know what he had in a horse like this, and Grace was happy a more deserving person won. The princess got Galileo for $300,000.

"I want to meet her," Grace said to Don when he passed her on the way to the viewing circle, where the press surrounded the young foreigner, who had just put Galileo in the record books as the most expensive horse in the world.

When Grace entered the small arena, where the new owner stood next to her prized stud, the press went crazy. Grace's arrival was unplanned, of course, but the princess was gracious, and she and Grace spoke for several minutes. Pictures were taken of Grace petting the horse; one particularly splendid picture was of both women with their delicate hands planted on the flanks of the powerful animal. Grace couldn't remember when she was this thrilled.

"Can we have dinner?" the princess asked. "I was just a teenager when your husband came to Brunei to meet with my uncle. My cousins and I hid under the dinner table all night, listening to the talk. My uncle found us under there the next morning, asleep."

"Was he angry?"

"Not at all; he was stunned. It's the longest, he said, that he'd ever known the five of us to be that quiet."

Grace smiled. "What a marvelous story."

"Forgive me," said the young woman, "but I had such a crush on the late president."

Grace laughed. "You weren't alone." As Grace was about to gladly accept the princess's dinner invitation, something moved in her peripherals. She knew him before their eyes met. His smell, his countenance, the way the air shifted—so familiar to her, yet so foreign.

She'd forgotten, or so she thought.

He wore black—black shirt, black jeans, and a black leather jacket. A clear, inconspicuous earpiece sat in his ear and disappeared into the collar of his shirt. He was clean shaven, and his hair was cut short and styled professionally, rather than shorn military-style—like when he worked for the Secret Service. It was hard to view John Marin in any other capacity. She'd blocked out the three weeks they had together, and then the five days in London, in which she attempted to get through to him before he tossed her out of his life. His eyes had lost some color, and they shone now like shards of ice. He'd gained most of his weight back, she was glad to see.

I'm no good for you. You're better off without me.

As if he'd been in any position to decide—physically or mentally.

He'd been a broken man; a proud, broken man. Doc warned her. *He doesn't want you to see him this way.* Stupid woman, she was, believing that all it would take to bring the stubborn man around was a bit of love. She'd handled it wrong; she'd handled *him* wrong. She thought she knew; she thought she was in charge.

You were warned, he'd written in a note attached to flowers he sent to her offices the next day. The last time she saw him, he'd collapsed in her arms.

And now here he stood, like none of it ever happened. But it had. The ache in her heart told her so.

He wore the flat countenance typical of someone being paid to protect. She'd seen it before, but never to this degree on this particular man. It had been six months since the shooting, six months since she'd kissed him, six months since she'd made love—to him, or any man. He looked good, strong. His jaw was firm, he stood straight, she saw no pain in his eyes. In fact, she saw nothing in his eyes. He looked dead inside.

Until he recognized her.

"Can you get us a couple of waters?" Princess Alyra said to the formidable man, and Grace brought her fist to her mouth to stifle a giggle when he simply looked down at his charge and said not a word, nor did he move. Why such a thing struck her so funny amidst such pain, laced with shock, at seeing him, was unfathomable.

"Ugh! Fine. Jesus," the young princess growled. "I'll be right back." When the woman stalked away, Grace looked up at John Marin.

"Huh." She fought back a smirk—unsuccessfully.

"The dinner?" he said.

"Yes?"

"You'll turn her down." Marin looked straight ahead when he said it.

"Hello to you, too." She buffed her nails on her shirt. "I might not want to turn her down."

"But you will."

"I like her."

"You'll say no."

"We could go club hopping." Provoking him seemed better suited to her personality, the new *her*, than crying did. Or smacking him. It didn't make her feel good the first time.

"Grace."

"Pub crawling. Imagine? A real live princess, and...*me*."
Grace was suddenly enjoying herself.

"Keep it up, Duchess."

"Oh, thank you. I shall."

"And then I'll—" Grace felt the déjà vu of a previous
conversation between them that was remarkably familiar
and did not end well for her. Alyra returned with two ice
cold bottles of water, saving her from Marin's veiled threat.
"Here you are," she said, handing one to Grace. It wasn't lost
on her that she didn't think to bring her bodyguard one.
"Now, about dinner..."

Suddenly, Grace didn't like this girl much, for she was
just a girl, with whom she had little in common. "I've just
looked at my schedule and I'm afraid I can't."

"Oh." The woman gave a pout as only a twenty-some-
thing can. "Well, shoot. Well, okay..."

"Another time, perhaps. You never know when our paths
will cross again. We have something lovely and very unique
in common." Grace glanced up at John Marin.

Alyra nodded and stuck out her hand. "It was a pleasure
to meet you." She pumped Grace's hand once, turned on her
heel, and walked away, with John Marin—*her* John Marin—
on her heels.

Grace fell back against the wall as her breath returned.
She believed she was over him. She'd moved on. But clearly
six months wasn't long enough to get over the love of one's
life. Ordering her to refuse the princess's invitation, as if
he...as if he...*owned* her, or something.

She stood in the doorway of the arena and watched
Marin put his charge into a large black car while minions
loaded the most expensive horse in the world into a trailer.
She watched until the car and the trailer were out of sight.

OF ALL THE gin joints in all the world...

Goddamn woman! It never occurred to him that he'd run into Grace Coolidge in Vermont, and it was only when he saw her enter the arena and sit down that he remembered her parents lived here—an 1810 farmhouse in Chester on a few hundred acres, if he remembered right. *Windstorm...Windchester...* The rich sure loved to name their estates.

Marin sat in the backseat in silence as Alyra tapped away on her phone. She never looked up from the damn thing, it seemed, and he'd been surprised that she hadn't found reason to be on it while in the presence of the former first lady. He'd not have put it past the spoiled young woman. She was a decent enough kid who'd never been taught, or forced, to look past her own navel. Thank God they were on their way to the private airport in Killington, where he'd offload his client to another group who would see her to Boston, then on to Brunei. Had he been forced to spend one more night in Vermont just so this spoiled brat could be seen in public with Grace Ashton Coolidge, he'd quite possibly have ended both their lives.

Jesus, Grace looked good. Not much had changed in six months except, somehow, she was even more beautiful. John Marin didn't know how that was possible. Her hair was longer, to her shoulders now. He loved that look, too. She smelled amazing, and she had an air about her that told only those who knew her well that she'd had a rough time of things. She seemed to get over him quickly enough, he noted. He hadn't come close.

The three weeks behind closed doors with Grace and

the special prosecutor yielded indictments and no need for an open hearing. Much of what happened, who exactly was responsible, and what their futures held was still being, for the most part, kept from the public due to 'national security'. John Marin, and all who worked closely with the government, knew what a line of bullshit that was. No matter; his only concern, from the day they came and took Grace away, to this very day, was Grace herself—physically and mentally. That she was in Vermont, in the bosom of her loving family, laying low, told him she was in recovery mode. Seeing him, and him seeing her, didn't help. All it brought up for him was a dull ache somewhere deep. Running Marin and Associates, which he'd acquired again in November, after allowing himself to fully let Grace go, was enough for him. He took the jobs he personally wanted, and kept his people employed and happy. Taking on the Sultan's niece had been a mistake, but he'd done it as a favor, and just for her time in the states. It was all he'd tolerate of her.

As Marin stood in the doorway of the tiny terminal and watched the princess's private plane take off, he decided maybe it was time to go home, for a little while at least.

"WHAT IS IT?" Delilah Ashton reached across the glass and wicker table and took her daughter's hand. At sixty-one, the woman was still vibrant and beautiful, retaining the fresh, outdoorsy look the Duke of Wight fell in love with thirty-eight years ago. In fact, mother and daughter were often mistaken for sisters, which Delilah loved, and Grace merely tolerated. "What did you lose?"

"Whatever do you mean?" Grace asked.

"The last time you had that look, Matt had just been

killed. What did you lose?" This time Delilah over pronounced her words and pierced Grace with sparking green eyes that communicated that she would not be stonewalled, eschewed or rebuffed on the subject, no matter that Grace Elizabeth Ashton Coolidge was a grown woman.

"God...Mummy." Grace blinked back tears as she stared out at the beautiful gardens and the green grasses for acres beyond the yard. Their tea grew cold between them as Grace searched for where to begin such a tale. A light breeze blew along the covered porch of the stately farmhouse, and in this moment, despite the third degree, Grace wished to be no place else.

"His name is John Marin."

And then Grace told her mother everything.

"YOU DUMP PRINCESS AIR HEAD?"

"That isn't nice," Marin said into the phone.

"Yeah. Sorry," Brian Dean said. "I'm still wondering how you got stuck with that one. She was more suited to Deeter."

"The Sultan asked me to." Marin knew Dean well enough to time the eyeroll and the jerkoff motion he'd make with his hand at that pronouncement.

"Ah, well then..." was all Dean offered verbally.

"What about you? You taking off anyplace for Easter?" Marin asked.

"Karen has a book signing in Los Angeles and then we're going to Mammoth."

"Nice." They made quite a pair, the romance author and the elite protector. Marin could only shake his head, and then he remembered what he had with Grace. His chest hurt.

"Yeah. Can't leave her alone two minutes. I told you she had a stalker—had him on her for over a year, which she didn't bother to tell me about until a few months ago."

"You set her straight on that, buddy?"

"You know I did. Sonofabitch fell off the roof of an apartment building watching her."

Marin laughed. "No kidding. Dead?"

"Dead."

"There you are, then. Success. Give her a kiss for me."

"I will. What about you?"

"I think I'll go home."

"Good idea. Do you good."

"Yeah." There was no need to tell his best friend he'd seen Grace. Not a thing was going to come of it. "Have fun, buddy."

"You, too, asshole."

Yeah. No need to say a word.

APRIL CHILL HAD RETURNED to Vermont after days hovering in the seventies. Grace's ride today had been beautiful, the morning chill exacerbated by an unexpected dusting of snow that threatened to send the crocus and daffodils back underground.

She guided Annabelle up the path toward the stables and saw the unfamiliar car in the drive. Steve, the farm's stable man, was talking to someone. The Range Rover was nowhere in sight. It would be just like Governor Paul Kinney to come all the way out to Windswept to discuss the U.S. ambassadorship to Great Britain Bannish spoke to her about last February. That the man, twice divorced, had let his feelings about her personally be known more than once, made it very likely that the visitor was he, and the ambassadorship was an excuse to spend time with her. And it wasn't like she wasn't flattered. Paul Kinney was a very handsome man, and he was positioned for great things; she saw it in him like she'd seen it in Matt Coolidge years ago. But twice divorced? And a *democrat*? Bloody hell. Still, she couldn't help but feel flattered, no matter his motive. That she was even considering *perhaps* dating again was a surprise to her. It was time. She needed to let herself love again. Seeing John Marin at the auction didn't help. Who knows? Maybe it did. Maybe seeing him was all the motivation she needed to finally move on. She wanted to get married again; she wanted children.

"Dammit," she hissed. Annabelle nickered in agreement. "I am not quite ready for this, old girl." The mare snuffled in indignant support.

Grace brought Annabelle up the hill at a trot and pulled her to halt fifty feet from Steve and the visitor. And then her heart dropped.

"Bloody fucking hell," she murmured.

"Say the word," Steve growled, not taking his eyes off the visitor. He was a third generation Vermonter and had worked for the Ashtons for two decades. Knowing Grace well, and aware of all she'd been through, the man was in protection mode now. That John Marin still leaned casually against the sleek black vintage Jaguar with his arms crossed and one corner of his mouth turned up, spoke volumes about his opinion of Steve. Two alphas about to piss on the same tree. This should be good, she mused.

"I think I'll be fine, Steve."

"Your folks went for a drive," he said.

"Yes," she said. "Would you be so kind as to do the same?"

"You sure?"

"Quite."

Marin waited until the dust settled from Steve's departure. "You came out here without a coat on," he said.

Grace nodded. "As did you."

"You took off without telling anyone."

"Yes. I wished to be alone."

"Now that we've recapped the morning..."

Grace smiled at the familiar conversation, one that led to a significant change between them back at Shannonfield on that crisp October morning when they'd almost made love atop a horse. But all of that was in the past.

Marin pushed away from the car and took Annabelle's reins. "Get down."

That familiar dominance, that hubris, that uncanny ability to send hearts fluttering and panties flying off hips of their own free will, was on full display. Sadly, Grace was weary of it all.

"Not this time," she whispered.

He stared up at her as Annabelle shook her head in an attempt, Grace believed, to rid the air of tension. Marin held her firm, as he seemed to with all women who grew disagreeable.

"I'm sorry," Marin finally said.

"For what?" Grace leaned over and rubbed Annabelle's neck to settle her.

He was quiet for a long time before he said, "Doc told me I'd heal faster if you stayed around."

"You should have listened."

"You didn't deserve that."

"You're a proud man."

"I was stupid. I'm sorry."

Grace looked up at the clear sky and shook her head,

willing the tears not to fall. She'd been so good, so damn good about the tears and the emotion, the dreams, the fantasies of a moment just like this, where he comes back to her, and she forgives him.

"I'm fine," she lied. "I'm over it." She would never be over it. She knew that now. "Why are you here, John?"

Marin sighed. "Get down. I'm not going to talk to you looking up."

"Unfamiliar position, I know." For reasons Grace would analyze later, she swung off Annabelle and stood before her visitor. She saw it then; she saw it in his eyes, the look that warmed her from their early days together months ago. Love was there, and so was dominance, and the certain belief that he would be obeyed. His broad body under a thick rust sweater, black jeans that fit him just so, the black boots moist with dew along the toes—it all worked for her.

Marin shook his head and stared at the fluttering leaves of the old oak that caught a sudden breeze. "I dropped my client and was on my way to Montpelier to catch a flight to Jackson."

"Windswept is a long way from Jackson."

"What is it about you people and naming your homes?"

"Ancestry and family titles mostly. Is that why you came? To discuss the many quirks of the British?"

Marin shook his head. "No. Seeing you the other day at the auction was a surprise. I thought I was over it. But I've had this pain—" He twirled his finger in the vicinity of his heart. "Angina, maybe a heart attack this time…"

"Stop it."

"It hurt. It wouldn't go away. Oddly enough, it's gone now, just like before."

"I don't think—"

"I came to tell you, Duchess, that I haven't been happy

since October 23rd. I decided, after I regained conscious-
ness, that it was all for the best. I convinced myself that
there was no room for me in your life, and I convinced
myself you weren't worth chasing after—you had a lot going
on, and your life was plenty full without me in it. Biggest
fucking lie I've ever told myself."

"What's changed?" she asked.

"I have." He moved a step closer. "Not a day has passed
that I don't think of you."

Grace shook her head. "It isn't enough. All those issues
still remain."

"I know. Hear me out." He lifted his hand to her face and
caressed the apple of her cheek with his thumb. "I love you,
Duchess. I've loved you since..." He scratched his eyebrow.
"Since you twisted your damn ankle on my dock. The only
time I've ever gone against myself, broken the rules, is
with you."

"Perhaps I should spank you." Her delivery was so
sedate, so lacking mirth, that he chuckled. And then his
cock stirred.

"Not how I play, Duchess," he whispered. And then he
kissed her. The kiss was soft, tentative at first, and then it
deepened, deepened until he'd crossed the line from *hello* to
possession. Grace knew in that moment that she would
never again settle for being kissed any other way.

"I'm sorry I sent you away," he whispered, his forehead
resting against hers. "I'm sorry I let things get out of hand.
I've missed you so much."

"Your heart," she said, placing her hand there.

"Yes. It's better now." He put his hand over hers. "I don't
know what your plans are, Grace, but I'm hoping there's
room for me. I want to be wherever you are."

"That might be London. Bannish wants me as ambassador."

"Wherever you go. That's what I want." And then he kissed her again. Annabelle nickered, and Grace giggled into his mouth.

"Where's Steve when I need him?" she smiled, glancing over at her new acquisition.

"About Steve," Marin asked. "Is he housebroken?"

"He'll get there. He's very protective."

"Well, you're used to that."

"Only from you."

"I love you, Duchess."

"That is very gratifying." She smoothed the front of his sweater after gripping the wool in her fists during that last kiss. "I thought you were Paul Kinney," she said.

"Do you wish I was Paul Kinney?"

"Not really, although he's quite handsome." Grace wiped some lip gloss from the corner of his mouth with her thumb. "Twice divorced, so that's a mark against him."

"Do I need to worry about Paul Kinney?"

"I don't think you do, no."

"Good."

"Do you know who Paul Kinney is?"

Marin shook his head.

"Do you care?"

Marin shook his head. "Don't mention him again, please."

"All right."

"Or any man, unless it's your father."

Grace giggled. "All right."

"Ambassador, huh?"

"Maybe. We'll see. Do you mind?"

"I said I didn't. When does this happen?"

"Early next year, I predict. Until then, my plans are fluid."

"Then maybe we make a few together."

"I'd like that."

The Duke and Mrs. Ashton didn't see their daughter for three days.

EPILOGUE

June, 14 Months Later

The view from the ridge spanned thousands of acres, but it was the beautiful emerald green meadow next to the ten-acre natural pond, fed by a flowing river, that Grace could not stop looking at. At present, a crew was erecting tents and setting out chairs. The gazebo they would be married under tomorrow was being looked over by an efficient woman who had been given her marching orders a month ago. Beyond and to the left, atop another ridge, sat John's family home and the main residence on the Big Five resort. Cabins, stables, barns, corrals and a boathouse dotted the landscape. The resort would open a week late in order to host The Wedding of the Year, John's mother, Kathryn Marin, joked.

It did not take much for Grace to fall in love with John's family. He was a remarkable man, and remarkable men tended to have remarkable families. She was thrilled that the wedding would take place at his home; in two days they would be off on a honeymoon to Spain, and then back to London and Winfield House.

Her future husband was a strong man. He had fully recovered from his injuries of a year and a half ago, and according to Doc. John Marin was the very worst of patients. Grace warned him that the 'for better or for worse, sickness and health' part of their vows should be amended to include in-home care by a burly, and handsome, male nurse should he ever get truly injured or ill again. He had the nerve to remind her that he'd reinserted the word 'obey' into their vows, and threatened to bring back 'MAN and wife' if she got too mouthy.

"Is it bad luck that we're standing here admiring our wedding plans instead of keeping out of each other's sight until tomorrow?" Grace mused.

"You're too old fashioned," Marin answered.

Grace whipped a brow up in shock. "I am old fashioned? Whose idea was it to stick himself in one of the resort cabins until after the 'I-Dos'?"

Marin bent and kissed her tenderly. "Trying to teach you a little self-control, Duchess."

"I see."

"Are you happy with all this, Future-Missus-Marin? Or is it Ambassador Marin?"

"Lady Marin. I like that." Grace settled her hand on her stomach. She would tell him tomorrow. And then she would tell the president. She knew of no ambassador who gave birth while holding a diplomatic post. Oh, she was sure one, possibly more, existed. It might serve her well to do a little research on that before she got too settled in her new role as U.S. Ambassador to the U.K. The man standing next to her, and his child, were all she cared about. They were the priority now.

"So do I. First a lady," he said. "Always."

"Indeed, darling—a lady first."

ACKNOWLEDGMENTS

Writing is lonely work, and the smart don't go it alone. From day one so many have had my back, and I hope always to return the favor in bold and in subtle ways.

To Chief Kenneth R. Lewis (Retired), who took a chance on an unknown author years ago. He read my first detective novel, *Testarossa* (*A Deadly Legacy*), asked me if I was a cop, and then published the book through his own Krill Press. It's still selling.

To Staci Taylor, who took a chance on a first-time romance author. I had no idea what I was doing; she told me I was just fine, and then published my first three books through Lazy Day Publishing.

To Alta Hensley, who always takes my calls, and never ignores my texts. I want to be you someday.

To my publicist, Heather Roberts, and her staff at L. Woods PR, you make me look good. Thank you so much.

To KR Nadelson at Epic Romance Editing ~ you have an eye, and I appreciate the time, attention and feedback. Working with you was...well, EPIC.

To Celeste Jones, an old pal. We'll outlast all of them, kid, you wait and see. Thanks for taking a look and for being hard on me. And for pointing out that the most impossible (what can and cannot go around a woman's waist) can actually work with the smallest tweak. The Olde Jaol again someday, eh? I'll buy.

To all my fellow authors, scattered about—we come together for an event here or there, and I always enjoy seeing you and getting to know you better. We're in an amazing and very exclusive club, and I wouldn't change a thing.

"What matters most is how well you walk through the fire".
~ Charles Bukowski

"Your story is boring. It's the writing that makes you great".
~ Jack Grapes

ALSO BY JADE CARY

To Love A Woman

Bella Rosa

The Point of it All (Series)

The Point of it All

Days With You

The Reason for It All

Return to Big Sky

Stubborn Pride

I'd love to keep in touch with you! Join my newsletter so that you never miss out on a thing!

Join here: http://bit.ly/2IMNHBA

ABOUT THE AUTHOR

Jade Cary wrote elaborate fantasies in her head from the time she was a small child. The fantasies included strong men and strong, loving relationships. She discovered romance novels quite by accident. Desperate for something new to read, she picked up The Other Side of Midnight by Sidney Sheldon. After that, she found Scruples, by Judith Krantz. A whole new world opened up, and she buried herself in everything these authors wrote. She was fascinated with how the stories were able to capture her and take her to another place. But, more than that, she paid attention to how the words, the writing, made her feel.

She discovered a talent for writing later in life, after careers were had and kids were moving about on their own. She falls in love on a daily basis with her characters, and hopes readers will do the same.

Jade lives in SoCal with her family.

Please keep in touch with me via email! I'd love to chat, any time. *jadecaryromance@gmail.com*

Made in the USA
Middletown, DE
09 September 2018